A MECHANICAL LIZARD . . .
WHAT ELSE?

LATER, SOME WOULD SAY THEY SAW IT, CAUGHT it in a blink as it slid, quivered, rustled down the back of Finn's cloak, a blur of shiny metal, a splash of brass and copper in the sun, a thing they all agreed, quite agitated, clearly disturbed, not at all pleased with the turn of events.

Only seconds after that, no two men agreed they'd seen the same. One saw iron claws rake across his boots, tearing them to shreds, one saw his trousers disappear under snapping silver jaws. One later said he was sure a razored tail had whipped about his crotch, not an inch from his precious private parts.

Everyone agreed they'd heard a rusty crackle, heard a rattle and a hiss, heard a croak like a saw ripping through a sheet of tin. Many saw and heard things that never even happened at all . . .

The

TREACHERY
OF KINGS

Neal Barrett Jr.

Bantam Books

New York Toronto London Sydney Auckland

THE TREACHERY OF KINGS
A Bantam Spectra Book/August 2001

ISBN 0-553-58196-1

Published simultaneously in the United States and Canada

Bantam Books are published by Bantam Books, a division of Random
House, Inc. Its trademark, consisting of the words "Bantam Books"
and the portrayal of a rooster, is Registered in U.S. Patent and
Trademark Office and in other countries. Marca Registrada. Bantam
Books, 1540 Broadway, New York, New York 10036.

PRINTED IN THE UNITED STATES OF AMERICA
OPM 10 9 8 7 6 5 4 3 2 1

WITH LOVE, AND ETERNAL
GRATITUDE FOR HIS FRIENDSHIP TO
HONORED YOUNGER BROTHER PIERCE WATTERS
AND WITH ADMIRATION AND RESPECT
TO DAVE GROSS, WHO FIRST
BROUGHT FINN TO LIFE

The
TREACHERY
OF KINGS

Chapter

ONE

I WOULD LIKE TO GET A SUGAR-PEAR, LOVE," SAID Letitia Louise, nearly shouting in his ear, "and fatpie-and-nettle, if there's one to be had, with so many folk about. Oh, and corn on a stick where the pepper runs down."

"That you shall have," Finn said, catching a word now and then, "all three and more if we can fight our way out."

It was nearly impossible to hear oneself speak, much less another soul as well. Sound, in a meadow, will dispel itself nicely on the wind. The clamor and the roar, trapped within the royal courtyard, merely restored itself time and time again.

Not that many seemed to care, Finn thought to himself, for the heat and the racket and the foul emanations of their neighbors scarcely dimmed the joy of the folk of County Ploone.

Besides the booths and stalls and the varicolored tents, each crowded one against the next, sites that offered tortes, cakes and sour thistle pie, colored beads and spells, mead and silvered glass, there would also be more family fun, late in the afternoon. For every creature there, human, Newlie and even the dead, knew SpringFair Sunday was also the Chopping of May.

And, this day, it was rumored about, commoner and noble alike would meet their fates. One, the Prince's

Keeper of the Mead, it was said, would face a new
and cunning device. Maybe, more horrid than the
Grapnel and the Snip. Which, of course, was a favorite of
all, for the victim seemed to last a great while. One could
see the fair, eat a tart or two, and drop by to watch at any
time.

Not, indeed, like Old Mug o' Lead, which was over in
a blink. If you didn't watch, you missed the whole thing.

More and more these days, many good people, folk like
Finn himself, felt this a grim celebration, a shameful practice in an age when reason was beginning to sprout, when
the Light side of nature seemed to have some sway over
the Dark.

Still, it was wise to keep such thoughts to oneself, for
many looked forward with great anticipation to the grim-
mer aspects of the day.

It was, indeed, a time when even the humble, those of
scanty means, those most stricken by the dark and hurtful
deeds of family and friends, could forget, for a moment,
their own drab lives, their debts and their hunger and
their fury at the world, and enjoy the miseries of others for
a while.

And, besides, it was no great secret that the Prince took
enormous pleasure in these events as well . . .

IT'S PERFECTLY AWFUL, IS WHAT IT IS," LETITIA WHIS-
pered, clearly guessing Finn's thoughts. "Crime and gross
offense must be punished, I suppose, but they don't have
to be so dreadful about it. And they don't have to do it out
here."

"They seem to think they do, dear. In a fearsome manner, where all may come and see."

"A lesson, then, for those who'd consider some misdeeds themselves?"

"Depends on who you ask . . ." Finn said, glancing toward the dark, dreary heights of the Keep, where the doomed awaited their final day.

". . . and, most certainly, when."

"I suppose," Letitia sighed, pausing, again, to press the oaken cask safe against her breast, to dab a lacy sleeve against her brow. She didn't want to show it, but her nerves were wearing thin. The day was steamy hot, the crowds were closing in. The blare, the bray, the clatter and the din were nearly more than she could bear.

Many folk there, Letitia knew, would revel in this most oppressive scene. Humans seemed to love it, and even many Newlies thought it fun. A noisome pack of Bowsers trotted by, yapping and snapping at everyone in sight. Each wore those awful straw boaters and silly little ties. A hefty pair of Snouters, in lilac and blue, headed for a crackle-pie stand.

Letitia's folk, though, had come from different stock indeed. Before the Change, they had lived in peril all their lives. Any sound, any shadow, had set them fair a'fright, sent them fleeing for the safety of the dark.

Letitia was not what her folk were before, but she was part of what they'd been. The swarm, the frenzy, the harsh assault of sound was, she feared, about to take her down . . .

"Shouldn't be long," Finn said, craning above the crowd. "There's a tent over there and they're pouring cool beer. That and a fatpie should serve us quite well."

"Yes, fine," Letitia said, no longer sure it all sounded as good as it had before.

Finn reached back and grasped her arm as he pushed his way forward through the crowd. He was close enough now to catch the tang of bubbling cheese, freshly baked bread, and, an aroma all its own, the heady scent of ale. There were benches, just beyond the tent, in the shade of the castle wall. If he could squeeze them over there, find a place to sit—

This thought had scarcely touched his mind when Letitia made a tiny sound, a little cry, not a major thing but enough to cause alarm.

He turned, quickly, and found an enormous, unwashed lout looming over Letitia, a brutish fellow with hair in his ears, teeth black as cinders, and pale, cesspool eyes. His nose was a horror, like last year's potato, and, as far as Finn could tell, he had no lips at all.

These, then, were the fellow's finest features, hardly worth notice, next to the ugly, quite unsightly aspects of his face. There, great red cankers, boils, lesions, blisters, whelks and suppurations of every sort had taken hold. Finding not a hint of healthy flesh, nothing but a dank field of pits, craters, vile and nasty pores, these gross eruptions had formed a nation of their own.

Finn took in this disconcerting sight in a blink, and, as the lout brushed Letitia with a vile and brutish hand, Finn struck the man with the hard edge of his palm.

The man gasped and blinked his watery eyes. He stared at Finn, unable to move, unable to voice his pain. Frightened, for sure, but clearly more astonished that his hand had gone numb, every muscle locked, shocked, frozen somehow, refusing to answer his call. And all because this man had merely *touched* him, scarcely more than that.

"Enough?" Finn said. "Think you can behave yourself now, keep your filthy hands to yourself?"

"Aga-gapa-yaaaa!"

"Not what I asked, now is it?"

"Yes, all *right!*" The man paled, nearly went to his knees.

Finn let go and moved a step away. The man took a breath, caught himself and stood aright. Finn noted it didn't take long for anger to fill his eyes again.

"Magic, that's what you done. Some kinder spell."

"No," Finn said, "I did nothing of the sort. Don't ever

come near her, fellow. Never even think about touching her again."

"You had no cause fer doin' that, wasn't even fair."

The man looked at his wrist, searching for something. Sometimes magic left a sign.

"Didn't mean nothing, wasn't doin' any harm."

"Fellow, you did exactly what you meant. You know that as well as I. And, if ever you should do it again, I won't use my hand, I'll take a blade to you."

The man looked warily at Finn, took in the sword stuck in the belt about his waist. Let his eyes linger there, let them flick away. Then, because he couldn't help it, because his mind was set in evil ways, let his gaze rest upon Letitia again.

Let them, for an instant, linger on her small and slender form, on her lips, on her eyes, eyes that held a dark and iridescent light. And, once again, for he truly was devoid of all restraint, searched every hollow, every grace. Pried, meddled, poked. Assaulted, with his filthy thoughts, every secret place he'd missed before.

Letitia shuddered, drew in a breath, for she could feel him, as surely as he'd touched her, as surely as his hands had stroked her flesh. . . .

THE MAN CRIED OUT, STARTLED TO FIND HIMSELF flat on his back. He looked up in wonder, and tried to recall just how he'd gotten there.

"Get up," Finn said. "You're clearly a fellow with only half a wit. I'll try to explain this again."

Stumbling to his feet, the fellow rubbed his jaw, spat out a tooth, and looked curiously at Finn. Then, as if to further irritate his betters, he turned to Letitia again.

"I'm askin' your pardon," he said, backing off a step with half a bow. "I hope you'll be forgiving a poor unlettered fool, Missy, what's got no proper ways, but I was borned in Sessia-Troat, where there's many a Mycer folk, as I'm certain that you know.

"That's why I acted how I did, for your kind's got a way of heatin' a fella's fires. A sinful thing it is, but the head can't stop what the body's set to do—"

"Kettles and Pots, that's more than enough of you!"

Finn came at him, hand on his hilt, ready to give the lout the flat of his blade, to see him on his way.

"Stop him, help me," the man cried out, stumbling back in terror, arms flailing at the air. "Murder it is, an' I've done no harm at all!"

The act was a poor one, worse than Finn had seen in some time, but it took no talent to draw a good crowd on such a day.

"Murder, you say," said a farmer stopping by, "who be killin' who?"

"The ugly one, there, he be the one gettin' kilt," said a merchant with a great enormous nose. "That's what I heard him say."

"The other one goin' to murder him."

"I believe he is."

"One gettin' kilt, he ugly for sure."

"I seen folk dead an' buried a week, lookin' better than him."

The merchant was bald as a stone. The farmer had a thatch of yellow hair, cut, it appeared, by a madman with a saw.

In scarcely a moment, the pair were joined by another, and another after that. Finn was appalled to see that he and Letitia were suddenly surrounded by a curious, and somewhat surly crowd.

"All right, clear a way, please," he said, "no one's killing anyone, nothing's happening here."

"You hear him," the ugly said, "you hearin' what he say? Don't listen to him, friends, look what he done. *Look what he done to me!*"

With that, the fellow thrust one grimy hand at the crowd, poking the thing in their faces so everyone could see.

The folk there gasped and rolled their eyes, shrinking back from the awesome sight. Some grabbed their amulets, thrusting them at Finn.

For an instant, Finn was stunned as well. The brute's hand was no longer a hand—suddenly it appeared to be a twisted, broken thing, fingers frozen at tortured, horrid angles, a talon, a claw, caught in the throes of death.

"Damn me," he said beneath his breath, "this fool's a better actor than I thought . . ."

"This man is a trickster," he called out to the crowd. "There's nothing wrong with his hand a little work wouldn't cure. He's a lowborn fellow who lives by his wits, while the rest of you follow an honest trade."

"And what do *you* do, sir," the farmer with exploding hair wished to know. "How do you earn your bread?"

"Rumbley-rumbley-roo . . ." the crowd added to that.

"Hah!" shouted the lout, making his hand even uglier than before. "I'm the trickster, am I? Look at what he did to me. There's your trickster, good friends, there's your seer, for he did this with merely a single touch!"

"Nonsense! Foolery!" Finn said, his words quickly lost in the anger of the mob.

"And is that not enough? Is there more to this we've yet to know? There, men of County Ploone, is the rest, right there, behind the villain who's crippled me for life."

With that, his twisted hand stabbed out at Letitia Louise. The crowd surged forward, each man stretching for a look.

Letitia, who'd stood behind Finn, near paralyzed with fear, praying this horror would vanish quite soon, suddenly found herself the center of it all. Faces white as moons, moons with raggedy mouths and crater eyes, seemed to take her breath away, seemed to block out the sky.

"Finn," she said very softly, "may we leave now? I fear I don't want a sugar-pear or corn on a stick anymore."

"Easy, dear," he told her, "stay right beside me, I'll let no harm come to you."

He hoped she didn't notice he was not near as confident, not near as bold as he might sound. He was good enough with a blade, good as any man with an honest trade, but there was quite a pack now gathered about, more than a throng, say, less than a horde. Still . . .

"Back now," he said, loud enough for all to hear, only

the slightest irritation in his speech, "there's no trouble here, clear away, if you please."

"Clear away, is it?" The pock-faced rogue stepped in Finn's path, close enough to loose a foul exhalation, a stench, a rank and awesome thing that could bring a strong man to his knees.

"There, you see what I'm saying? The pretty hiding behind him there? I swear to one an' all, I seen him touch her in a sinful way, I did. A Newlie, mind you, a Mycer girl!"

The crowd came alive, a storm appearing from a clear and empty sky, a beast, aroused from sudden sleep into unthinking ire. Finn scarce had time to draw his blade fore they were on him, pounding on him, kicking at him, knocking him about. He shouted a warning to Letitia as they drove him to the ground.

"It's him what ought to be hangin' today," the grimy lout crowed, "oughta be *him* on the Grapnel and the Snip. Consorting with a beast is a crime against nature, a mortal offense, a—*Rawwwwwk!*"

Later, some would say they saw it, caught it in a blink as it slid, quivered, rustled down the back of Finn's cloak, a blur of shiny metal, a splash of brass and copper in the sun, a thing, all agreed, quite agitated, clearly disturbed, not at all pleased with the turn of events.

Only seconds after that, no two men agreed they'd seen the same. One saw iron claws rake across his boots, tearing them to shreds, one saw his trousers disappear under snapping silver jaws. One later said, he was sure a razored tail had whipped about his crotch, not an inch from his precious private parts.

Everyone agreed they'd heard a rusty cackle, heard a rattle and a hiss, heard a croak like a saw ripping through a sheet of tin. Many saw and heard things that never even happened at all. . . .

· · ·

Finn GOT TO HIS FEET, AND HELPED LETITIA OFF THE ground.

"I trust you're all right," he said, brushing her off as best he could. "I'll see someone is severely punished for this, I promise you that. The Prince himself will hear of this, love. If a person's not safe in the royal courtyard . . ."

"Finn, stop it, will you? Just quit!"

She smiled, pushing his hands gently aside, fussing with her gown. "I don't need any help, I can brush myself off. You look like a fool doing that."

Finn shrugged. "I would, perhaps, if there was anyone about. We're quite alone, it seems."

He was right, of course, she'd have to admit to that. SpringFair was crowded as ever, but there was a visible gap where a pressing mob had been before.

"I find that a great relief," Letitia said. "For a moment I was not at all certain we would make it out of there."

"There was never really any doubt," came a rasp, came a creak, from under Finn's cloak. "My senses, as ever quite acute, read that brute's intentions the moment he appeared. I would not have let him do any harm."

"Fine," Finn said. "You certainly let everyone in the county know you were there. Only no one asked for your help, Julia, no one asked you to make a spectacle of yourself."

"Please, don't shower me with gratitude. I cannot abide that."

"She did help," Letitia put in.

"I could have handled the matter myself. In scarcely a moment, those dolts would have melted under my will."

He glanced at the great clock in the royal tower overhead. "We have important things to do, and we've scarcely time to grab a bite to eat."

"If it wasn't for me," said the raspy voice again, "you'd likely have a hole in your belly, and no place to keep your lunch at all. . . ."

"Quiet," Finn said, "I didn't ask you."

"What else is new?" said Julia Jessica Slagg. "You hardly ever do . . ."

Chapter

THREE

AFTER ALL THE FRACAS, AFTER ALL THE FRAY, fatpie-and-nettle seemed to lose its taste. The ale was flat and warm by the time he got a mug, and Finn was extremely out of sorts.

Julia had been quite helpful, and that was part of the aggravation, though he'd not admit to that. The rest, of course, was the incident itself. Why, on a day such as this, when he must complete a most important task—why, with hundreds of others about, did that gross collection of sores, cankers and other eruptions have to chance upon *him*? Why not another fellow, why not anyone else? What if he'd been severely hurt, maimed, crippled for life?

There was no sound answer, of course, nor did Finn expect there to be. It was his belief the Fates had a measure of misfortune to dump on mortals every day, and there was little one could do to get out of the way.

"I trust," he said, to whoever might hear such pleas, "that you're finished with this for now . . ."

I MUST SAY," LETITIA SAID, WITH A HAND TO HER breast, "I have never been so dreadfully high. The view is lovely, but it takes my breath away."

"Indeed," Finn said, "there is no place like it in County Ploone, or in the whole country, as far as that goes. Unless one counts Mount Spleen, which, of course, is a natural site, and should not be compared to such as this."

"I should love to see a mountain sometime. Not merely Mount Spleen, though that would be fine. You've worked very hard, dear Finn. Perhaps we could take a vacation after this. Get away from home, leave our worries behind."

Finn gave her a startled look. "Our last vacation was a total disaster, have you forgotten that? I can't imagine you'd care to risk your life again."

"It wouldn't be the same, and you know it, love. Really, now. What are the chances we'd run into lunatics and demons and horrors such as that? We had a string of bad luck, is all."

"Bad luck, you say."

"Yes, that's precisely what I say. Most people never run into that sort of thing at all."

"There's that," Finn agreed, for it was certainly true. Most people merely bored themselves silly looking at historic old things and eating bad meals. Buying ridiculous items they'd throw away the moment they got back home.

Still, the idea of leaving The Lizard Shoppe, leaving the safe, familiar scenes of Garpenny Street, gave him the shudders, as it did every time it crossed his mind. There must be a reason people were where they were. Very likely, this was exactly where they were intended to be.

INDEED, LETITIA WAS RIGHT ABOUT THE VIEW FROM the Prince's Keep. Past the crowds in the royal courtyard, past the massive gatehouse and the guards, the way led through the inner court and up a dizzying set of stairs.

From there, high atop one of the four great towers, he could see beyond the banners and the pennants, past the ragged crenels and the thick curtain walls, far past the bounds of Ulster-East, past County Ploone, to the borders of Fyxedia itself.

The castle, Finn felt, though surely a wonder, was a testimony to excess. Its turrets, loops and parapets had served a purpose in ancient times. Now, this monstrous structure was merely decoration, and a costly one at that.

War was still a fearsome thing, but was no longer fought as it had been in ages past. From where Finn stood, he could see, in the distance, a most disturbing sight, one that never failed to knot his belly up tight. Above the River Dill, the brassy sky was filled with dark balloons of war, a terrible array of fat, distended hulks painted in cheerless shades of dun, gray and a noxious tone of brown.

Hanging from each of these ungainly vessels—though Finn couldn't see them from such a great distance away—were coarsely woven baskets full of men. Men from the Green Fusiliers and the Crimson Cannoneers. Home Guards, Royal Guards, Lilac Lancers and the Prince's Dragoons. Men from the bold, ever-colorful, Balloon Grenadiers.

Each, Finn knew, was headed for the battles raging in the west, and each, to a man, was very likely doomed. Doomed, as so many others who'd gone before, fighting a war that had lasted more than seven hundred years.

And what, exactly, was the war all about? You could ask around, but no one seemed to know.

Not for the first time, Finn thanked whatever gods there be that he'd been born a craftsman, fit for something better than the ghastly warrior trade.

Many a soldier went to war, but few returned alive, or wholly intact. Coldtown was filled with the shades of poor fellows who would never find rest.

.   .   .

Finn, I do believe your mind has been
a-wandering again," said Letitia Louise. "Some new marvel, I'll wager, some wondrous device that is scarcely
imagined by ordinary men."

"Why, you are unbelievable, my love," Finn said, covering his somber mien with a smile. "It's quite uncanny
how you can manage to read my every thought . . ."

LONG BEFORE HE CAME IN SIGHT, THE HIGH Chamberlain's boots sent reminders of his presence, harsh resonations striking one wall of the long corridor and then the next. Finn had long suspected that the Count VanDork nailed small bits of metal to his boots to produce this irritating sound. This, along with the six-inch heels, the less than subtle buildup in his soles, made the gawky fellow seem somewhat taller, and certainly louder, than he actually was.

"Ah, Master Finn, how very fine to see you again," the Count said, accepting what he felt was a less than fawning bow.

"And you too, Miss," he added, with a look that did little to hide the base suggestion in his watery eyes.

"Honored, sir," Letitia said, "my privilege indeed."

She lowered her head to hide the rising color in her face. She didn't like the man, loathed him, for a fact. He would not, in the presence of his peers, acknowledge his attraction to a mere Mycer girl, a creature, in his mind, beneath the notice of humankind. He would, though, grope her if he caught her alone in a corner somewhere, she had no doubt of that.

"You have it there, I see," VanDork said, speaking to Finn, nodding at the cask Letitia held in her arms.

"Wonderful. I'll take it, please."

VanDork reached for the cask. Finn held up a restraining hand.

The Count looked startled. "Really, Finn, what's this?"

"I'm grateful, sir, and honored indeed. I feel, though, that His Greatness might take offense, might, somehow, imagine a slight, might, I can even see, think I have failed in my craft, that I have asked you, in my fear, to present something less than worthy, instead of me."

"You do? Is there something wrong with it, then?"

"No, sir, I assure you there is not."

"Well, then . . ."

"You have always shown me kindness. I would not, in any way, want some deficiency, if it was seen that way, to reflect upon you."

"Yes, of course." A smile spread across the Count's bony face. "You're quite correct. You should most certainly make the presentation yourself. The Prince would be pleased with that."

"If that is your wish," Finn said.

"Oh, it is. It is indeed. Come now, he'll be ready for you soon."

VanDork brought a purple hankie to his beak of a nose and sniffed. "He has just signed the warrant for his cousin's execution. Baffleton-Kreed. Irritating fellow. Should have done him sometime ago, you ask me. But no one ever does. At any rate, His Eminence will be in a jolly mood after that. A propitious time for you, Finn. I'd say it's your lucky day. . . ."

LUCKY DAY INDEED," LETITIA SAID, CERTAIN VANDORK was strutting well ahead. "You could have been badly hurt out there, dear. I should think the least the Prince could do would be to offer some protection to a guest like you. You're not just anyone, you know."

"Yes, Letitia, that is exactly who I am. Just anyone. Please don't think I'm more than that."

"You are, too. You are a master of your craft, a most respected person, even beyond Fyxedia itself. Besides, the Prince owes you his life. He cannot have forgotten the Count Onjine affair."

"Princes have short memories, my dear. They seldom last through the day."

She wanted to move close to him, then, touch him, show her affection, but of course she didn't dare. Not with someone like VanDork around. She wouldn't be the first Newlie to share a very close, very intimate union with a human, but it wasn't something one paraded about. Not if one wished to avoid the neighbors' scorn and keep to the letter of the law.

"The Count is a horrid, despicable man," Letitia said, under her breath. "He cares not a whit for you, nor anyone else unless they serve his needs. How do people like that gain high position, Finn? It's frightening to know such a brute is so close to the Prince himself."

"That is exactly how they do it," he whispered, well aware that sound carries very well in a corridor of stone. "A ruler is ever on the watch for men with the qualities of a Count VanDork. Men with a sly demeanor, men who practice dishonor and deceit. Men who are desperate, men who are defilers, men who are debased."

"Heavens, Finn. How could a Prince begin to trust a man with such disgusting traits as that?"

"They are the only ones he *can* trust, Letitia. For these are the qualities he knows so well in himself."

Letitia shuddered and drew in a breath. "I hope this doesn't take long. I feel I need to get home and take a bath."

"If I can be of any help in that matter, I hope you won't hesitate to call."

"You'll be the first," she said, "be certain of that."

"Do I have to listen to this?" Julia muttered, from under Finn's cloak. "Can't you two contain yourselves a while?"

"What you can do," Finn said, "is be thankful I don't toss you in a tub and watch you rust to death. Don't think it hasn't crossed my mind a number of times."

Finn stopped at a hollow in the wall, drew Julia out of his cloak, and set her down.

"Now. You'll stay quietly here. Don't move, don't speak to anyone at all. Don't do anything, sit perfectly still."

"It's a blessing to have your trust," said Julia Jessica Slagg. "My kindest regards to the Prince."

"The Prince," Finn said, "has less regard for you. Be grateful you're not going inside. . . ."

T WO LARGE PIKEMEN STOOD STRAIGHT AND TALL outside the high, arched entry to the Prince's Great Hall. As the Count VanDork approached, each pounded the butt of his weapon loudly on the floor.

Noise in excess, Finn thought, seemed essential to the royal process. Princes liked the sound of boots, pikes, cannon going off and the like. They gained some pleasure from the roar of large crowds.

Finn had been in the Prince's exalted presence before, but not with Letitia Louise. And, she would surely not be there now, if the Prince's neatly flourished scroll hadn't set her name there as well. It was a matter that had delighted Letitia, and caused Finn to lose a night's sleep.

Nothing his sovereign did could put Finn at ease. The Prince was, as Finn had told Letitia, a mirror of his minions, only much more shrewd and devious than the lot.

A quick glance about the hall told Finn that the Prince had gathered a veritable herd of toadies, grovelers and spongers of every sort for this auspicious day. Each, of course, gentlemen and ladies, noble and commoner alike, was dressed in drab shades of dun, ash, umber and toast. Dull, somber and sad was the fashion in the presence of Aghen Aghenfleck the Fourth.

Finn had chosen an undistinguished brown for himself—somewhere in the liverish range—and a soot-colored gown for Letitia Louise. He was most relieved to see they both blended nicely into the dreary crowd.

AH, THERE HE IS, THERE'S A GOOD FELLOW," THE Prince shouted, bounding from his great carven chair. "Bless you, old friend, you've come to me at last!"

"I am, as ever, overwhelmed to be in your presence, sire," Finn said, bowing halfway to the floor, "a privilege unexcelled, an honor un—"

"Yes, yes, of course you are," the Prince said, dismissing Finn's praise with a wave of his hand. "And this, I'll wager, is your charming serving girl. Lavinia, is it not?"

"Letitia, sire," Letitia said, "though Lavinia will do if you desire."

"No, no, no, I won't have it. By all means, keep the name you've got. I'm sure you're quite used to it now."

"Thank you, sire."

"And, Letitia," the Prince said, with a sly wink at Finn that Letitia didn't miss, "do you serve your master well?"

"Though I strive to carry out my duties, I would not presume to answer, sire," Letitia said. "It is my master who must tell you that."

"Well said, girl, well said, indeed!"

The Prince applauded, and swept his gaze about the court to make certain everyone followed his lead.

An overly garish fellow at any time, Finn thought the Prince especially appalling on SpringFair Day. His cutaway was a lustrous, iridescent blue, his vest a vivid pumpkin, his breeches a bright domino in pink and tangerine. One shoe was lilac, the other vivid green. His dashing, wide-brimmed hat was topped with plumes of crimson, salmon and lime. Colors, incidentally, which mirrored the coat of arms of the Aghenfleck Dynasty itself.

Yet, Finn mused, nothing could disguise what lay beneath that rich array. The Prince was a handsome man of charming mien, a man of scarcely thirty years, yet there was something old, something wicked there. An essence, a nature, that set even the slyest, most dissolute members of the court a'twitch when Aghen of Aghenfleck looked them in the eye. . . .

"She is, then, a worthy servant?" asked His Grace, pleased with his wit, determined to amuse his followers even more. "She is ever obedient, and answers to your will?"

"She is a good worker, sire," Finn answered, as if this sovereign were playing no games with him at all. "I have no complaints."

"Good. Nor would I, I'm sure." He turned his eyes on Letitia again. "I shall speak to you more, my dear. At a later time. There is little I know of the Mycer folk, and you could help me learn about your kind."

"Yes, sire. . . ."

Finn felt a sudden chill at the Prince's words. He saw Letitia pale and quickly turn away.

"*Apples and Stones,*" he muttered beneath his breath, "*what indecent thought is churning through that foul and odious head of yours now?*"

Chapter

FIVE

F INN, HOW VERY GOOD TO SEE YOU. IT'S BEEN
some time, I fear."

Finn turned at the familiar voice. An older man with
thinning hair and kindly eyes stepped from the crowd and
gripped Finn's hand. He, too, glanced at Letitia, but there
was no lechery there, only a gentle smile.

"Lord Gherick, a pleasure," said Finn. "Indeed, it has
been a year or more."

"Closer to two," Gherick said. "I'm getting stouter,
and you're getting slim. You must come and dine with me,
we'll soon take care of that."

"At your will, I'll do it, too."

"Gherick, I didn't know you were here," the Prince
said, no little hint of irritation in his speech. "I thought
you were going to the country for a while."

"I did, sire. And, with your pleasure, I'm back again."

"Yes, I see that you are . . ."

Though Finn knew full well the two were brothers, it
was hard to see how one could be remotely kin to the next.
Like air and water, they were, like fish and fowl. More, to
the point, like night and the light of day.

Gherick, the Prince knew, was the only man among his
various kinsmen—and kinswomen as well—who did not
lust after his throne. Thus, he was wary of his brother,
and had him watched at all times.

"I must apologize for this most unseemly interruption," Gherick said, easily sensing his brother's ire. "We'll talk another time, my friend."

"No, no, stay," the Prince said. "You have been too long from me, brother. Your presence, and your counsel, is sorely missed in Fyxedia, and in the royal house itself."

"It is gracious of you to say so, sire." Gherick bowed, fully aware there was no one in the court, most especially Aghen Aghenfleck himself, who believed a word of drivel such as that.

"Well, then," said the Prince, clasping his fingers in a knot above his chest, "we are here for an occasion, are we not? You have brought me a craft of your making, Master Finn. I believe the lovely Newlie person is clutching it to her, ah—to her breasts, is she not?"

"She is, sire. If you will permit . . ."

"No, no, no," the Prince said, waving him away, "you may bring it to me yourself, my dear."

Letitia had the good sense not to glance at Finn, not to hesitate at all. With a graceful step, she bowed and set the wooden cask in the Prince's hands. Somehow, Aghen Aghenfleck managed to brush his fingertips across hers.

"Open it, if you will, then. And set the contents on the table there."

Letitia obeyed, opened the crafted lid and gently set Finn's work on the marbled table before the Prince.

Muttered whispers greeted the marvel. Courtiers crowded forward to get a better look, each one giving the illusion they were quite familiar with what there was to see. Each, however, holding smiles or frowns at bay, waiting for the Prince to lead the way.

The Prince, alone, did not move at all, but only studied the object with his eyes. Shifted his gaze from the left to the right, from the bottom to the top, then started all over again. He muttered and wheezed, cleared his throat, rolled his tongue about his cheek.

Finally, he said, without looking away, "I am astonished, Master Finn. Truly I am. It's a marvel, a wonder, a
miracle of the age. I find that I am stunned, stupefied,
awed at your genius, partially impressed. What, sir, exactly is it, then? You must tell me that?"

The Prince, then, let the hint of a smile escape his lips,
enough to draw approval from the crowd.

"Why, it is a timepiece, sire," Finn explained, with all
the patience at his command. "A timepiece in the shape of
a lizard, if you please. As you ordered, sire. The lizard,
you will note, is rampant, upon its hind legs. In its right
foreleg, it holds the banner of the House of Aghenfleck,
and in its left, the pennant of Llowenkeef-Grymm. Its
snout is agape to display its silver teeth and red-enameled
tongue.

"Its eyes are set with emeralds, and each individual
scale, on the body and the entire surface of the tail, is
crafted of gold. The timepiece itself, as you see, is set in
the belly of the lizard. The numbers are formed of rubies
and sapphires, and the hands are carved of precious shell.
The whole of the face is protected with the finest crystal
glass. The delicate works, the tiny cogs and gears, the
wires and the hummers and the wheels, are deftly packed
inside.

"It is, I trust, as Your Grace intended it to be. Or,
surely, as close as my poor talents can come to the vision
you conveyed to me."

"Hmmmmmph." The Prince scratched his chin.
"What do you think, Count?"

"Quite nice," VanDork answered at once. "As Master
Finn says, I believe he's caught at least a bit of Your
Grace's creative drive, a flame of your inner fire—"

"Yes, indeed. Go sit somewhere. And do something
about your breath."

"I believe that simpering fool Llowenkeef will like it,"
the Prince told Finn. "Fellow's daft about clocks. They

say he's got clocks everywhere. Eats with clocks, goes to *bed* with clocks. At any rate, it's his bloody birthday, can't forget that."

The Prince frowned. "How does the thing work, how does it go?"

"One sets the tail in motion, sire. It acts as a pendulum, swinging back and forth. Upon the hour, the jeweled eyes roll about, the snout opens, and it makes a, ah—crackly sort of sound. If Your Grace will allow—"

"No, do nothing of the sort. I abhor things that move or make any kind of sound.

"I will say, Finn, it's a pleasure to see you making a rather decent-looking lidert these days. . . ."

"Lizard, sire."

"Yes, what I said. Not at all like that nasty creature you carry about. The one, you'll recall, that tried to bite my leg. I am still displeased about that."

Finn showed no expression at all. Julia Jessica Slagg had, indeed, reacted to the Prince in much the same manner as nonmechanical creatures. In other words, she loathed His Grace on sight, and somewhat lost control. Finn had managed to stop her in time, and, thus, likely preserved his head.

"It was the most regrettable moment of my life, sire. A tiny mote of dust where none should be. It would never happen again in a hundred lifetimes, I hope Your Grace understands that."

"Better *not* happen again," the Prince muttered. "Best you confine yourself to liderts that do something useful, Finn. Like swabbing out muskets, grinding trash and such. Making things that tell the time, right?"

"I could not agree more, sire."

"Good, good," the Prince said, shaking his head so the plumes atop his hat swayed in the breeze. "One thing more, Finn, and I'll see you on your way. A thing of great import, a duty to your Prince. A—What, what the devil do you want, Count," the Prince said, scowling at VanDork, "I'm quite busy here."

"Your pardon, sire, indeed." VanDork leaned close to the Prince's ear. In an instant, the Prince broke into a merry smile, stood up straight and threw his hands in the air.

"Here, all of you, come see. They're going to mush old Baffleton-Kreed!"

Chapter

SIX

A VOLLEY OF CHEERS ROSE FROM THE ROYAL sycophants. If Lord Gherick had not appeared at that moment, Finn was sure he and Letitia would have been trampled beneath the crowd.

"Quickly," Gherick said, drawing the pair aside. "You'll be safe over here."

"Safe from what?" Letitia asked, bewildered by the sudden turmoil in the hall.

Gherick didn't answer, but urged them on until they were up against the far wall.

Finn drew in a breath. In an instant, the great room was empty, for everyone there had followed the Prince to the gallery that overlooked the courtyard below.

"Can't we see too?" Letitia complained. "I didn't understand, dear. What is it they're going to do?"

"If I'm not mistaken," Finn said, "it's something you very much want to miss."

Gherick's expression told him he was right. The Prince's brother glanced at the ceiling with a sigh.

"They're executing His Grace's Keeper of the Mead," Gherick said. "Aghen's been out of sorts with the fellow for some time, though I can't see why. Nothing wrong with his ale, near as I can tell."

"Oh. Oh, my," Letitia said.

"Chopping Day is a strain on everyone, Miss. My

brother *will* have it on SpringFair, though. Says it keeps the people on their toes, and I suppose it's so."

"I'm not sure it's worth it," Finn said, "just for crackle pie and cheese. Letitia makes it better than anyone here."

"How kind of you to say so, Finn."

"It's quite true. And the tarts are doughy here as well—"

Finn's voice was lost as a terrible, desperate wail arose from the courtyard below. A cry of such pain, agony and torment the hair nearly stood straight up on Finn's head.

"I'm going to be ill, Finn."

"Don't," Gherick said. "You mustn't do that here. Aghen doesn't like that sort of thing at all."

"I'll be fine," Letitia said.

"Please do. If I'm anywhere around, he's inclined to blame me."

"Why should he do that?"

"Why not? Why do you think I stay out of town?"

"Good reason, I suppose," Finn said.

"Damned if it isn't. Pardon my language, Miss."

"No offense. You are most kind, sir . . ."

Finn looked up to see the Prince returning from the gallery, the crowd all a-chatter at his back. Count VanDork whispered something in his ear, and the Prince broke out in a hearty laugh. More than a chuckle or a snort, close to a guffaw.

"Exhilarating, marvelous! Make a note, VanDork, we must have another mushing quite soon. Next week, no later than that."

"Wonderful idea, Your Grace. I'll see to it."

"Finn, should have had you out there, something a fellow doesn't see every day. You should stay for the show tonight. We're roasting old Bechidal, my worthless seer. Fellow can't cast a simple spell anymore."

"You're too kind, sire."

"True. I am indeed. Now . . . Oh, back to you, then. One more thing and we'll have you out of here. VanDork, that what's-his-name. The, uh—Damn your hide, do I have to do everything myself? Get him in here!"

VanDork disappeared. Finn could see the Prince was clearly on the edge of irritation. Gherick had told him more than once—and everyone else appeared to know— that Aghen Aghenfleck could not pursue the same subject more than a moment and a half. If he did, sweat began to form on his brow and dangerous thoughts popped into his head. As His Grace turned on Finn, it looked as if that might be happening now.

"Do you see what I have to put up with, Finn? I have to do everything myself. None of these—worthless louts can lift a finger if I'm not—not—You see? Nothing's happening, everyone's just *standing* there, waiting to see what *I'm* going to do. Why can't I have a simple trade like yours, Finn? Why? Why—can't—I—ever—be—*me!*"

The Prince pounded out his words on the arm of his chair. Gherick muttered something that Finn couldn't hear.

Then, as quickly as this murderous mood had struck, it was just as quickly gone, as something new appeared before the Prince's eyes.

A collective sigh swept through the crowd. From an anteroom behind the Prince's chair, a giant, a pillar, a mountain of a creature came into view. Save for the monstrous Grizz, the Bullie was the largest of the Newlies, the nine beings changed from the animals they'd been before.

And, like all of the Newlies, the Bullie kind retained some reminders of their past. This fellow was tall, hulking, broad-shouldered, immense across the chest. His neck was thick and his eyes were the color of muddy glass. Short, stumpy horns were nearly lost in his braided hair.

His great arms were covered with lewd tattoos, and he wore a golden ring in his nose, some rite from ages gone.

"Ah, here's the one, Finn. Enormous brute, is he not? What's your name again, I can't tell you fellows apart."

"Bucerius, sire."

His voice seemed to come from some great hollow in his chest. It was clear from his expression that he didn't like the Prince at all, and didn't care if anyone knew.

"You hear him, Finn? His name's Bucerius. I expect you can remember that."

"Why, yes, Your Grace," Finn said, puzzled at the question. "I'm certain that I can."

"Good. Yes. Well, I—believe that's all, is it not? You may leave now, Master Finn. I have much to do and—Damn you, VanDork, now what?"

"I would merely remind Your Grace . . ." said the Count, bending close to the Prince's ear.

"Ah, yes. Well. Here's the thing, Finn. You and what's-his-name here, you will deliver this timepiece gadget of yours to King Llowenkeef-Grymm, in Heldessia Land. Personally, mind you, no nattering dolts and hanger-on types like VanDork here. Right into that miserable person's hands."

Finn stared. "Heldessia? Sire, we're at war with Heldessia. How could I possibly do that?"

"Of course there's a war, Finn. There's always a war. You telling me I can't send a birthday present to that damned oaf because there's a *war* on? Are you daft, or what?"

"Sire, how could I possibly get to the King's court? I mean, if you were truly serious, and this wasn't a magnificent bit of humor on Your Grace's part?"

"Easy, friend," Lord Gherick said, so softly no one else might hear.

"Why, the same way everyone gets there. By balloon, of course. Master Finn, I fear you're not listening to me."

Indeed, at that moment, Finn could hear nothing at all. Nothing, it seemed, but the terrible silence where his heartbeat used to be. . . .

> *slice 'im up*
> *cut 'im up*
> *rippity-split!*
> *crack 'im up*
> *rack 'im up*
> *chop 'im up a bit!*

HAND IN HAND THE CHILDREN DANCED, DANCED in dizzy circles, danced around their fires, danced in the shadow of the great high towers, danced in the gloom of the fast-approaching night. Happy little urchins, cheery little waifs, raggedy-muffs with runny noses and bright shiny eyes. They danced and they sang and they circled about in the empty courtyard, round and round and round and round about . . .

And, when the story was done, they all fell down, screamed and wailed and thrashed about. Choked, croaked, stuck their tongues out in horrid parodies of death. Laughed till they cried, shrieked with great delight. Got up and started all over again. . . .

FINN SCARCELY NOTED THIS GRIM EVENT, WAS hardly aware of the empty stalls and tents, the clutter and the waste, the foul and odorous remains of SpringFair and the Chopping of May.

His mind was so numbed, so fuddled and stunned, he was greatly surprised to see they were very nearly home, back in Garpenny Street.

Indeed, he had been so angry and distressed, he'd forgotten to retrieve Julia Jessica Slagg from the niche outside the Royal Hall. It was Letitia, then, who had no choice but to still her own fears, who stopped to retrieve the lizard herself—the lizard, and that damnable clock, which had cast a dark shadow over all their lives.

Farther from the castle, Letitia let Julia down to scuttle along by herself. The lizard croaked and complained about that, for as quick and agile as she surely might be when such a need arose, Julia knew that walking was not her most graceful attitude.

"You mustn't be upset," Letitia said, determined to break the silence Finn wore like a cloak about himself. "He can't *make* you do this, Finn, you don't *have* to go."

Finn stopped, shaken, for a moment, from his dark and desolate thoughts.

"He can't? What on earth gave you an idea like that?"

"There are laws, you know. Laws and rules and regulations of every sort. You're a citizen and a—a human, Finn. You have certain rights like everyone else."

"That's partially true."

"You can be heard. You can declare a grief."

"A grievance."

"I just said that, didn't I?"

"Yes, and I believe you chose the better word, not I."

"Well, then. It will be all right, I'm sure. They certainly can't send you somewhere in an awful balloon. I know you. You'd be scared out of your wits up there."

"I'm scared out of my wits right now, and I'm standing in Garpenny Street on solid cobblestone. Letitia, love, do you recall our conversation, as we were approaching the Royal Hall?"

"Of course I do. Why would I forget what we talked about, my dear?"

"We discussed how Count VanDork was a despicable person, and that the reason he is, is that he mirrors the equally despicable character of his master, the Prince. The Prince, with the help of a veritable horde of vermin like VanDork, makes the laws and rules and regulations. These laws do not apply to them. They do apply to us."

"But Finn . . ." Letitia bit her lip, her voice no longer firm, no longer bold. Doubt, now, seemed to slip in and push resolution aside.

"You're not a vagrant, you know. You're not of common folk. You're a—a master of your craft is what you are. You know people of quality like Lord Gherick, brother of the Prince."

"Yes I do."

"Well, then?"

"I don't like to say it, but we can't be sure Gherick didn't know about this."

"Surely not. He's such a nice man, Finn."

"He made himself absent as soon as Aghenfleck gave us the news. I turned around and he was gone."

"They're not really close, are they?"

"Aghen Aghenfleck isn't close to anyone, as far as I know."

"He certainly wasn't close to that other relation of his. That . . . oh, dear, Finn."

"His cousin, Baffleton-Kreed. They grew up together. Inseparable, I understand."

Letitia looked up at Finn. In the near end of the day, her eyes seemed enormous pools of liquid night. And in those pools, he saw a reflection of himself, an

image blurred by a tear, which Letitia quickly wiped
away.

"I'm not being rational, am I," she said, turning from
him then. "I'm making up pretty endings in my head."

"Somewhat, yes. But there's nothing greatly wrong
with that."

"It is, yes. If it holds no truth at all. Oh, Finn . . ."

He held her, then, and in a moment she simply turned
and walked quickly across the street and opened the latch
with her key. She appeared for an instant, before the dim
lantern in the hall, and then she was gone. A moment
later, Julia squeezed through the portal and followed
Letitia inside. There, but a few steps from the door of his
house, Finn felt as if he'd never been so utterly, completely alone. . . .

Chapter

EIGHT

WITH DARKNESS CAME THE USUAL SOUNDS of night, the boots of a pair of guardsmen on Greenberry Street up the hill, the rattle of a blade against a studded belt. A shout from a fisherman, working on his nets, perhaps, on the river below.

And, at the end of Garpenny Street, a drift of wispy figures, disembodied souls, phantoms in ragged disarray. One might run out of ale in Ulster-East, Finn reflected, or sacks of wheat meal, but there was never any shortage of the dear departed in town. Foul deeds, pestilence—and, of course, the war—took care of that. The pale and spectral lights of Coldtown were a grim reminder that death was truly an alternate way of life.

Someone down the street, likely the Wheelcrafter's wife, had left food out for the Coldies that night. For though the dead no longer fed in the ordinary way, they ever hungered for the savor, the essence, the joyous scents of suppers past.

Letitia might have remembered to leave them something herself, especially on SpringFair, had the day not lingered so long and ended on such an unpleasant note.

A WARM EVENING WIND MADE ITS WAY DOWN the hill, past Wesser and Doob and Winkerdown Square, on into Garpenny Street. The sign above Finn's head began to creak, and he knew he ought to grease the thing and give the carven lizard a coat of green and gold. Such thoughts had occurred a dozen times before, and somehow the work was never done.

Truly, it was a task worth his time, for it was the symbol of his trade, and folk judged a craftsman by what they saw *outside* his shop, not what was done within.

It was not a fair appraisal, of course, for many of the signs on the street that pictured swords, pies, ale and mead and spells, did not reflect the quality of goods and services offered inside.

Take Bickershank the Booter, for one. A man would do better to walk unshod on broken glass, than to trust his feet to the torturous wares of Master Bickershank. Once, Finn had caught a glimpse of the fellow's own bare feet, and he had never passed the shop again. . . .

He paused, then, cocked his head and listened, certain he had heard a sound that didn't belong to the ordinary noises of the night. A shuffle and a scrape, a rattle and a shake, something such as that.

Still, after a moment, when it didn't come again, he decided he was simply out of sorts from the misadventures of the day.

And what would be so strange about that? Who wouldn't feel adrift after what I've been through?

And, worse still, the fear, the awful trepidation, the lurch in his belly, the knowledge that tomorrow would be a hundred times worse than today.

As much as Finn loathed Aghen Aghenfleck, he found it hard to work up righteous anger at the Prince. In the face of such unthinking folly, such total unreason, it was like getting mad at a solid stone wall. You could kick it, curse it till you were blue in the face, and the damned thing still didn't know you were there.

Millions of men had died, and death would claim untold numbers more in the brutal, senseless war between Fyxedia and Heldessia Land that had dragged on more than seven hundred years. Finn had no idea what they were fighting for, and had never found anyone who did.

Yet, in spite of the carnage and destruction, the maimed, the mutilated and the dead, Prince Aghen Aghenfleck found the time to send a gift—a birthday present, mind you—a golden lizard with a clock in its belly, to the horrid, despised King of Heldessia, Llowenkeef-Grymm himself.

"Why?" he said aloud, and answered himself at once. Easy enough, as the words were his own, loosed not long before. "Because neither law nor reason applies to princes and kings. They do as they will, and damn the rest of us poor bloody souls!

"And, if a craftsman should tell a prince he does not wish to waste his precious time making lizards with clocks in their bellies, he might find himself some fine holiday on the Grapnel and the Snip.

"Or," he added, "a *mushing*, whatever sort of horror that may be. . . ."

"Someone told me once, that he who talks to himself is conversing with a fool. I suppose there's truth in that."

Finn didn't bother to turn around. "I told you that, as you know. I have also said that every adage, every saw, every chestnut of advice, contains its own exception to the rule."

Julia Jessica Slagg gave a rusty cackle and waddled into sight.

"The exception being when Master Finn babbles to himself. I think I see now."

"You don't, and no one asked your opinion, as far as I can tell."

"No one ever does."

"And might that tell you something? Might it be some kind of clue? Julia, what are you doing out here? Do I appear lonely, in need of company tonight? Is this what's whirring about in your head?"

Julia opened her silver snout and showed him a row of razored teeth.

"I was somewhat anxious. I simply couldn't sleep."

"Of course you couldn't sleep. You're not supposed to. You're a mechanical device."

"We've discussed this before. You say I don't, I say I do. Finn, I have to tell you Letitia is handling all this much too well. She fell into bed, went right to sleep. She hasn't let herself believe what is happening here. Our imminent departure, the gravity of the event, the danger most apparent in such a voyage, has yet to fully hit her. When it does, I strongly urge you to be prepared for weeping and wailing, hysterics of every sort."

Finn shook his head. "I had no idea you were qualified to give medical advice."

"Play me for a fool if you like, but tell me I'm wrong. Tell me she will take your almost certain impending demise with perfect ease."

Finn looked Julia in the eye. In a set of ruby, unblinking eyes, as it were.

"I grant your concern is well founded. Still, I believe she'll handle this better than you think. And, on two grounds, Julia, I have to say you're quite wrong. One, in spite of the fact that it's suicidal to even get *close* to a balloon, I intend to survive and get back here intact.

"Two, you mentioned *our* departure. It's not our departure, it's mine. You're not going, you're staying here."

"What?" Julia gave a rude and horrid squawk, like the howl of rusty iron.

"You're joking, of course. You'd be daft to embark on such a treacherous journey without my presence. Why, you wouldn't last a day without me at your side. You've lost your reason, Finn, what little wit you have, you—"

"Stop. Right there." Finn raised a restraining hand.

"There can be no argument here. None. Stop squawking for a minute and listen to me. Yes, this is a fool's journey, I've the wit to know that. I feel I'll throw up a lot, and risk death a number of times.

"I could surely use your help. But I need you more here. I'll regret these words the rest of my life, but it's true you have uncanny senses, beyond the ken of any human or Newlie alive. You can hear things, smell things, see things no other creature can.

"What you can do is protect Letitia Louise. Warn her of danger, and fight all intruders, if it should come to that. This is why I need you here. I'm sure you understand, now that I've made it perfectly clear."

Julia flicked her brass tongue. Her scales seemed to quiver, though the air was perfectly still.

"What I see," she said, "is what you'd have me believe. What I'm thinking, is that while I am truly invaluable and superior to fleshly creatures in every way, Letitia is intelligent, resourceful, and completely capable of taking care of herself. You have left her alone before, and never mentioned any great concern. What greater threat do you feel is lurking about Ulster-East now?"

"You weren't there, or you wouldn't ask."

"Wouldn't ask what?"

"The Prince. Aghen Aghenfleck. His eyes drank her in, Julia. Tasted her with his filthy gaze, as if she were some fine exotic wine brought to court for his pleasure. 'I will speak to you more, my dear, at a later time,' he tells her. 'You could help me learn much of the Mycer folk,' he said."

"Surely a creature like the Prince befouls every female he looks upon," Julia said.

In spite of a warming breeze, Finn felt a sudden chill. "Surely indeed. And many get more than a glance, and have no wits about them when the Prince has filled his needs. That will not happen to Letitia Louise. And, if I'm not thinking better on this on the morrow, I'll not take this damned mission at all. I will take you and Letitia and leave behind everything I've worked for here, and flee to some other land."

"And where would that be?" asked Julia Jessica Slagg. "Where are the kings and princes wise? Where are the nobles truly noble, Finn?"

Finn, gazing off into the darkness of the night, had no ready answer for that. . . .

INDEED, AS JULIA HAD SAID, LETITIA WAS DEEP IN peaceful sleep when Finn finally cast his thoughts aside and quietly joined her in the small bedchamber above The Lizard Shoppe.

Slipping out of his clothes, he snuffed the single candle and slipped in beside her in the dark.

As ever, Finn was awed by the touch, by the presence, by the magic of this lovely creature who shared his bed and brought joy to his life. *Fate,* he thought, not for the first time, *bestows its wonders in ways no mortal can comprehend.* Less than a year had passed since Letitia had come into his home as housekeeper and cook, someone to do those tasks that needed doing while he spent long hours pursuing his craft.

It was clear, when he hired her, that she was a most attractive Newlie, a charming Mycer girl with dark, iridescent eyes, small, but pouty lips, and a rather pointy nose that turned up nicely at the tip. Her ears rose to delicate points beneath her ashen hair, and her skin had the soft, downy texture of her kind.

All these qualities he noticed, but cast them in a corner of his mind for the time, most of his head being crammed, jammed with thoughts of silver wheels that whined and hummed, golden wires thin as gnat whiskers, tiny cogs and gears, and gems no bigger than poppy seeds.

Then, on a day much like the one before that, when a lizard that peeled potatoes didn't seem to work at all, he suddenly looked up and saw her standing there, holding a cup of clover tea.

Finn was struck dumb at the sight, dazzled by her opalescent eyes, eyes that seemed immersed in dark and fragrant oil. Stunned by the way every beam of sunlight shimmered in her hair.

That moment of wonder passed; nothing was said or done, nothing for a time. Letitia, though, felt a flush at Finn's glance that began at her toes and nearly exploded through the top of her head. For she had fallen for him the instant she walked into his house—and, until that moment, was sure he'd seldom looked at her twice.

Misadventure and dread, fearsome times kept further declarations at bay. But, as fortune would have it, these dire events seemed to bring them closer still, and, finally, toss them into one another's arms, and they had seldom been far from one another since. . . .

How COULD I HAVE BEEN SO BLIND?" FINN HAD asked her a hundred times since. "I should have known at first sight you were the love of my life."

"The important thing is, you *did* come around, my dear," she told him. "And, often, love takes its time to strike."

Especially for the male, who has to be struck in the head before he can open his eyes . . .

They WOULD EVER PAY A PRICE FOR THEIR DEVOtion, and both knew it well. They might be husband and wife to one another, but never in the public eye. Any sort of intimate relations between a human and a Newlie was forbidden by the law. While many folk no longer cared just who did what with whom, others were filled with righteous gall, wouldn't stand for habits different from their own, and handed out dread judgment in the dark of night.

Would it ever be different, Finn often wondered, or would the world always be the same?

THE "CHANGE" HAD TURNED THE WORLD UPSIDE down, and many Newlies—as well as humankind— thought turning beasts into something similar to Man had brought great sorrow to everyone.

Shar and Dankermain, the seers who'd done this deed three hundred years before, had paid for their crime with their lives. The spawn of their sin, though, were left behind to breed in a world where they didn't belong.

Now, as well as Mycers, there were Bowsers, Snouters, Foxers, Yowlies and Grizz. Vampies, Bullies, Dobbins and Badgie kind, strewn all about the known world.

And, if the Mycer folk were one of the Chosen Nine, and if a man named Finn fell in love with a being who was, truly, not solely a person at all, what was he to do— shut out his feelings, or sleep with one eye open, in case some loony decided to "purify" them both some dark and sorry night?

And you, Finn thought to himself, not for the first time or the last, *why did you do the same, and break such laws as well?*

For, much like the two mad sorcerers themselves, he had flouted nature himself, giving life to Julia Jessica Slagg, a creature not of flesh, but brass and copper, gold and iron and tin. More that that, he had given his creation the brain of a ferret, a poor creature caught in a trap and nearly dead.

And why? He had answered that question long ago. Though his was no act of magic, he had done this deed for much the same reason as the seers: Because he had the talent, the flair. He had dared the act of creation because he could.

UNABLE TO PUT SUCH THOUGHTS ASIDE, FINN SAT up, eased himself out of bed, and walked to the window to peer out into the dark. The sky was clear and a million stars blazed with a cold and fearsome light.

To the west was the river, dark except for a few dim lanterns on the masts of fishing boats. Finn could imagine the men and Newlies there preparing their nets for the day, and wondered what life was like for those who plied their trade on the twisting waterways.

Not far from the river, up the rise upon the hill, were the heights of the royal palace. Bright lights always burned there. Sometimes one could hear their reveling far into the night. Princes and their toadies didn't have to work the next day; there were lesser fools hired to do that.

Finally, Finn forced himself to look to the east. There was the glow of the Royal Balloon Yards, a pale, threatening cloud of dirty orange, and below, an eerie yellow light.

The light, and the pall of dirty smoke, meant the Grounder Crews were stoking the coals in the great hot furnaces there, pits of fire that never went out through the rains of summer or the howl of winter storms. The work went on under the high, timbered roofs, work that never ceased because the war never stopped, and the great balloons must rise every day. Rise, and float out across the river, past the swampy land where the enemy's balloons waited to meet their foes.

There, men would fight and men would die. Men would come back bloody and maimed, missing an arm or a leg. Some, who clearly had no luck at all, would live to fight another day.

And what will I lose, if indeed I do not lose it all? An eye, a toe? An arm or maybe two? A fine lizard-maker that'd be. . . .

"Scones and Stones," he said softly, gripping the sill and staring into the night, "if I'm not whole, I'll not come back at all. I will never burden dear Letitia with some gross and mutilated creature, some piece of a man who drags his poor shell about the streets, begging for a pence or two. By damn, I will not. And if I've not the limbs to do myself in, I'll hire some fellow for the job. I'll do that before I'll—

"Huh? What's that?" His wretched thoughts slipped away, and he quickly found his wits, instantly aware of the hulking figure looming against the night down below. And, with a chill, he knew at once it was a Bullie peering up at him in the dark, for nothing in Ulster East could match the creature's size. "You, what do you want?"

"Don't fear, little fellow," came the deep, yet scarcely heard whisper from below. "I means you no harm. Be coming down here if you will."

"It's—Bucerius, yes?" Finn said, searching for the name. "I have that right, do I not?"

"Close enough, human."

"I'll—I shall be right with you, then."

Finn quickly found his trousers and slipped into a shirt. His boots were not in sight, and he decided to do without. Letitia stirred in her sleep, and Finn prayed she wouldn't wake up.

"Shall I come with you?" said Julia Jessica Slagg from the dark.

"And do what? Wrestle him to the ground?"

Julia didn't answer. Finn hurried quickly down the stairs, slipped the lock on his thick oaken door—a door he had always felt secure, until this very night.

"You being at the balloonin' place," the Bullie announced. "I sees you there when the sun be rising again."

"Did you come here to tell me that?"

"No."

"No. Then what?"

"We be goin' to Heldessia Land. If fortune be with us, we be comin' back as well. I be tellin' you this. I am not liking human persons at all."

"All right, I guess I can live with that."

Finn stared up at the Bullie. The sky, the stars, the universe itself had disappeared. There was nothing else to see but the monstrous, somewhat odorous form, that blocked out the night.

"If you don't like human—persons, why do you work for the Prince? Why don't you do something else?"

Bucerius shrugged, a major event in itself.

"Business is business. Money be talkin', and a Prince be no worse than anyone else."

"Point well taken," Finn said. "Sunrise then, all right? I feel we're off for a really fun time."

"That be a humor, is it not?"

"Sort of, yes. Close enough."

"Don't."

"Don't what?"

"Don't be doin' it again. My folk isn't likin' joke, whimsy, slappers of any sort. You be joking, keep it to yourself."

"Fine, I will," Finn said. "You have a nice night."

"Be watching good, human. Might be trouble you havin' before it get light."

"What? What kind of trouble, what are you talking about?"

"Something bad. Something like this maybe coming here again."

"Something like what?—"

Finn froze in his tracks. The enormous creature reached down behind him, lifted up a big potato sack, then another after that. When both of these burdens hung snugly on his shoulder, he turned back to Finn.

In the dark of night, Finn was uncertain if what he was seeing was real. The two potato sacks seemed to squirm, seemed to wiggle, refuse to sit still. Something in there shuddered, something in there *moved*. More than that, vague, incoherent sounds came from the sacks as well.

"When sun comin' up, you bein' there," the Bullie said. "We be leaving, catching the easterly wind."

"Yes, fine. Easterly wind . . . Look, I don't feel you answered my question about what trouble might appear. And something, I guess you know, is stirring in your sacks."

Bucerius rumbled, deep within his chest. His features twisted in disgust. "Human person don't be listenin' at all. Fellow you be fighting with, fellow be ugly, even for one of your kind. He comin' here with a friend. Goin' to be doing you in, is what he got in mind."

Finn felt the hairs climb the back of his neck.

"That lout at the fair . . . He's in your, uh—"

"Might be he gots another friend, might be he don't. You be where I'm sayin', all right? Don't be messing up my business, human person. You hear?"

Finn didn't answer. He stood on his doorstep, stood very still. He watched, as the Bullie hefted his sacks more easily on his shoulder and stomped down Garpenny

Street toward the river way. He wanted to ask what his shipmate, his ponderous companion, his new best friend—who didn't care for whimsy—intended to do down there. On the other hand, he didn't really want to know at all. . . .

Chapter

TEN

FROM AFAR, FINN HAD SMELLED THE NOXIOUS fumes when the wind was from the west, heard the clamor, heard the roar of the great eternal fires, seen the ruddy glow against the night. Never had he felt the slightest need, the least desire, to go near the horrid place.

Never, and that included now.

A horde of men and Newlies swarmed about, shouted, bellowed, cursed one another, caught in seeming chaos, total disarray. Some clutched ropes that dangled from the sky, lines that held the great, sluggish war balloons in tow.

Some manned the endless complexity of valves, flues, nozzles and such affixed to the pulsing, swollen tubes that snaked across the grounds. The tubes themselves emerged like multilimbed demons from the fiery sheds where coal, through some alchemic means, conjured itself into gas that fed the ever-hungry balloons.

Then, having had their fill, these giant, bloated creatures could scarcely be contained upon the ground. It took much effort, strength, and obscenities as well to keep them from breaking their tethers and rising into the tainted air. . . .

"You be gettin' a move on, human person. We runnin' out of wind, runnin' outta time!"

A shout, coupled with a ferocious grip that nearly took his shoulder off, shook Finn out of his thoughts.

"If we miss the wind, then what?" Finn said. "We don't have to go?"

"Not be *goin'* to miss it, you hearing this, you unnerstan'?"

"Yes, I think I've got it," Finn said, fully grasping the Bullie's ire. "Perfectly clear to me."

"Good. You keepin' up now, I don' be askin' you again."

Without another word, Bucerius stomped off across the noisy, crowded flats, through the flurry, through the tangle and the maze of ropes and lines and nets, through the mud and the mire, the curses and the shouts, and the vast, bloated herd of captive balloons that overshadowed them all.

The Royal Balloon Grounds were a mix of human and Newlie alike. A crowd of Snouters leaped aside as Bucerius plowed through their ranks, scattering the fellows in his path. One went sprawling on his back, giving the others a hearty laugh.

They were stout, short creatures with ugly noses— noses that gave them their common name—beings with tiny pit eyes and scarcely any chins at all. Most wore the overalls of farmers, for this crew was bringing crates of vegetables and fruits to the balloons. To Finn's eyes, their merchandise was somewhat wilted and overripe, produce that shoppers in the market wouldn't buy.

Bullies, too, were all about, barely clad giants that loomed above the crowd, hefting loads of every sort upon their broad and muscled backs. Finn didn't fail to notice they all gave Bucerius a fierce and bitter glance, for his dress and manner said he didn't have to make a living with his back, the task so common to his kind.

Still, the Bullie was scarcely a dapper fellow in his plain, plaid trousers and worn high boots, but he did sport a butter-colored vest sewn with shells and shiny bits of glass. A garment, Finn decided, several ordinary creatures could use for a tent, in case a storm should appear.

For a moment, Finn was unaware that they'd left the massive war balloons behind and come to a section of the grounds reserved for merchant craft. Here, balloons of every shape and size gathered to await the morning winds that would waft them on their way.

While the war balloons were drab, dun, dull as burned toast, as colorful as lint, the merchants used the vast surfaces of their craft to picture their wares, their names in graceful, cursive script, scenes of mountains and rivers, groves of sturdy trees, all in the tackiest, most lurid colors they could find. Finn was reminded at once of the carnival shows that came to town from time to time, gulling children and grown-ups alike.

Perhaps, he thought, such showmen took to balloons, once their acts had played too long on the ground. It was, he knew, a question he would keep to himself.

There were balloons aground here from near and far, some from friendly lands, and some that clearly were not. Finn saw, in fact, three craft from Heldessia itself, loading wine and bolts of cloth, ready to catch the morning breeze.

And, no doubt, there were balloons from Fyxedia over there, ready to return upon the night.

"Ironic indeed," Finn said aloud, to no one at all. "It's a sad and bitter thing that we hurl our cargoes of death at one another each and every day, as well as silk for ladies, and jars of thistle wine."

And I, he said only to himself, *I am risking life and limb to carry a blessed clock to Heldessia's King, whose warriors would slaughter me at will without the blink of a witless eye.*

*The world is a'tilt, I fear, and reason is spilling like syrup
over its treacherous edge . . .*

"Human person," Bucerius said, his blunt features a
mirror of disdain, "dream on your own time, but be
lookin' alive on mine!"

FINN HAD MANAGED TO SET HIS FEARS ASIDE, PUT
them out of sight, shove them in a corner in the attic of his
mind. Now he faced a terrible moment of truth, for the
sight before him was no mad fancy, but a real and awesome
device. The instant he came near this horrid apparatus, he
was sure he was looking at the instrument of his death.

In essence, the thing was a great, swollen sphere, some
sixty feet in height, its bulk enclosed in something akin to
a net. Attached to the sphere was a tangle of ropes,
shrouds, pulleys and lines. And, below that, tethered by
stakes and heavy cords, was the most frightening part of
all: a wickerwork basket, much like the one where folk
tossed their laundry for the wash. This basket, though,
seemed scarcely large enough to hold a child, much less
the bulk of Bucerius and himself.

"You are not serious, I presume," Finn said. "You can't
send us up in a crate like that."

For the first time since they'd met, the Bullie grinned, a
grin that spread his vivid coral lips to the cratered nostrils
of his nose, to the wrinkles on his lightly furred skull that
led to the faint suggestion of latent horns.

Finn prayed the Bullie would soon return to his grim
demeanor, and never smile again.

"You be findin' joy in the skies," Bucerius said, finger-
ing the ring in his nose. "Even a human person be havin'
the sense to see that. There's free up'n there. There isn't
be free down here. They is only little shits like princes, an'
folk thinkin' Newlies not good as nobody else. Thinkin'
Bullie got a strong back and nothin' in his head."

"I don't think that at all. Really, you mustn't feel I do."

"You don' talk. *I* talkin' to *you*." Bucerius made his point with a finger to Finn's chest, a finger the size of Finn's hand.

"You gots a nice Mycer girl. So you be smarter'n most human persons, I s'pose. You keeps bein' smart, I be gettin' you over there an' back. You acting dumb, like maybe you piss on yourself we gettin' up there, you be dizzy or something, you maybe fallin' out."

"Wait a minute," Finn said, "that sounds a lot like a threat to me. I don't care for that."

"You think I gotta do a threat? Gotta scare you, little man?" Bucerius looked pained. "What I sayin' is so. There be danger up there, you don't know what you doing. That's what I tellin' you.

"They's even more danger you gets to Heldessia Land, I be sayin' that. Them human persons be crazier'n the ones you got here. Meaner, too. Make that prince an' his mushin' and skinnin' look like a bunch of chil'ren pullin' legs offa ants. You want to be a-climbin' inna basket now, you wanna be whinin' down here? Whichever you doin', be doin' it pretty damn quick. . . ."

Chapter

ELEVEN

AS THE SUN, WITH A FIERCE AND DOGGED sense of will, heaved itself over the rim once more, as indigo faded to a blushing pansy blue, Finn, Master Lizard-Maker, late of County Ploone, now, truly, shorn of any grip on the precious earth at all, peered down upon the most fearsome, breathtaking sight he'd ever seen.

As if the day star had sounded a call, sent its brilliant heralds far and wide, the winds above the earth began to stir and come alive.

At first, a gentle breeze, playful puffs of air, then, of a sudden, hearty gusts that swept the balloon up high, high and higher still.

The wicker basket wobbled and the lines began to sing. Finn closed his eyes, thought of Letitia, thought of happy days that would never come again. Then, when he dared to face the world once more, he found he was mostly intact, though his stomach remained several hundred feet below.

Bucerius, along with many other merchants, had loosed the tethers of their craft only moments before the Easterlies arrived. Now, Finn saw the wisdom of this move. As if some trumpet had surely blown, all the plump and hefty monsters, all the great balloons of war, began to rise at once. . . .

"Great Socks and Rocks!" Finn said. "What a muddle, what a mess!"

Why the military should choose disorder as a plan, as a ploy, Finn couldn't say. The Bullie, though, working his pulleys and his lines, noted Finn's words with a rumble of disgust, deep within his chest.

The horde began to rise, swiftly now, upon the lofty winds. Ten, a dozen, twenty, fifty, more than Finn could count. Some like clumsy sausages, puffers, floaters, blind worms bobbing about. Some like swollen melons, ready to burst in the heat of the sun.

Each, and all, seemed distended this way and that. None could claim a color more enticing than mud. Each was a hodgepodge, a muddle of canvas, linen, and sacks, patches of calico, patches of pants.

And, 'neath each of these behemoths, some a good hundred feet long, hung a tangle of webbing, a jumble of cords, a covey of baskets chock-full of pikemen, dragoons and fusiliers. Lancers, sappers, archers and doomed grenadiers.

Some of these craft carried loads so heavy they were lashed together in sixes and fours. Still, many seemed scarcely able to rise above the ground.

Even as Finn watched, two great bulbous creatures—seven gasbags in one, four in the other—collided some fifty feet above the ground. Lines tangled, baskets tipped, and spilled their hapless troopers about.

Finn closed his eyes against the sight, but he could still hear the screams, hear the rips and the tears as the great crafts tore themselves apart.

And this is the beginning, this is just the start. We've yet to even taste the war . . .

And, as confusion reigned supreme, as disorder held sway, Finn had visions of these bloaters, these lunks bobbing against the sooty pall below. As much as he wished the picture would go away, it was hard to dispell the image of a great, airborne sewer, with a multitude of turds all about. . . .

. . .

Bucerius' CRAFT, WHICH CARRIED NO CARGO AT all, except for Finn's clock and a goodly stack of food, sailed well ahead of many of the merchants, and all of the cumbersome military craft.

Below, the River Gleen quickly gave way to the awesome Swamp of Bleak Demise, which stretched all the way to the Prince's foes, Heldessia Land. The swamp, as every schoolchild in each of the warring nations knew, was the reason both combatants had turned to balloons.

No army could cross the Swamp of Bleak Demise. If there was to be a war at all, it had to take place on reasonably solid ground. Thus, more than seven hundred years before, the lords of both domains had chosen the small, agricultural province of Melonius, an island of plenty surrounded by the swamp on every side, for their mutual battleground.

It was no longer known as Melonius, for the folk there had long been driven from their homes. There were no trees there, and no trace of crops of any sort. Now, it was a barren plain of death, where nothing, not even the hardiest weed, dared to grow.

Finn HAD LITTLE DESIRE TO PEER OVER THE SIDE OF the craft, for his stomach was yet to catch up with the rest of himself. And, when he chanced to look below, there was always the sight of tattered balloons that had not made it past the swamp or back. Many, Finn imagined, had rotted and disappeared into the darkness years before.

Toward noon, Bucerius brought out hard bread, a large wedge of odorous cheese, and a jar of stale beer. He offered to share with Finn. Finn was surprised, and grateful as well, for he had forgotten to bring the fatcakes and berry sandwiches Letitia had carefully prepared.

Though the Bullie had scarcely said a word since they'd
begun, he seemed more amiable after his belly was full.

"I see you be lookin' down there," he said, shoving a
whole pickled potato in his mouth. "It don't be a good
idea to bother them what's down below."

"And who would that be?" Finn asked, for he couldn't
imagine who the fellow could mean.

"Coldies, what you think? There's seven hunnert years
of the dead scattered round down there. Many a soldier's
falled to his doom 'tween here and where we be headed
for."

"I hadn't thought of the dead, though you're right as
you can be. I think, though, if I were a Coldie, I wouldn't
stay there. I'd get out of the Bleak Demise as quickly as I
could. Get to a town, a decent city somewhere."

Bucerius looked aghast. "You never *been* down there.
Isn't no one be findin' they way outta that. You dyin'
there, you stayin' there. Even a human person ought to be
knowin' that."

"I, ah—suppose. Though I've always found the dead
like their comforts as well as the living do. And they
clearly have plenty of time to search about. They've nothing else to do."

Bucerius muttered under his breath, clearly not
pleased with Finn's opinion on the matter. Finn had to remind himself that Bullies, by nature, found it offensive if
others had opinions contrary to their own. Not unlike a
great many beings of other races, as far as that was concerned.

When the meal was done, Bucerius tossed a few bites
of food over the side, and Finn did the same. If any of the
dead were down there, they would surely enjoy the
essence, the emanation of these remains.

Finn knew it was likely better to leave things as they
were, but there was little to do until they fell to their
doom, and death was much upon his mind.

"You think, then, there is such a thing as the afterlife? You think we go somewhere else?"

Bucerius frowned. "What you be meaning? We just talkin' 'bout that."

"I mean after you're a Coldie. After that."

"Isn't no *after* that. You be dead, that's that."

"Some say different. There's churches tell you there's a hereafter place to go."

"Here after what?"

"Somewhere different. Somewhere you go after you're dead for a while. I talked to a Coldie once said it's so. Fellow used to be a barrister, so he might know. Said there's seers tell you if you act right after you're dead for a time, you can do something else."

"Huh." Bucerius spat in the wind, narrowly missing Finn.

"That be what seers an' magician folk is for, you livin' or you're dead. Get you to *buy* somethin' from 'em, get you to spend your last pence on some stupid spell."

Finn gave the Bullie a curious look. "Your kind don't believe in magic, then? I never knew that before. Plenty of Newlies do."

"'Course we believes in magic. What you think, you better'n me?"

"Certainly not. As you have pointed out, friend, I'm united in bliss with a Mycer girl."

"Don't mean you got any concern for my folk—or any other creature what isn't humankind."

"You think what you will. My feeling, simply from being with you a very short while, is that it is you who have little affection for any but your own. And I'm not certain of that. I saw how those Bullies back at the Grounds looked at you. And how you looked at them."

For an instant, the cords in Bucerius' massive neck tightened, and his broad nostrils flared. Then, turning away, he began to busy himself with the shrouds of his balloon.

"Don't be botherin' me, human person. You be wavin' at the dead down there. Preach at 'em all you like. I got work to do. . . ."

B Y LATE AFTERNOON, THE WAR BALLOONS BEGAN to catch up a bit, though none passed the fleeter merchant ships. If any of the military craft had collided or fallen in the swamp, Finn couldn't tell.

Closer, he could see crewmen swarming about the dizzy heights of the portly craft, loosing this, possibly tightening that. Many, he noted, were Yowlies, Newlies with flat, ugly faces, pumpkin-seed eyes, and mean dispositions. Still, their great agility was valued on ships at sea, as well as those in the air.

Before the Change, before the erring seers had brought them up from beasts, the ancestors of the Yowlies had viciously hunted down the ancestors of Letitia's kind. Finn could scarcely blame Letitia for her fear and dislike of such beings. Their fierce appearance and disturbing cries were enough to set anyone's nerves on edge. If any creature changed from beasts lived up to its name, Yowlies took second place to none.

T HE AFTERNOON SUN CAUGHT THE BIG BALLOONS in its glare, and Finn noted their swollen flanks were no longer entirely bare. Now, magic symbols in garish shades of yellow, violet and green were smeared on every side.

This rite, he had heard before, was performed only when the craft were in the air. From the distance of Garpenny Street on the far side of Ulster-East, Finn had often seen vessels returning from the west with such markings, but never on any as they rose into the skies.

"Not too surprising," he muttered to himself, "for the

more disaster, mortal fear and death are involved in a spell, the more effective they seem to be. . . ."

Many of the merchant vessels bore runic markings too, but Bucerius' balloon showed nothing but an archaic ß, a letter in the common tongue.

"You credit the magical arts to some extent," Finn said, "though I see no signs upon your craft. Would I be out of line if I were to ask why?"

"Out of line's not even be a start," the Bullie answered, without turning from his tasks. "Human persons be pokin' they ugly heads into ever'thing they got no business in at all.

"No, I got no signs or symbols on my craft, an' don't intend to."

He stopped, and abruptly faced Finn, the late sun narrowing his eyes. "That thing up there be snappin' a line or rippin' a hole, you try chantin' a spell while we be droppin' like a barrel of lead. What I believe is curses an' hexes can send this thing to the ground. I doubts there's a charm can hold 'er up."

Words, Finn thought, that made a strange kind of sense. Perhaps he, and this great—often smelly and disagreeable creature—shared a belief in kind: that he who depended on the strengths within himself possessed a power greater than magic spells.

"At least," Finn added, "I'd like to think it's so . . . ."

Chapter

TWELVE

YOU MUST PROMISE ME YOU WILL TAKE CARE of yourself, my dear. I know you are a fine, capable, and courageous man, and responsible in every respect. Still, I urge you to take extra caution at all times. You will be alone in an alien land, and have no one to depend upon but yourself."

"I promise, Letitia. And I will, indeed, make every effort to keep myself wholly intact, and return as quickly as I can."

"Oh, Finn, I have no doubt you will."

"And I must tell you, love, and I mean this in the highest regard, you are showing a braver face at my departure than anyone could truly expect. You know I am embarking on a voyage that is rife with hazard, and danger of every sort. Yet, you do not falter, you do not yield to the fear, the dread, the torment that is tearing you up inside. I think no other could show such mettle as you are showing now."

"I know you will come back, Finn. You have faced adversity before, but you always come through."

"Yes, that's true. But *this* venture, you understand, is somewhat more treacherous than any I've faced before."

"Ah, you'll persevere. I have no doubt of that."

"You don't?"

"You are skillful, deft, cunning to a fault, my Finn."

"I suppose I am, that's true, but anything could happen, you know. I don't wish you to worry, but—"

"I won't, really."

"Won't? Won't what?"

"Worry. Not truly, I mean."

"Well, you should, if I may say so, Letitia. It may be you are taking this all too lightly. As a fact, it would not be unseemly if you were—greatly concerned. Certainly, more than you seem to be now!"

"Give us a kiss here in the hallway, love, where no one can see and turn us in for lust between Man and the spawn of the beast, and be on your way to your balloon. The sooner begun, the sooner done, as some wise sage has said. Or if he hasn't, he very likely will . . ."

THIRTEEN

I T ISN'T AS IF I WANT HER WAILING AND THRASH-
ing about," Finn mumbled to himself, noting that the sun
had dropped farther behind a crimson veil. "But I do feel
she could have shown a bit more fervor, anguish and remorse. I don't think that's too much to ask. . . ."

"What now? What you be mumbling over there? A
human person's got such a weaky little voice, they might's
well not be talkin' at all."

"I was talking to myself, Bucerius. I would have spoken louder if my words were meant for you."

Finn was surprised he'd let his attention wander so
long. The war balloons were closer now—much too close
for his liking, and too many of them to boot. Was there
any reason they had to huddle together like a school of
bloated fish? There was plenty of room to move about, a
whole bloody sky.

Some, he noted, had vented their balloons, letting their
craft sink rapidly down. Others tossed over bags of sand to
rise higher still. The skies were near smothered with clumsy
craft, rising up and sinking down. Through sheer dumb
luck, most seemed to pass each other with room to spare.

"Fate is truly kind," Finn said, "or we should see a
dozen dire disasters before our very eyes—

"Kites and Mites," he suddenly shouted, squeezing the
wicker rail, *"look out, you damn fool!"*

No one heard him above the constant shriek of air. Bucerius saw it too, and cursed beneath his breath, jerking a line that sent his vessel swooping dizzily away.

It happened in a wink, in the blink of an eye. A great, dun-colored sausage, patched, pasted, fiddled and darned, rose straight up into four enormous spheres, linked together as one. It struck the wicker baskets suspended from the vessels, struck them cruelly hard, and sent grenadiers, archers, fusiliers with purple pantaloons, crimson-clad dragoons, shrieking down in a deadly colorful array. Some went straight to the ground, some bounced once, some bounced twice on other balloons, before they went down. Several poor fellows plummeted through another craft and disappeared.

As one cart collides with another on the ground, as each slams another, and another after that, so it is with vessels of the air. Finn looked on in abject horror as one balloon tore itself apart and spun dizzily to the ground, a basketful of doomed soldiers trailed by a string of tattered rags.

A tragedy greater still occurred then, one that stunned Finn above the rest. A large balloon exploded, its fabric set ablaze. Finn covered his eyes from the blast as a gaseous ball of fire blossomed nearby.

Before it was done, he counted nine of the monsters down. There was no way to tell how many men had perished as well.

"Have you—have you ever seen this happen before," Finn said, staring at Bucerius. "Whales and Nails, it's not *always* like this, is it?"

"Isn't bad. I be seein' worse."

"Worse?"

"Trouble is, there be plenty of *bold* balloon pilots, but there isn't no *old* balloon pilots. If a captain don't die his first trip, he don't be ever signin' on again."

"You seem to make it, all right."

"I be a business person. I'm not some kinda fool what's fightin' in a war."

Bucerius looked at Finn with a mix of scorn and pride. "War be for human persons. Killin' be what they like to do."

"There are many brave Newlies who have joined our forces to fight with valor in the war."

"Uh-huh. They be stupid, too."

And that, it appeared, was that.

AS IF ON SOME SILENT SIGNAL, THE CLUSTER OF merchant balloons rose higher still, higher than they'd risen before. Finn peered over the side and saw the reason why. There, far below, lay the dread, desolate province once known as Melonius. The only dry land in the midst of the Swamp of Bleak Demise, it was now the battle-ground where warriors from Prince Aghen Aghenfleck and the King of Heldessia, met to slaughter one another as they had for seven hundred thirty-nine years.

Finn was glad they had risen so high. The balloons of Fyxedia and those of her foe, which had just arrived from the west, were disgorging their troops on the bare and blackened ground—those that had survived the journey there. The gaily decked officers and somber-clad men were much too far away to appear more than blotches to Finn's eye, and he was most grateful for that.

Beyond, the swamp took hold again, and, past that, the onset of the night.

"I see the sun is nearly gone," Finn said. "We can hardly have more than an hour more of light. Where will we stay for the night?"

"What?" The Bullie scratched the little nubs where horns had appeared among his kind in the past.

"Where would you *like* to stay, different from where you bein' now?"

"Why, down there somewhere, of course. Surely you wouldn't attempt to sail this device in the—in the dark?"

Finn felt a sudden chill, for he could see the answer in the Bullie's glassy brown eyes.

"No, truly, that makes little sense at all. We can't very well remain aloft unless we can see . . ."

"An' what'd you like to do? Set 'er down there among that poor lot? By damn, if you'd stop thinkin' 'bout your Mycer lass, you'd see what be a'happenin' outside your fuzzy head . . ."

Chapter

FOURTEEN

THE MOMENT THE SUN VANISHED UNDER A purple haze, two frightening things occurred. First, the dark flowed in so quickly, Finn felt some heavenly scribe must have spilled his ink across the skies. And, with the coming of night, the breeze that had driven them steadily from morning's light suddenly disappeared.

Bucerius' balloon began to sink like a stone. Finn drew in a desperate breath and held on tight, waiting for the dreadful impact with the ground.

Why hadn't the Bullie mentioned they'd never had a chance at all? That would have been the proper thing to do.

Instead, the fellow grabbed Finn's shoulders, bellowed out instructions that nearly left him deaf in one ear.

In an instant, he was tossing out sandbags as quickly as he could, watching the ground rise rapidly in the dark. Behind him, Bucerius was yanking at his infernal array of lines, shrouds, pulleys and vents, actions which seemed to have no effect at all.

Then, of a sudden, all was well again. They weren't moving fast, and they surely weren't sailing very high, but they were still in the air and not crushed upon the ground.

"Would you mind," Finn asked, feeling as deflated as a capsized balloon, "telling me what that was all about? I thought we were doomed."

"That isn't no word in the tongue of my folk. That's a human-person word, be what it is."

Finn knew better than to argue the point. And, in time, Bucerius explained that surely Finn recalled that the Easterlies blew in the morning and the Westerlies in the night. It was night, as anyone could see, and now they would have to sail low, to catch what wind there might be, wind known, of course, to veteran pilots like himself.

Finn accepted the Bullie's answer, and wondered, not for the first time, if there might not be some better way to navigate the air than hanging below a bag of gas, hoping it would go where you wanted to be. He vowed, when he could, to give the matter more thought. There might be some way to craft a lizard for such a task. He would certainly take it up with Julia Jessica Slagg.

He quickly swept away those thoughts, determined not to bring them up again.

"And when will we reach Heldessia?" Finn wanted to know. "Sometime soon, I presume."

"If the wind be willing. If it not, it be later than that."

"Later than what?"

"Later than when we'd be if it wasn't. You wants to run this lovely device, let me be gettin' some sleep?"

"No, I wouldn't care to do that."

"Wouldn't care for you to try. I got some good years left to be."

So do I, Finn thought, *and if I come home safe, I swear I'll not risk the time I've got on something as foolish as this. . . .*

He searched the sky for other balloons of the merchant fleet, but if they were there, it was too dark to see. The ground swept by perilously close below, and Finn could smell the foul stench of the swamp, the fetid odor of stagnant water and rotting vegetation, the scent of some loathsome, unknown creature of the night.

Either that, or the stupefying, deadly emanations from

Bucerius, who had eaten great quantities of turnips, whistle beans and mackerel cheese. Finn thought of the jelly sandwich and fatcake he'd left behind, the supper Letitia had packed. Even his favorite foods had no appeal now.

"Sweet Letitia, how I wish I was with you now. Though it's clear you're not as worried, not as anxious or disturbed as I feel you ought to be, I would overlook that if only you were near . . ."

"What's that? By damn, what you be a'mutterin' now?"

"Not a thing, Bucerius. I was talking to myself. As you so kindly mentioned before, it's a thing that human persons do."

"It be one of the things. Not all of 'em, for sure. You wantin' some of this cheese?"

"No," Finn said, holding his breath as the Bullie loosed a ripper again, "but it's kind of you to ask."

UP, GET UP, DAMN YOUR HIDE, ON YOUR FEET, NOW!"

Finn came awake at once, suddenly aware he'd been dozing, and wondered how he'd managed that.

"What is it? Nothing of great matter, I hope."

"Just hold on to those lines. Don't be lettin' 'em go."

"Something's amiss, I can tell. Whatever it is, I want to know."

"We be landin' soon, is what it is. Them lights down there? That's Heldessia. Just south there's the royal grounds."

"Say, that's fine." Finn peered over for a better look.

"Isn't fine a'tall."

"It's not?"

"You listenin', human person? *Not* bein' fine, there's Bowsers everywhere. Place be swarming down there. They already snaggered a balloon, or I'd never spotted 'em at all."

"What? Why would they—"

Finn's words were lost as a volley of musket fire rang out in the night. A lead ball thunked into the wicker basket, close to Finn's head. Another whined overhead and snapped a line.

"What do they want? What's going *on* here!"

"I shoulda remembered, damn me," the Bullie said. "It's Thursday again. Tuesdays and Thursdays, they be try an' kill the King . . ."

FINN HAD A GREAT MANY QUESTIONS, QUES-
tions he felt called for answers at once. Panic, chills, fear
of urination, gastric irritation, swept all thought from his
head.

Shouts, howls, bellows and barks reached them from
below. Discord, clamor, and harsh resonation filled the
night. The flare of muskets, the smell of powder, the din
of leaden shot stung his eyes, split his ears and burned his
nose.

Then, with a terrifying, sound, a sound more fearsome
than the rest, the fat sphere above ripped asunder, from
the bottom to the top, burst its vaporous innards with a
great unearthly fart.

Bucerius roared in anger as the basket gave a sickening
lurch, tipped on one side and nearly tossed the pair to the
ground.

Finn hung on for dear life. From the corner of his eye,
something big, something dark, something more solid
than the night rose up at him in a blur. The basket jerked
to a stop, snapping wicker, shredding cords, slamming the
Bullie into Finn, squeezing him nearly flat.

As he struggled for a breath, Finn saw a chimney rush
by, saw the shattered basket fill with brick and soot, felt the
clatter and the rattle as they slid down the steep-sided roof.

For another awful moment, they were airborne again.

Then, wicker, brick, lines, an avalanche of slate, came to a wrenching halt on the ground. A shroud of fabric settled gently over the Bullie and Finn.

Finn rubbed his stinging eyes, spat a mouthful of soot. Wondered how he could possibly be alive.

"It is no way short of a miracle," he said to himself. "And even then, I have my doubts. . . ."

"Don't be a'gabbin', keep still," Bucerius muttered, lifting him easily out of the mess. "You not be entirely livin' yet, lest we hauling out of here."

"Thank you, friend. I'm terribly grateful for your help."

"Take a care, watch it where you step."

"What? Pots and Pans, what am I stepping *on*?"

"I fear we be smushin' a fair lot of chickens. More like a herd. Somethin' bigger than a flock. Doubt anyone be thanking us for that."

As if in answer, a florid face, round as a moon, appeared in a window overhead. The fellow shouted and flailed his arms about, cursing in a gruff, unknown tongue, a language that seemed to greatly rely upon spit.

Before the man's wife could join him, wide-eyed in a tasseled nightcap, Finn and Bucerius were out of the yard and into the dark, Bucerius stepping ahead, Finn doing his best to keep up, clutching the carefully bundled clock against his chest.

EVEN AS THE PAIR REACHED AN ALLEY SOME DIStance from the scene of their imperfect descent, it was clear there were deadly pursuers still about, determined to track them down.

Barks and yelps resounded from the street just ahead; Finn and Bucerius crouched in the dark and watched them pass by.

They were, indeed, Bowsers, as Bucerius had noted before their craft struck the ground. They were short, tall, bony, stout and lean, as Bowsers tended to be. Some had oversize noses, some had puglike features, perfectly flat. Most had tufted ears, and all had sad and droopy eyes.

Finn, though certainly no bigot where Newlies were concerned, didn't care for Bowsers at all. He found them irritating at best. Some were quite friendly by themselves, but the moment they came together in a group, in a horde, in a pack, they seemed to become mean of spirit and intense.

He had crossed their path before in a misadventure across the Misty Sea, and didn't care to meet them again.

All of these fellows, he noted, wore varicolored pantaloons, natty striped jackets, red bow ties and straw boaters tipped at a rakish angle atop their heads. Wherever Bowsers seemed to settle, one nation or the next, they all preferred this ridiculous attire. And, if Bucerius was right, and they were after the Heldessian King, Finn thought their clothes seemed improper for assassination wear.

"Why do they seek to do in the King?" Finn asked quietly, when the noisome bunch had passed. "And why, in all reason, on Tuesday and Thursday night? That seems peculiar to me."

"They be doin' it 'cause someone paid 'em to," Bucerius explained. "Bowsers don't have lots of goals of their own. They be inclined to strong drink, filling their bellies an' gettin' lots of sleep. Someone'll give 'em all that, why, they'll hire their ugly selves out to whoever comes along."

"And who do you imagine is behind these louts now?"

Bucerius looked astonished at Finn's remark.

"Now how'd I know such a thing? Don't no one care for kings, I thought you be knowin' that."

"I suppose so," Finn said. "That sort of thing goes on, wherever one happens to be."

Bucerius didn't answer. He listened in silence for a moment, then led Finn down the darkened street. Far ahead, Finn could see a few pale, flickering lights above the high battlements of the palace of King Llowenkeef-Grymm.

Before they had gone too far, Bucerius discovered the shattered remains of a balloon in a small public square. The square was silent as a tomb. Shutters in every house were closed tight. No one, it seemed, dared to risk the streets with the Bowsers about.

Finn waited while the Bullie walked through the wreckage. His clenched fists, the rage barely suppressed upon his stocky features, told Finn what the giant had found.

"Sysconditi. He dealt in gems, which mostly be fakes. Never cared for the fellow, but he be a merchant, same as me."

Bucerius stared past the crowded block of structures to his right, where a fire glowed against the sky.

"There be another one down over there. It'll take some doing to get to it from here. Not that anyone'll be alive. These louts'll pay dear for this night's work. They know we be traders, an' not ships of the King. We got no part in the royals' fight."

"Could some be bandits, and not assassins as you say? Intent on loot from the goods merchants bring?"

"Could, I reckon. Bowsers, they got to eat regular, eat till they throwin' up they guts. They need to, I guess they'd be turnin' to this."

"I don't know why the King's troops haven't shown up before now," Finn said. "Or at least the city guards. Why, lawlessness seems to be unchecked in this land."

Bucerius showed Finn his second curious grin of the night.

"You be new here, human person. There be a lot you don't know 'bout Heldessia. Things you maybe wish you didn't know 'fore you get home . . ."

Finn was near certain it was on the tip of the Bullie's tongue to add *if* he got home, but he'd kindly held the words back. . . .

B EST WE BE CROSSIN' HERE. WE GOING ANY FAR-ther, they'll likely spot us for sure."

Finn could see his companion was correct. They were closer to the center of the city, now, near a deserted market square, the close-packed houses and shops that hugged the walls of the palace itself. Bucerius wanted to reach the spot where the merchant balloon had burned, but knew they had to take the long way around.

"I be crossing first. Wait till I gets there, you hear? Count a couple times. No Bowsers seem about, you be coming too."

"Good luck, then."

Bucerius showed him a scowl. "We be talking 'bout that before. Human persons not even hearin' what any-body says. Luck's got nothin' to do with me running over there. I be getting there or not."

"Fine. Just in case—"

The Bullie was gone. For a giant, for a creature that easily made three of Finn, he seemed to move remarkably well, swiftly and silently across the cobbled street, vanish-ing into the dark.

Finn waited. Looked, listened, and counted as well. Taking a breath, he crouched low, staying in shadow as best he could, running quickly toward the spot where the Bullie waited in the narrow alleyway.

You can toss Fortune aside if you will, my fine enormous friend, but I wouldn't mind the Fates looking down and lending me a hand. I wouldn't mind if someone tossed me an amulet now, or cast a simple spell—

The light was as bright as a small and angry sun, the sound a crack of thunder after that. Finn felt the ball part his hair, heard it sing, heard it whine like a hornet as it struck the wall over his head and showered him with dusty bits of stone.

Luck, chance, instinct or what, made him duck, veer to the right, as the second blinding flare came quickly on the heels of the first.

The missile drilled the empty air, directly where he'd been—that was enough for Finn. He tucked the clock to his chest, went to ground and rolled, felt his hands and knees scrape the rough stone, smelled the foul odors of the street, odors that could trace their families back for years.

The Bullie shouted, somewhere to his left, words Finn couldn't hear. He came to his knees, scrambled to his feet. Heard the yap, heard the bark, heard the irritating howl. Looked up and saw them, not a dozen yards away, big Bowsers, little Bowsers, straw-hatted Bowsers short and tall, five of the brutes in all.

Two carried muskets, old-fashioned arms with barrels flared like silver hunting horns. Heinz-Erlichnok .47s, Finn guessed, relics of the Love Wars, eighty years past. Old, but awfully good for maiming, laming, tearing off a limb.

The others carried blades, loping ahead, while the gunners charged their weapons again.

All this, Finn perceived in the barest snip of a second. Scarcely time to blink, time enough to spare,

time enough to rise, slide his hand in a practiced fashion
to his left, grasp the hilt of his sword and take the proper
stance.

Or, as it happened, grasp empty air, and wonder if his
blade was on the roof of the fellow with the pumpkin-
sized head, shattered in the basket, or possibly among the
dead and wounded fowl . . .

Chapter

SIXTEEN

THIS CAN'T BE," FINN SHOUTED, STANDING HIS ground, staring at his foes. "Where is it written I shall be shot and skewered by Bowsers in a dark and fetid street? I can't accept this at all!"

"Zhooot 'im, zhooot 'im in zuh haid! Zhoot dis perzon ded!"

"No you don't, fellow. I'm not armed, can't you see that? It's simply not the thing to do—"

An ancient weapon blossomed with a tongue of scarlet fire, with a stink of black powder, with a horrible din. For an instant, a dark plume of smoke obscured the Bowsers, sending them into choking fits.

"Valor delayed is courage yet to come," Finn said, and turned on his heels and ran. "Someone said that, I can't remember who."

He chose the first alley to his left, praying it went somewhere, anywhere at all. It did, but only to a narrow, twisted maze of sewers, sumps, garbage bins and dumps. Somehow, he'd stumbled on the septic tank of the city, found it all alone, without the aid of a map.

Left, right, it didn't greatly matter. It was nearly pitch-black. He could barely see his hand in front of his face.

"I could smell my way out, if I knew where one odor stopped and the other one began. . . ."

Light, a pale reflection off a grimy brick wall. A torch, and the throaty yelp of Finn's foes.

"Zere, zere 'e izt! Komen vit ze Svord, Zhep!"

"*You* getz 'im, Mahx. Izt schmellin' in zere."

"*You* gotz ze Svord. I beze shtayin' here!"

Finn searched about in the dark, setting the damnable clock aside. Soot, smut, broken bottles and pots. Things he hoped never to touch again. No fine blades, no weapon of any sort. His hand found something round, something short: the broken handle of a shovel or a hoe.

A head appeared out of shadow. Finn could see very little, but the white straw boater floated like an apparition in the dark. The Bowser went down without a sound. The crown of his hat collapsed atop his head, while the brim formed a collar about his neck.

"What a witless thing to do," Finn said to himself, "blundering in without a torch. Why didn't the idiot wait for his friend?"

No need to hang around for an answer. He scrambled about, looking for the fellow's blade—

—found it, hefted it in his hand. More like a bludgeon than a blade. Short, heavy, dull as the opera "Bob" Letitia had dragged him to.

Still, a blade for all of that, one step up from a stick.

And, found in the nick of time, as it were, for the Bowser with the torch stepped around the corner, a tall, solemn fellow with droopy jowls, checkered vest, red bow tie, and a blade very much like Finn's.

"You be geshtoppen vere you izt, hooman. Dropen you veapon now!"

"Huh-uh. You be dropen yours," Finn said, lashing out with a jab that snipped a button off the fellow's vest.

The Bowser didn't care for that at all. The button was imitation pearl, and difficult to find. He muttered an oath in the harsh, irritating tongue of his kind, slipping Finn's blade aside, going for the gut.

Finn stepped deftly to the right, his left foot squashing something vile. Then, instead of pressing his adversary, the Bowser backed off, assuming a formal stance, designed for defense, rather than attack.

Finn didn't stop to ask why. Feinting to the left, he whipped his blade high and came in swiftly from the right.

Too late, he saw his mistake. He'd paid no attention to his enemy's torch, intent on the dangerous blade. Now, the Bowser ducked low, and with his left hand thrust the burning brand in Finn's face.

Finn cried out as the heat scorched his brow. He heard his hair sizzle, felt his lashes curl.

This time, the Bowser followed through, leaping in fast, flailing away with wicked strokes while Finn was still blinking from the light. He fought back blindly, shouting at the top of his lungs, fought with such anger at his own near-fatal blunder, that the Bowser was startled, stunned by such a sudden, mad assault.

Finn cut him once across the chest, ripping the checkered vest. Cut him once more below the throat, a move that unraveled the red bow tie, and brought a gasp from his foe.

The Bowser raised a hand to his neck and stared at Finn. A gold-rimmed monocle dropped from his eye and onto the sodden ground. Finn had ever thought the monocle an odd conceit among these folk, for it didn't seem likely all their people had defects in one eye.

Once more, the Bowser leaped forward, whipping his weapon about. Finn moved in a blur, turned his blade around and struck the creature across his pointy nose with the heavy, weighted hilt.

The Bowser sagged and went down atop his companion, still moaning on the ground. Finn took a breath, and had little time for that. The third of his foes, with a comrade at his back, was yipping for his blood, scraping through the narrow alleyway. Finn was grateful the passage was a very tight squeeze. Grateful, too, that both the Bowsers wanted through at once.

And where, pray, was his large companion all this time? Had the Bullie found a jug of ale and settled down for the night?

"Prinz, here! Ze hooman's kilt dem both! Getz in an' zhoot 'im now!"

The Bowser in the rear crowded his companion aside, raised his enormous weapon and aimed it at Finn's head.

Finn backed off, came up against a sodden wall with nowhere to go. The immense, flared barrel of the musket looked a quarter mile wide. There was little metal showing, as most of the aged device was covered in rust and soot.

"If that is a Heinz-Erlichnok .47 as I suspect," Finn said, "I'd take a care if I were you. The trigger tends to stick on that model, especially in weather like this. If that lock you're using comes from the Sandow Works, which I believe it does, the weapon will likely freeze after two or three shots. From the noise you fellows made, I expect you're past that. If it truly fires, I'll wager it takes *your* head off instead of mine."

"Vhat?" Prinz, for that was the short, chunky Bowser's name, looked curiously at Finn, then back at his weapon again.

"You zhink he bein' a vizeass, Phydo? Nuttin' zeems wrong to me."

"Zhoot 'im, don' talk vit 'im, phool!" Phydo bared his teeth, snatched the weapon from his friend, blew a cloud of soot from the lock, and aimed the thing at Finn.

"Hold it," Finn said, his belly clenching up in a knot. "You look like reasonable fellows, let's talk about this."

"Lezz nhot. Be shtillen, hooman. Don' be jerkin' round—*whuuuuk!*"

As if by sorcery, a strange, unnatural act of some kind,

both of the Bowsers rose up off the ground and into the darkness above. They flailed, kicked, quivered and thrashed about. The musket went off and lit up the night.

In its sudden glare, Finn saw Bucerius on the roof overhead. His legs, stout as young trees, were spread wide. With scarcely any effort at all, he hauled the two Bowsers up into the night, bits of strong line looped about their necks. He dangled them there for an instant, watching them kick hopelessly about, then dropped his lines, and let the pair sink limply to the ground.

The Bullie jumped lightly to the alley floor, caught Finn's expression, and turned up his mouth as if something tasted bad.

"They isn't dead, though it wouldn't trouble me none if they was . . . "

Finn could scarcely fault the Bullie for his thoughts. Bucerius hadn't forgotten the merchant he'd found in the downed balloon, and those who'd likely perished in the flames they'd seen some blocks away.

"There might be others out there. We'd best have a care."

"Isn't no one bein' out there now," Bucerius said, peering at Finn through the dark. "I haven't been takin' no nap, in case you didn't know . . . "

THROUGH THE ALLEY AND OUT IN THE OPEN street again, Finn saw a Bowser sprawled on his back. And, farther down the block toward the square, they passed two more, moaning and holding their heads. Finn understood why the Bullie had been delayed. He'd had things to do.

Finn scraped dirt, soot and something soggy off the sacking wrapped tightly about his clock. Cleaned his trousers and his cape as best he could.

"Still got the pretty, do you? You be hangin' on to that thing. Don't be leavin' it lying in a alley somewhere."

"Do you think I would indeed?" Finn answered, not a little annoyed by the Bullie's lofty attitude. "You think I embarked on this voyage, floating about in a deathtrap with a—with a giant that farts like a typhoon, you think I came here to fight a herd of yapping maniacs? No, Bucerius, don't tell me how to hang on to my goods. It is a coarse, vulgar, common piece of crap, but I can handle it very well."

"Thought you be makin' the thing."

"I did. So what?"

"So why you makin' crap? You no good or what?"

Finn stopped in the darkness and peered up at the Bullie.

"I *am* good. I invented lizards in my head. No one else

in the world even thought of that but me. I am the finest craftsman you'll ever meet. No, in all modesty, I am more than that. I'm an artist, friend. I'm the best.

"And that's why I made this ugly, base, despicable clock. Because, if you live in a land that is governed by a tasteless Prince, you had best make a tasteless, golden lizard with a clock in its belly, if that's what he desires. If you do not, there is little chance you will be around to create finer things, things that people can use, things that people will admire because of their beauty and craftsmanship.

"You think Aghen Aghenfleck is a greedy, worthless lout and so do I. Yet, you work for him as well. Now why do we suppose you do that?"

Bucerius, in spite of himself, seemed taken aback.

"He be what you sayin', all right. But he also be sittin' in a castle, not me."

"Exactly. I have never understood how such a thing happens, but it seems to be the same, everywhere one goes. There is always someone at the top of the heap, and, more often than not, they scarcely have the sense of the most witless fellow in town. Yet, we let them stay there, and tell us what to do."

"That's the way it always been," Bucerius said. "I figure that's how the world's suppose' to be."

"I can't believe we're all as ignorant as that. There must be something missing here. Something we simply fail to see . . ."

THERE WAS NO MORE TIME FOR IDLE THOUGHT. A howl and a clatter arose from down the street. Finn and Bucerius stepped into a shadowed entryway. The swinging sign above the door read GREENS.

"Snouter runs the place," Bucerius said. "I know him. This is farm country 'round here. You be seeing a lot of grocers in Heldessia Town."

"You know a lot of folk here?"

"Why you askin' that?"

"No reason at all."

"Don' be askin' me stuff you haven't got to know. Come on, them Bowsers has turned off the other way."

Finn had known Bullies here and there. Few of them, though, had risen to Bucerius' status as a trader. Most seemed content to use their great strength to make their pay. None—laborer or no—were keen on manners or social grace. Maybe, he thought, it was some sort of cultural trait. Or perhaps if you were that big, you didn't have to be civil at all.

Bucerius became more cautious as they left the side streets and approached the broader avenues. Even in the dark, one could see the houses and shops here were of a grander scale, some three and four stories tall. At the far end of the tree-lined boulevard was the gate of the palace itself.

Finn felt a sense of relief at the sight. Three, maybe four more city blocks, and they would be off the streets, safe from the rabid Bowser bands.

"Huh-uh, keep movin'," Bucerius said, guessing Finn's thoughts. "You don't be seeing anyone, don't mean they isn't there."

Finn didn't answer. He followed the Bullie past the avenue into yet another side street, much like the ones they'd left only moments before.

Finally, Bucerius stopped, looked about and sniffed the air. Finn smelled it too. Burned varnish, scorched fabric and smoking wood.

"That balloon. The one that went down . . ."

"On ahead," Bucerius muttered. "We was east of it, passed it right by."

"I know the folk here fear the Bowsers, and rightly so, but I'd think the King's Guards or someone would stop this horror. Why, these ruffians could take the whole town, and no one would stand in their way. . . ."

"Stop your gabbin', human person. This way. Over there!"

Bucerius broke into a run, moving faster than Finn would have imagined of a creature of his size. When he stopped, at last, Finn came to a halt as well, and saw the terrible sight.

There was scarcely any way to tell the thing had been a ship of the air. Fabric, lines, and the wicker basket itself had completely disappeared. The fire had burned with such intense, unforgiving rage, that there was little left to see. Not even embers remained, only scattered mounds of ash.

"It's a death pyre's, what it is," Bucerius said, great fists clenched at his side. "Didn't no one be gettin' out of this."

Finn guessed the gasbag had ignited somehow, then exploded, incinerating the craft and anyone inside in less than a blink. The thing had gone up so quickly it hardly charred the stone walls on either side of the street.

"And no one bothered to help. Not a one of these worthy citizens came out to lend a hand."

"Lend a hand an' do what, even if they'd had the guts to try?" Bucerius was clearly on the edge of reason, caught up in fury and despair.

"What you figure they be doin', sweeping up soot, patching some poor crispy together again? Damn me, if human persons aren't as simple a creature as there be!"

"Me? Why, you're the most vile, crude, offensive being it has been my displeasure to meet. You drive me crazy with your vulgar manner, your vexing ways."

"Manners, is it? That's your complaint, I don't be actin' *nice*?"

Bucerius roared, a great and hearty guffaw that started deep in his chest, burst into life, and rattled windows on every side.

"Manners be what them Bowsers got, with their fine little hats and bow ties. They was bein' *mannerly* like, when I stopped 'em blowing your fool head off. Might be I should've waited a minute or two."

"I thanked you for that. I don't intend to do it twice. Besides, I think I could have handled the situation myself."

"How? You gonna hit 'em with your clock? Scare them louts with your fancy city talk? You gonna—"

"Hold it right there, buckos. Make a move and I'll fair drop you on the spot. . . ."

Finn and Bucerius turned as one, staring at the man who had silently stepped out of shadow, taken them unawares, and now aimed a pair of pistols squarely at their heads.

"Sir, we mean you no harm," Finn said at once, "we're merely passing by."

"No, we *aren't* just passin' by," Bucerius said, sending a furious glance Finn's way, "now put those toys down, you ol' fool, 'fore I stuff 'em down your craw."

"Easy," Finn said softly, "if I'm not mistaken, that's a very fine pair of matched Wesley-Grovenhalters. Back-action, side-lock. Notch rear sight. Sliding safety catch. Sixty caliber, I doubt I'm wrong in that."

"Fifty-seven," said the stranger. "You've got an eye for arms. Not many thugs of your sort can tell a fine weapon from a brick."

"I assure you we are not—"

"Stop! Another step and you'll be singing with a Coldie choir!"

The man didn't look to be a danger—seventy, eighty if he was a day, and clearly walking with a limp. A pale, stringy fellow with scarcely any flesh on his bones, a bristly chin, and hardly any teeth at all. His eyes seemed enormous behind the thick spectacles that perched on the bridge of his nose. A nose, Finn noted, with a prominent wart on the end. A wart so big, it might well have grown a wart itself.

Looks, though, could be most deceiving, Finn reminded himself. Large-bore weapons had a way of enforcing respect, even among the aged, the ugly and the lame.

"You got no cause to point them things at us," Bucerius said, with less defiance than before. "We're not a couple o' thieves. I be a respectable businessman, and this human person's a master of clocks—"

"Lizards," Finn corrected.

"Whatever. Anyhow, it oughta be clear we isn't no bein' ruffians or felons of any sort."

"What you are," the old man said, the weapons still steady in his hands, "is arsonists, torchers, flat maniacs. Heartless brutes what burns a man's ship of the air, and nearly murders him to boot!"

Bucerius stared. "That thing was yours? And you got out alive? I'm not believin' that. Anyone was in that thing was burned to a cinder 'fore they could blink an eye."

The old man showed them a nasty, double-toothed grin.

"If you was *in* it when it catches, that's so. If you had the sense to get out, that's something else again. And what's it to you? You care if an old man fries?"

"You got out before it . . . Damn me, I never thought of that. Who are you, what's your name, then?"

"Devius Lux. What of it?"

"Devius Lux. I heard of you somewheres."

"I expect you have. Devius Lux, purveyor of antiquities and such. Ancient brushes, curries, combs. Items for those who take an interest in hair care of the past. My shop is next to Gaxiun-Froon, the seer who sells plain water and swears it'll turn any female into a savage of desire."

Devius frowned. "Who in hell you be, sir? I expect you best tell me that."

"Bucerius. A merchant like yourself. I be dealin' in,

ah—a number of things. It was the filthy Bowsers what brought you down, not me."

"They got us too," Finn added. "We're lucky to be alive ourselves. I feel our fall was cushioned by chickens. Otherwise, we would not have fared as well."

Devius Lux looked dubious, not wholly convinced.

"You know who I am, all right. That doesn't prove a thing, and I never heard of you. You could be in league with those Bowser kind. No offense, but you're a Newlie yourself."

"Damn you, then!" Bucerius' chest began to heave, like an enormous bellows, intent on stirring up a fire.

"Patience," Finn said again, "those Wesley-Grovenhalters can do a great deal of damage, even to a fellow your size."

"Pistols or no, I won't be insulted by a dried up old man sellin' combs."

"They are not everyday combs, they're combs from ancient times."

"A comb is a comb to me!"

"Stop it, both of you." Finn stepped between the two, facing the brace of pistols himself.

"Bigotry and bile have no place here. You are both tradesmen, and quite aware that commerce goes beyond racial and political bounds. It's foolish to stand here and argue while a pack of ruffians is very likely on our trail. This is a time when we must all—"

"Get out of my way, or I'll blast you and the beastie both!"

"Wait, now listen, please!" Finn felt his heart leap up in his throat, felt his mouth go dry as toast. Knew, in an instant, from the light in the old man's greatly magnified eyes, that he wasn't listening at all, didn't give a flop about race, religion or anything else.

What he wanted to do was *shoot* someone, anyone at all, with his brand-new Wesley-Grovenhalters, for what's

the good of costly, quality arms, if you keep them in a
drawer with your socks somewhere?

"Put those down or I'll have your head for it," Bucerius
said. "I won't be askin' you again."

"Sticks and Bricks," Finn said, "that's not the way to
handle this at all. We're all civilized here."

"*He*'s not," the old man said, taking a bead on the
Bullie's head. "He's a creature, nothing more than that."

"—and so am I, Devius Lux, and you harm either one
of those two, especially the man I love, and you'll answer
to me!"

"*Letitia?*"

Finn drew in a breath, certain that a vision, a fine hallucination, had appeared before his eyes. "Is that really
you, or am I in a bizarre and happy dream—"

Before he could finish, Letitia stepped out of shadow
and rushed into his arms. Tears of joy stung his cheeks,
and they weren't all his alone . . .

Chapter

EIGHTEEN

DEVIUS LUX, WHO DIDN'T LIKE SURPRISES AT all, especially those that included any form of bliss, stared in wonder and disgust at the joyous scene. Stared, but only for an instant, until a glitter, a gleam, an errant flash of silver in the shadows caught his eyes.

A shiver crawled up the old man's spine, crawled up and raised the half dozen hairs on his head. A monster, a demon, an unholy thing scuttled out of the alley, clacking its teeth and winking its ruby eyes.

"Gibido, Fibido, something-something Blik!" he said in a quavering tone, too frightened to remember the spell for such events.

Instead, he took careful aim, raised his pistols, and fired them both at once.

Twin explosions shook the street. Gouts of fire burst from the barrels, followed by a pall of black smoke. Devius Lux staggered back, stunned, his arms going numb. Bucerius grabbed the empty weapons, and cursed beneath his breath.

"Julia!"

Finn and Letitia shouted as one, loosing their grips on one another and rushing to the lizard's aid.

Finn gagged, waving smoke aside, certain he would find a horrid sight, a lizard blown to nature's basic bits, iron, copper, silver and tin, scattered about like dust. Ghostly hints of cogs, springs and golden gears.

"Julia," he cried, with wonder and relief, "why, you're all right, you're perfectly intact!"

"On the outside, yes," Julia said with a rusty croak. "Inside, I'm a'quiver, a total nervous wreck."

"You don't have any nerves. That's all in your head."

"Now you don't know that," Letitia said. "I expect she's upset quite a bit."

"I made her, my dear. I know what's inside. There aren't any nerves to quiver, just a bunch of wires, hardly the nervous system of a creature of flesh and blood. The animal brain has some activity, yes, but there are no *nerves* that extend any farther than that."

"I feel better already," Julia said, scratching a copper scale. "It's helpful to have someone who knows *everything*."

"That old bastard couldn't be shootin' hisself in the foot," Bucerius said, bending down to stare at Julia Jessica Slagg. "You did a fine job on that fellow what bothered the Missy here in the Prince's courtyard. Like to see you have a go at one of them Bowsers sometime."

"I think," Finn said, knowing how flattery turned Julia's head, "I think we'd best be getting out of here. That noise could bring the yappers on again.

"Letitia, love, there's much we need to talk about. I left you and Julia safely on Garpenny Street. Now I find you wandering about Heldessia with a crazed old coot. I am eager to hear how this came about."

"As you so wisely said, I don't think we have the time for that. I'll be happy to explain when I can. Perhaps you'll forgive my rash decision when you understand why I came."

"Did I get it, did I kill that evil thing?"

Devius Lux peered around Bucerius' enormous form, his face no more pleasing covered with flecks of black powder than it had been before.

"I'll have those weapons back, fellow, you've no right

to take a man's arms—Great Stars, the horror's still there, somebody stomp on the thing!"

"I'd be taking a care, old man," the Bullie said. "Us beasts has got primitive ways. Isn't no tellin' what might set us on a spree . . ."

I GOT FRIGHTENED, IS ALL, I TRULY DID. YOU WEREN'T gone a minute 'fore I got to thinking about the Prince and his sly and lowly ways. What might he do? Would he dare molest me while you were gone?

"You know how he looked at me, dear, you heard what he said. And he *is* the Prince. I suppose he can do whatever comes into his head. At any rate, I recalled Miz Hammiter-Prin? The lady on Rattlebone Street who runs the little shop, the Doorstop Exchange? I knew she had a cousin who'd married a trader in Thistles and Weeds, and *he* sent goods by balloon all the time . . ."

". . . And he just happened to know an old coot who carried cargo to Heldessia," Finn added, "and, luckily, was leaving at dawn, with the rest of the merchant fleet. What a remarkable coincidence, Letitia. Not only to recall Miz Hammiter-Prin's relations, but to meet such a kindly, good-natured fellow as Devius Lux, who'd be most pleased to carry a lovely Mycer girl and a lizard in his balloon."

"Well, it wasn't *exactly* like that, I don't suppose," Letitia said, glancing off at the darkened sky.

"Not exactly."

"No. Very close, though."

"How close, indeed?"

"Not as close as that, I have to say. You know, of course, from his somewhat violent reaction that I failed to mention Julia was stowed safely in my satchel during the trip."

"One might gather that. And the rest of it, love?"

"The rest is simply that I, ah—slipped away a moment after we returned from the palace, and began my arrangements then."

"I see."

"Yes, I feel you do."

"You didn't waste a lot of time."

"I didn't *have* a lot of time, dear Finn. And it was, truly, only good fortune and the hand of Fate that I was able to bring it all about.

"Oh, don't you see? I simply couldn't let you go on such a perilous voyage alone. I had to be with you. I had a most terrible feeling that if I didn't follow on your heels, I'd never see you again."

Finn, though still not appeased by Letitia's tale, could not resist the tenderness, the caring in her voice, the very real concern in her dark and iridescent eyes.

"You could have been killed yourself. I could have lost you, Letitia. You must have witnessed the same tragedy and horror I did."

"I did, yes."

"I don't know what to say. Of course I'm glad you're with me, but I fear for your safety here."

"Don't, love. Nothing will happen to me. We have shared adversity before. If need be, we shall share it in this far land as well."

"Yes, well. I suppose we will."

Letitia gave a grateful sigh and kissed him lightly on the cheek. "I must tell you, I thought I had taken this voyage in vain, when our airship fell dizzily into the street. Devius Lux *did* get me out before the thing caught fire, do give him credit for that.

"Then, when we heard someone approaching, we thought it was those terrible Bowsers, and the old fellow made me retreat into the alley, so he could fight them off. When I heard your voice—"

Letitia could say no more. Finn held her close, and had no desire to let her go . . .

B<small>UCERIUS AND DEVIUS LUX STOOD BENEATH THE</small> high stone arch of a house a mere hundred paces from the entry to King Llowenkeef-Grymm's palace—a great, looming structure that betrayed no more light than the rest of this city in the small hours of the night.

It was Devius who had guided them the long way around the palace walls, avoiding the Bridge Gate, the Royal Gate, and a number of lesser gates, as well. And, finally, to a stout wooden door that sat within the base of a sentry wall.

It was not through any concern that he had done this deed, but his great desire to hold his precious weapons again. Bucerius had sworn he would grind them to dust beneath his boots if the old man couldn't think of some way to redeem himself.

Now, the two waited, without exchanging a word, while a guardsman went to wake a friend who had done a bit of business with Devius before. What sort of business, the oldster wasn't prepared to say.

A<small>T LEAST, FINN THOUGHT, STANDING WITH LETITIA</small> some distance away, it was easier to see, now, why his love had shown less concern than he'd hoped for as they'd parted back in Ulster-East. Why, she could hardly say she'd miss him greatly, could she, when she knew she would be riding the very same Easterly winds across the swamp of Bleak Demise to Heldessia Land.

The thought brought a moment of relief, followed quickly by a pang of shame at his selfish need, when Letitia had shown *her* love in a clear, uncluttered manner by risking her very life to be at his side.

And, more shameful still, a thought he hurriedly banished from his mind, he wondered how many gold and silver coins Letitia had given the fellow to take her aboard.

I'm damned if I'll ask, he thought to himself, *and it's better for future bliss I never know . . .*

IT SEEMED A SMALL ETERNITY BEFORE THE STOUT door opened again. Finally, a nondescript fellow, a man of no certain weight or height, appeared and thrust a lamp into the dark. It was hard to guess his age, for his features were most ordinary, neither flushed with youth nor withered by the years.

It looked, to Finn, as if some being wore the costume of a man, dressed for a festive event. From this very first glance, Finn felt wary, on edge, plainly discontent. Letitia, at his side, grew suddenly tense as well. No surprise to Finn, for the Mycer folk had a far keener insight into things unseen than humankind.

"Well, what is it?" the man of no distinction said. He spotted Devius then and turned the fellow's way.

"Do we have business, Lux? I don't recall we do. And these others, are they with you?"

"They are, sir. And I have nothing to show you at this time, though I am expecting some very fine items, which should arrive from the Venomous Coast in a fortnight or so. There is one article, said to be used in ancient times to curl a maiden's hair—"

"Then we shall talk about that at the time," the man said, raising a hand to halt Lux.

"I am Dostagio, First Servant to His Majesty, King Llowenkeef-Grymm," he said, looking vaguely at Finn, glancing past Letitia and the giant at her side. "What do you want of me?"

"I am Finn of Fyxedia, sir. And this is my—house servant, Mistress Letitia Louise. This fellow is Master Bucerius, Trader and Balloonist, who guided us here."

"You know me, Dostagio," Bucerius said, "though I doubt you'd recall. I been to your court on business before."

"Yes, well, I'm sure," Dostagio said, paying the Bullie no heed at all. "You. Finn, is it? Must I ask you again? What are you doing here?"

"I came on the orders of Prince Aghen Aghenfleck of Fyxedia. I bring a gift from my Prince to your King."

"From the Prince? I don't expect His Grace will want it, but you may leave it here."

"No, sir, with all respect, I cannot."

"You cannot?"

"I cannot. I have express orders from the Prince to deliver the package you see here into the hands of the King himself."

"Yes, well. Come back in the morning. Go to the main gate in front. Leave your name with the Chamberlain Fourth Class. It will be added to a list. The list will be forwarded to an official in the palace, as it is every morning at nine."

"And may I ask which official is that?"

"That would be me. I will look at the list, scratch off all the names, and send it back to the gate again."

Finn looked greatly alarmed. "What, then, is the point in getting on the list, if you scratch everyone off?"

"I couldn't say. I believe it was your idea to come here, not mine.

"Devius Lux, when you have an item of particular interest, do come and see me then. Please, all of you, step away from the door, and go back wherever you belong."

"Wait. I'm not finished!"

"Yes, sir, you are."

The drab fellow stepped back. The guard appeared again and began to close the great door. Bucerius pushed Finn away and thrust his enormous foot inside.

The guard looked startled. He blinked at the Bullie's boot, staggered back and went for his blade.

"Don't," Bucerius told him, poking a big finger in the fellow's chest. "It be a bad idea, puttin' your hand on that."

"What is this, now? Remove your foot and leave at once!"

Some errant emotion tried to make its way to the First Servant's face. Struggled there a moment, and gracefully went away.

"Take this," Bucerius said, drawing something from the packet at his belt. "I shoulda give it to you 'fore we be talking at all. Doesn't nothing get through to your kind, all you got is rules."

The fellow scarcely looked at the Bullie. He took the item and withdrew a step into the light. Finn saw it was a very small scroll, sealed with a smear of purple wax.

"What's that, what did you give him there?"

"Royal Warrant. It's what you use to be getting past stuffy fools like him."

"You've got a Royal Warrant? From Aghen Aghenfleck himself?"

"Your hearing be all right, human person? Just said I did. All them noble types, they be despising each other, but they got to do business like war and peace and such.

"I be carrying a sack of these things from princes, kings, sheiks, nabobs an' tyrants you never heard of before. Can't get nothin' done in my trade, you don't be having one of these."

"Why didn't the Prince simply give it to me?" Finn

asked, somewhat taken aback. "I could have presented it as easily as you."

"Oh, now, he couldn't do that." Bucerius granted Finn a kindly smile that galled him no end, a smile reserved for infants and others too dense to comprehend.

"You could be havin' one of these, but wouldn't do you no good."

"Oh, and why is that? I think I have my wits about me, much of the time."

"Surely you do. What you don't know, 'cause you never be in the trade like me, is how many gold crowns you got to be stuffin' inside that scroll."

Devius Lux gave a hearty cackle at that, and drew a frown from Finn.

"I don't know why I should be surprised to hear this. There's no one more venal, more eaten up with greed, than the toadies at a royal court."

"None, as a fact. Unless it be the royals theyselves."

At that moment, Dostagio stepped into the entryway again. If he had heard the talk between Bucerius and Finn, he gave no indication of it now.

"Master Finn, I know I express the feelings of His Grace, Llowenkeef-Grymm, his esteemed family, and the royal court itself, when I welcome you to Heldessia Land.

"If you and your, ah, serving creature, will kindly follow me, I will see you to comfortable quarters now."

Bucerius hid a grin behind his big hand.

"I be seeing you again," he told Finn. "Have a care, friend. These fellows is all of noble blood, but all your nobles be thieves. That's how they get to be princes and kings."

Again, Dostagio seemed to have a deaf ear to anything spoken in his presence. Before Finn could bid the Bullie and the old man farewell, the door closed behind him, and he and Letitia Louise were within the walls of Heldessia's King.

Julia Jessica Slagg was there, too, but she was curled tightly against Finn's shoulders, under his heavy cloak. For once, she had kept her silence for a while, and Finn was most grateful for that. Getting in the palace was trouble enough. Explaining a golden lizard with silver jaws and ruby eyes was something else again. . . .

Chapter

TWENTY

"IT WOULD BE MY GUESS," FINN WHISPERED TO Letitia, as they followed Dostagio down the long hallway, "that these will not prove to be the jolliest folk we've ever met. When the decorator color is black, one cannot expect the circus to appear."

"It is certainly not inviting," Letitia agreed. "And I am getting a chill, dear. I wish I had a wrap of some kind."

"It isn't cold in here, it's really quite warm. You're likely just affected by the somber atmosphere."

"I am *cold*, Finn. Please don't tell me how I feel. This is one of your most irritating habits, dear. I believe I have mentioned it before."

Finn was taken aback by Letitia's sudden show of discontent. Nerves, likely, reaction to the day's quite troublesome events. Still, he had the good sense to keep this opinion to himself.

"I'm dreadfully sorry, Letitia, I meant no offense. You would surely know if you're cold or hot. Here, allow me to put my cape around your shoulders. That will take the chill away."

"You can't. Julia's under there."

"Damn. I quite forgot."

"It's all right. I'll be just fine."

She wrapped her arms about herself and walked on in silence down the gloomy hall, trembling now and then.

Finn felt as if he'd failed her somehow, and didn't know how to make amends.

Indeed, the atmosphere in this dreary place was enough to cause a chill. Gaudy, garish, daring decor were not the proper words for the dark granite floors, the drab, cyclopean walls. Faintly glowing torches, set in iron brackets, appeared now and then, but did little to lessen the pall, for the lusterless stone drank the very soul from every errant beam of light.

Finn tried to remember the many twists and turns of this cheerless maze, but soon was completely lost. Even their guide, Dostagio, added to the task of guessing true perspective, for he was clothed in black from head to toe, and often simply disappeared ahead.

When, at last, the fellow began to slow his pace, Finn had the feeling they might be back to the outer door where they'd begun.

"Your quarters are just ahead," Dostagio announced. "We don't have many guests at this time, so I am putting you in the Chamber of Celestial Bliss."

"Oh, that sounds very nice," Letitia said. "Do you think there might be blankets in there?"

Dostagio appeared not to hear. "There are four hundred twenty-two sleeping quarters in the palace," he announced. "I am not counting the Royal Wings, of course."

"No, of course." Finn wondered when the fellow would actually stop, for they had passed a good dozen dark and unadorned portals now.

"Four hundred twenty-two," Letitia said, in a hapless effort to keep herself warm. "Imagine that."

"That's a great many rooms."

"It is," Letitia said.

"And our quarters are called . . ."

". . . The Chamber of Celestial Bliss," Letitia finished.

"That could be—interesting, Finn." In spite of her discomfort, she managed a mischievous grin.

Maybe there *will* be blankets, Finn thought, delighted at her smile. Big, heavy quilts we can burrow under and generate heat among ourselves.

"We are here, then," Dostagio said, stopping before a door indistinguishable from the rest. "Just let me find the key. It fits every room, which makes it quite easy on everyone, guests and servants as well."

"Yes, it would," Finn agreed. "Can you tell us, sir, when we might be able to see the King? Early is fine, if that's the custom here. Though later is satisfactory as well."

"Later, I should think."

"Good. Very well, then," Finn said, thankful for extra hours of sleep. "So you would say—when?"

"Seven months, I believe. Seven months and three days."

"*What?*" Finn stared. "I'm certain I didn't hear you right at all."

"Yes, sir, I'm sure you did, Master Finn."

The First Servant paused, as if in thought, then gazed at Finn again. "May I ask your religious persuasion, sir? If I seem impertinent, bear with me if you will."

"Crafters Tabernacle, now. Though I was raised in First Hammer and Vise. Why do you ask?"

"You are a stranger in this land, sir, and it occurred to me you might be unfamiliar with our beliefs. His Grace and the Royal Family practice the rites of the Deeply Entombed. Toomers, as the common folk say, but I would never repeat that to the King."

"Toomers. I'm sure I never—"

"Clearly you haven't, sir, or you would not have appeared to be astonished when I mentioned it would be some time before you could expect to see the King.

"I realize, now, you thought you would see him *tomorrow,* which is absurd, of course, no offense, Master Finn."

"I will freeze in my very tracks in the next minute and a half," Letitia said, "if you don't get me out of here."

"Yes, well, I will. No question of that. We cannot simply—Sir, if you would just explain to His Majesty that while I do not wish to intrude upon his spiritual life, I will only require a moment of his time to present my gift. Then we'll be out of your hair, as they say, and on our way. All right? Can you tell him that?"

"I could, but of course I will do no such thing. The Deeply Entombed, as the words connote, are *deeply entombed,* sir. The name is derived from the practice. Just as *hastily attached* conjures a picture of something quickly added to, or hurriedly affixed.

"The Deeply Entombed show their devotion through sleep, quite a bit of sleep, as it were. This sleep is accomplished in the grave, for those who rule the Afterworld count these hours as 'dead time,' and thus grant their devotees a seventh of that time as bonus days in this life.

"Do you understand, now, sir? If there are any further questions, I shall answer them if I can."

"Seven months? These people are *sleeping* for seven months?"

"No, sir. Nine months, to be precise. But they will awaken again in seven months and three days. As I believe I mentioned before.

"This gift you bring. May I ask if it is topical, timely, in any way?"

"Timely, in a way. But not really, I suppose."

"Is it likely to spoil?"

"No. There is no way it could spoil. However—"

"Excellent, sir. Then we don't have a problem, do we? I shall do my best to make your stay at court a pleasant one. And you as well, Miss."

"Thank you, but I don't think so," Letitia said. "I can't

possibly stay in this place, and neither can Master Finn. Finn, there is nothing else to talk about, as far as I can see. This is absolutely insane."

"I know, Letitia . . ."

"So give him the birthday present and let's take our leave. Thank the dear man and ask him where we can find a nice inn somewhere. An inn with a fire."

"Yes, that's certainly the thing to do."

Finn looked past Dostagio, down the long and lonely hall, feeling a chill and a slightly dank breeze himself. Still, he was quite aware of the aches of the day, the growing fatigue that threatened to drag him down. And, one more glance at the drawn, weary posture of Letitia Louise convinced him the choices here were not as clear as they seemed.

"I know it's best we leave, Letitia. On the other hand, if we could simply stay over here, since that's where we are. Stay and try to get some sleep—"

"No. Don't even think about it, Finn."

"—and get an early start," Finn finished quickly. "I'll seek out Bucerius and urge him to find us another balloon. I don't think Aghen Aghenfleck, in spite of his lack of any reason at all, would expect us to stay in Heldessia seven months."

"Seven months and three days, sir," Dostagio corrected.

"Yes, of course."

"I don't like it, Finn. I don't like it at all."

"Nor do I. But it has to be two or three in the morning, dear, maybe more. We have no idea where we are, and we *don't* know if those damnable yappers are gone."

Before Letitia could answer, Finn turned on Dostagio again. "If it's not personal, may I ask, would we find all the citizens asleep in town? I mean, is everyone in Heldessia a member of this—Deeply Enwombed church of yours?"

"Entombed, sir. Deeply Entombed."

"Right. Well, are they?"

"Oh no, sir. It's not for the common folk. Or Newlie kind, if you'll forgive me, Miss."

"Believe me. I am not offended at all."

"Only royalty, then?" Finn asked.

"That is correct, sir."

"It's not your religious persuasion, then."

"Oh, no indeed, sir." Despite the fact that no sign of emotion had crossed his drab features, Finn felt the man was quite stunned by the question. "Despite my esteemed and honorable position, I am only a servant here, a member of the Gracious Dead . . ."

TWENTY-ONE

I'M SURE IT WAS ONLY A FIGURE OF SPEECH," FINN said. "He didn't mean we should take him literally, dear."

"Are you? I'm not, Finn. I had a most peculiar feeling about our good Dostagio."

"And what kind of feeling was that?"

"Don't pretend you don't know. I saw *your* face when the fellow first appeared."

Finn nodded. As close as they were standing, it was hard to make out Letitia's features, for there was only a single torch set in a niche in their room, just enough to see that the place was as devoid of color as the hall.

"I must admit I did. I don't know what you saw with that keen Mycer instinct of yours, but I saw someone who looked as if he were wearing a mask, to avoid betraying his features, his feelings, as it were."

"Cold," Letitia added. "Withdrawn."

"Not unkind, though. Indifferent, perhaps. Clearly, as I'm sure we both agree, he is neither *gracious* nor *dead*. It may be it takes a rather detached sort of person to work for people who sleep all the time."

"Or those who don't have to work at all."

"It's hard to imagine anyone that lazy, Letitia. Numb, petrified, perhaps. When you look in the fellow's eyes . . . there's nothing going on in there that would stir a garden slug to any fervid thought."

"I've seen more personality and charm in a roach," said Julia Jessica Slagg. "In a log, in a sock, in a sack of cement, in a—"

"Yes, we get the point. That's quite enough."

"He's awfully dull, is what I meant to say."

"Find some place and sit. It's irritating to hear you walk around. You sound like a bucket of nails."

"They don't have carpets, that's my fault?" Julia snapped her silver jaws. "I wasn't the decorator here . . ."

"*Finn?*"

"What, love?"

Without even looking her way, he caught the mix of anger, aggravation and despair in the way she said his name, the tone, the manner, of a person who was beat, frazzled, weary of the day.

And, when he turned, he saw she had swept the torch to the far corner of the room. The wall was standard decor, black, polished marble with no fresco, tapestry, nothing to relieve the chill, dark expanse.

Nothing, that is, except two niches, horizontal ledges carved flush within the wall.

Finn let out a breath. He was getting used to chills, tingles, hairs climbing the back of his neck, not the sort of thing he cared for at all.

"They could be shelves. Places to put your clothes."

"They aren't, Finn."

"Books. Books would go nicely there."

"Stop it, will you? Stop it right now."

"They appear to be vaults, Letitia."

"Crypts."

"Not a good choice of words, no better than mine. Sacks and Cracks, this is a tomb, not a room. I should have made it clear to that fellow we didn't intend to be here that long."

"Do you think this is funny? You feel I'm amused? We have been *buried*, Finn. This is a jest to you?"

"I wouldn't say buried. I don't imagine they think of it

that way here. And they're not serious, love. These people don't die, they take naps."

"Very long naps, as I recall."

"Nine months, I know. And that's ridiculous, isn't it? I'm certain we'll discover that's meant in a ritualistic sense. A sacrament, a penance, something of the sort."

"It's Finn, Master of Theological Thought," Julia said. "I understand it better now."

Finn pretended she wasn't there. He walked to the door, opened it, peered each way down the dimly lit hall, closed the door again.

"It isn't locked. We could leave any time if we wanted to. The accommodations here are most peculiar, I admit. It's not the way we do things, but in their eyes I suppose it's rather like an inn."

"A dead inn, if you ask me."

"Nobody did, Julia. If you have anything to say, keep it to yourself."

"She's on edge, just like we are," Letitia said, showing the lizard a weary smile. "And all that copper and brass, she's bound to have a chill."

"She is not cold, love," Finn said, silently counting to three, for this was not the first time this conversation had occurred. "Julia is a mechanical device. You know that as well as I. Why would she have a chill?"

"I am very tired, dearest, too weary to talk about science and other such matters tonight. I'm going to try to sleep if I can."

"I didn't think you'd—"

"I'm not. I shall sleep on the floor. I will not get into *that*. And if you wish to offer me your cloak, fine. I would not refuse to accept. . . ."

I DON'T REALLY CARE IF AGHEN AGHENFLECK DOESN'T like it, it's the only sane and reasonable thing to do. We leave the damned clock with whoever will take it. If no one will, I'll simply leave it right here with a note. Bucerius will back us up with the Prince, I think. At least, I hope he will."

Finn shifted his bony hips on the hard floor and frowned thoughtfully at Julia Jessica Slagg.

"Did it ever occur to you that good Bucerius never mentioned the odd religious leanings of the King? I'm certain he never did."

"I wasn't present on your trip. I suppose it never came up."

"We spoke of religious matters, but only in a general way. And after that, there wasn't a lot of time. I cannot imagine anyone fool enough to hang around in this— oversize casket, waiting for the King to turn over and yawn. Rocks and Crocks, seven months is out of the question. I wouldn't spend seven *days* here."

Julia swept her tail about. In the flickering light of the torch, her ruby eyes seemed to dance to a fiery beat. In the corner, in a very small bundle, Letitia moaned in her sleep.

"Who are you trying to convince, Finn? You, or me?"

"No one at all," Finn said, more than a little annoyed at her remark, which hit too close to home. "I don't have to convince anyone. It's just that this whole situation is so bloody irritating. The ways of this land make no sense at all."

"And ours do?"

"That's not the issue here."

"I suppose it isn't. I'll give you that."

"Gracious of you, I'm sure."

Finn glanced at Letitia. Even with his heavy cloak about her, he was certain she was cold. Weariness, exhaustion from the day, could scarcely overcome the chill of that stone, a chill so old, so primal, buried so deeply within its granite heart, it would never go away.

"If you had, to, Julia, could you find your way back through this maze, to the door where we came in? I know you were beneath my cloak and all . . ."

"Of course I could," Julia said, her bright snout swiveling about, as if to test the frigid air.

"As you well know, since it's your fancy gadget that whirls about in my gut. I know every path I've trod, though I don't see why I should. It would be more efficient if you could show me where I'm going instead of where I've been."

"If I could do that, I would swallow such a gadget myself. That *whirly gadget*, by the way, as I'm sure you recall, is a compass, Julia. It is used in navigation at sea and in the air, though it does little good in either place, as near as I can see. And you're right on one point, at least. If I'd known where I was going, I damn sure wouldn't be *here*."

T HOUGH HE SURELY COULDN'T TELL FROM A HOLE in the ground, it was likely nearly dawn. It seemed much longer than one dawn past since he and the Bullie had risen from the Royal Balloon Grounds, floated past the Swamp of Bleak Demise, the awesome battleground, and into a chimney in Heldessia Town.

Scarcely arrived, then, and eager to depart—a wish that was nearly as strong as his second desire, a decent hot meal.

Letitia, bless her, surely was starving as well. Only great fatigue would set her need aside. For despite her ever-slender form, Letitia Louise seldom strayed far from the chance for a tasty meal.

No use even trying to sleep now, Finn said to himself. *Morning will be upon us, and we'll be out of here.*

Where would he find Bucerius? The Bullie said he'd be around, but Finn knew he should have asked. There was a shop he'd mentioned, someone he knew. Perhaps the name would come to mind.

As for the clock, the birthday present, the most taste-less object Finn had put together since he'd thought of lizard craft—he would give it to that sober-faced Dostagio when he saw the fellow again. Maybe a note would be apt, he could surely do that:

> Dear King Llowenkeef-Grymm:
>
> Here is an ugly gift from your greatest foe,
>
> > Hatefully,
> > Prince Aghen Aghenfleck IV

Probably not the way to put it, but something like that.

Finn rose, and gently pulled the cloak more snugly about Letitia Louise. Julia stood perfectly still in a corner of the room, giving her imitation of a nap. Finn had told her repeatedly she did not have the ability to sleep, and Julia, of course, insisted that she did, pointing out that while she was, indeed, a mechanical device, she had a ferret's brain, and that was the part that slept. A bit of logic, there, Finn had to admit—but never to Julia, of course.

No use sleeping, but it wouldn't hurt to simply sit: ei-ther that or stand up all night. What he wouldn't do, couldn't do, on the floor that chilled him to the bone, was nod off. No chance of that. A man must take control of himself, despite the situation. Use his strength, use his will. Maintain vigilance, in spite of one's bodily needs . . .

—he woke, kicking, screaming, flailing about, grab-bing for anything that might hold still—burst up out of a dream where the earth shook beneath him, tossing him helplessly, this way and that.

Woke, and saw the dream was real, heard the walls

rumble, saw the veil of dust tremble from the ceiling to the floor.

Stunned, dazed and out of sorts, Finn came shakily to his feet and made his way to Letitia Louise. She reached out for him, her dark Mycer eyes full of fear.

"Quake, tremor, terrible disaster, I don't know," he shouted, "I wish we were somewhere, anywhere but here!"

He waited, then, holding her close. Catastrophes seldom stopped at one. Usually, you could count on three.

Nothing.

Everything was perfectly still. A tiny stone went *ping!* off Julia's golden scales, a sound that seemed much louder than it should.

"Is it over, is it done? Are we all right, Finn?" Letitia ran her sleeve across her mouth, wiping away the dust.

"I would think so. Whatever it was, it's apparently over for now. Nevertheless, subterranean quarters are not the place to be when the earth begins to shift about. You bring my cloak, Letitia, I'll get the torch. We'd best make our way out of here."

"A sound call, you ask me," Julia said.

"I don't believe anybody did."

Finn opened the heavy door, thankful the mysterious tremor hadn't jammed the thing shut. The long hallway looked just as it had before. Cavernous and dark, except for the torches, set wide apart on the wall.

"All right, we seem to be clear. Let's hurry on, now."

"Not that way," Letitia said. "We need to go right."

"Are you sure?"

"Quite sure, dear."

"She is," Julia said. "And there's someone else out here as well."

"What? Yes, Dostagio—I'm very glad you're here," Finn said, catching sight of the fellow now, as he stepped out of the dark. "We're about to make our way out. There was some sort of quake."

"Not really, sir. It wasn't a quake, it was the Millennial Bell. Shook things up quite a bit upstairs."

"The *millennial* bell, you say?" Finn was uncertain he'd heard the man right. "What's that all about?"

"Sir," Dostagio said, as if he hadn't heard a word, "If you'll follow me, you might wish to clean up a bit: we'll find you some proper clothes. Breakfast will be at eight. I expect His Grace will be there. He's always quite hungry after he's been dead a while . . ."

Chapter

TWENTY-TWO

N O, I'M NOT GOING TO ASK HIM THAT, AND you're not either, Julia. The King's got his church, and I've got mine. It's not our concern. It might be the fellow simply decided to get up early this time."

"He's right," Letitia said softly, for sound carried much too well in the vast stone hall. "I'm curious too, but perhaps someone will explain."

"If I'm not being too impertinent," Dostagio said, without missing a step, without turning about, "what is the nature of that thing wobbling about at your side? Is it yours? I don't recall seeing it before."

"It's a lizard, and no, you didn't have a chance to see it when we arrived."

"A lizard, you say?"

"Yes, that's what they're called. That's what I do. I make lizards of every sort."

"Very well, sir."

A TWIST HERE, ANOTHER THERE, WALLS, TORCHES, and a myriad of doors. Where these doors might lead, Finn couldn't guess, and wasn't sure he wished to know.

Finally, however, the grim, black-marble walls came to an end. In their place were grim, black-marble stairs, spiraling up from the depths. A warm, more comforting breeze wafted down from above, driving away the chill of the underground world.

"If I should lose my senses and leave the surface of the earth, ever again—I beg you, Finn, stop me, by whatever means."

"A promise, my dear."

JULIA, AS AGILE, QUICK AND SPRY AS ANY CREATURE OF flesh and bone, had met her match on the winding marble stairs. At times she simply stalled, iron claws spinning against the slick, unyielding stone. She moved in a blink, in a blur of motion, going nowhere at all.

Neither Finn nor Letitia made any move to help, or even notice she was there. If senses beyond either human or Newlie were a virtue, then pride was Julia's sin.

AS THEY APPROACHED THE TOP OF THE STAIRCASE, they could see, 'round the corner, not the dim flicker of torches, but the first, hopeful beams of nature's light itself. And, a few steps farther into the ascent, a dazzling dome of brightly colored glass came into sight.

"How perfectly lovely," Letitia said, squinting into the unfamiliar splendor overhead. "What a marvelous thing to see!"

"Finely crafted, indeed," Finn added, mostly to himself.

He noted, upon a second look, that a face was pictured there, a face of extraordinary beauty, features captured in an instant of unbridled joy, triumph and release.

"It is called *The Happy Dead*, sir," Dostagio said, as if

guessing Finn's thoughts. "One of our finest works of art. You will see, as we reach the final steps, it is the first of such wonders made to light the Hall of Lengthy Termination, the Holy Place of Emperors, Tyrants and Kings."

"Oh, dear!" Letitia, first on the heels of their guide, clasped a hand to her breast, as if she could scarcely breathe. "Never have I seen such a marvel in my life. Finn, I can't believe my eyes."

Finn, too, was stunned by the sight. He felt a pang of both envy and pride, for the artisans who had created these masterpieces clearly possessed skills unsurpassed.

Each magnificent statue stood atop a solid, polished obsidian base. The works themselves, carved of the whitest, purest marble Finn had ever seen, stretched down the long passageway in seemingly endless array, the whole brightened by still more dazzling colored domes arching overhead.

The marvel of these pieces lay in their extreme sense of detail. Each gem-encrusted crown, each fold in a ruler's cape, each vein, each feature of royal countenance, was sculpted with most exquisite care.

And so many, Finn thought, such a long line of kings! Prince Aghen Aghenfleck's forebears, he knew, could be traced for many generations, but nothing so ancient as this.

"His castle isn't that grand, either," Finn whispered to Letitia. "I wonder if the arrogant fool knows what his foe has over here?

"I must say, Dostagio, I have seen fine art in a number of lands, but these marbles of your kings are most notable, indeed."

"Oh, no, not *marble*, if I may correct you, sir," Dostagio said, pausing to face his charges there. "Crystallization, as it were. Deanimation, wherein one is shifted to an unresponsive state. Awfully painful, I understand, but nobility has its ups and downs, you know. Are you all right, Miss? Can I get you a goblet of water, perhaps a cup of tea . . . ?"

Chapter

TWENTY-THREE

LETITIA LOUISE, QUEASY, SLIGHTLY OUT OF SORTS
and weak in the knees, completely forgot about petrified
potentates and calcified kings the moment they reached
the top of the twisted stairs.

The sight before her was spacious, immense, though
neither word could describe the beauty and grandeur of
the place. Another, even greater dome of glass arched a
good hundred feet above the floor, and was easily twice as
wide. Countless delicate shards of fractured glass clung
together in spiderwebs of lead. Unlike the brighter hues in
the Holy Place of Emperors, Tyrants and Kings, the glass
here was a thousand, muted shades of amber, rose, coral,
saffron and tangerine. And, scarcely there at all, lest keen
eyes searched them out, pale breaths of lilac, lavender and
beryl-blue.

The startling effect of these colors was a light that
painted every surface, infused the very air, with the subtle
magic of golden dawn.

Yet, there were still more marvels in this wondrous
room. From the base of the dome, from depths as azure as
the sea, sprouted shadowy lengths of stone, impossibly
thin columns that rose on tapered stems to blossom into
broad, graceful petals, shapely lily pads.

These elegant circlets were of different heights, some
stretching nearly to the top of the dome itself. Fifty or so,

Finn guessed, and maybe more. The giant stems were made of alabaster, olivine, milkstone and quartz. Opal, onyx and jade. Finn stared in disbelief at these structures, for he knew such stones, minerals and gems couldn't possibly stand under the stress of this magnificent design, even if such staggering amounts of these materials could be found.

"Yet, it is there, indeed," Finn said aloud. "And though I've found it wise to question many things I see, I believe there are a great many people eating breakfast here, and they don't look dead to me."

"If I were deeply entombed," Letitia said, "I feel that I'd get hungry too."

"It smells good as well," Julia said, with a rusty sigh. "I've already separated seventeen individual scents, all of them edible, eight of which I wouldn't touch if I were you."

"I would rather decide that myself, if it's all the same to you. A mechanical device that doesn't eat is not the best judge of fine cuisine."

"Do the words 'toxic,' 'venomous,' 'poison,' have any meaning to you? Consider 'fatal,' if you will."

"Come now, sir and Miss, and lizard, I believe," said Dostagio. "I shall find you a comfortable table at a level suited to your class, and see that you're served dishes I am certain will please and delight, and do you little harm at all . . ."

NARROW, CIRCLING STAIRS TWISTED AROUND THE sides of the dome, now and then leading to fragile, hanging bridges that joined one pad to the next—frail, swaying spans that looked more decorative than useful to Finn.

"Don't look down," he said. "You'll likely get queasy, nauseous, feverish, and dizzy as well. You may suffer chills, diarrhea or fits."

"How do you know, Finn?"

"Because four of those things are happening to me, and I expect the others will as well."

"If you fall, dear, I'm eating your breakfast. Think about that."

Julia Jessica Slagg, certain she could easily cross this span herself, came across in Letitia's arms, chuckling with a sound like rocks rattling about in a can.

I CANNOT GET USED TO THE DISPARITY, THE CONtrast here. As you say, these persons of the Toomer persuasion lie in the chill, dreary depths of the palace, then pop up for lunch in this marvelous place. Letitia, look around you. I doubt there's a structure on earth that can claim such a blend of art and architectural beauty."

"I wonder if we can ever get a waiter over here. Everything smells delicious, and I'm starving, Finn."

"I'm certain someone will be along. You've noticed, I guess, that Dostagio was right. Seating in this place is clearly determined by rank. Those folk in cheap, clashing colors directly above us are courtiers, toadies, parasites of every sort. I can spot their kind anywhere. They all look like Count VanDork at Aghenfleck's court.

"The ones directly above them are of noble birth. They all look very much alike, for they are related to one another in various ways. No chins, bad hair. Folk who wear satin and have someone tie their shoes."

"And up in the heights," Letitia finished, "where we cannot see, that would be the King, above all the rest?"

"Indeed. You can rest assured the royals will be just out of sight."

And, Finn noted, even if one couldn't see the King and his family and his favorites gathered about, they would look like kings were supposed to look, for sure. Cunning, sly, with penetrating eyes and a practiced smile. And,

though they managed to follow a train of thought sometimes, not overly bright.

As he watched, craning his neck to see the sight, something hurtled down from the heights—a single object,
then another after that. The first was half a cake, plummeting end over end, a chocolate comet trailing dark
crumbs in its wake.

The second was a blur, possibly a peach. It came very
close to the edge of Finn's alabaster pad, then splattered
on the diners below. A lady cursed, but was quickly
hushed, for it was clear the missive came from royal hands
above.

THE FOOD WAS DELIGHTFUL, OR SURELY FINE
enough for Finn and Letitia, who had not had a morsel
since they'd dropped on this land in ill-fated balloons.

As far as Finn was concerned, their server was much
too close a match to Dostagio. As if, like the other, he too
was decked out to play a role at the ball.

"There seem to be quite a few of them about," Letitia
said, mopping up a lake of eggs, squashberries and mush
with a heel of poppy bread.

"You don't believe what Dostagio told us, do you,
dear? I mean, how he's one of the Gracious Dead."

"No more than I believe the King actually dies for nine
months, then comes up for lunch. No, it's a religious rite
of some sort, and a very peculiar one at that.

"Do I believe they believe it? Oh, yes. You certainly recall our misadventure among the Hooters and the
Hatters. A zealot, a loony, can hound you to death,
whether his faith is real or not."

"If I were you, Finn—and I'm only a mechanical device—I would keep my voice down a bit, as several of
those zealots and loonies over there are giving us the eye."

"Yes, well." Finn pretended to gaze at something else

nearby, and saw that Julia was right. Two stocky louts, with coal-black beards and brows that sprouted like hedges above their eyes, were indeed scowling Finn's way. Both wore brown waistcoats, full pantaloons, ruffled collars and plume-bedecked hats, all in colors that assaulted Finn's eyes.

"Thank you, Julia, I should have taken a care."

There was little Finn despised more than admitting Julia was right, and he couldn't resist the chance to take a little back.

"It might be, however, they have simply never seen a lizard before. I'm sure I wouldn't know what to make of you if I hadn't thought you up in my head. I expect I'd be appalled at the sight."

"More likely awed, amazed, I should say. Stunned, astonished at such a marvel before your eyes. Rapt, totally overwhelmed—"

"Dostagio didn't seem impressed at all," Letitia added, reaching across to fork a puffball or two. She wouldn't touch the carp, for Mycer folk did not eat things that had once been alive.

"Though that surprises me not at all," she added, "for whatever the First Servant might be, he and the others of his kind, he is not like any human I've come across before. It's not a Newlie behind that somber face, I'll tell you that."

"Julia?" Letitia set down her fork and gave the lizard a thoughtful look. "With all your extraordinary senses—"

"Extraordinary, indeed, Letitia, in nearly every way. But I don't sense anything in the fellow. I can't get past that somber mien. I've tried, but I cannot."

"Nothing?"

"Nothing. It is much like trying to penetrate a stone."

"Damned peculiar, I'd say," Finn said.

Letitia sighed. "I don't know if you can use such a word in a place like this. *Odd,* and *unusual,* seem quite ordinary here."

"I'm not sorry I got the chance to see this marvelous sight," Finn said, "but I won't be sorry to finish what we came for, and get out of here. The peace and serenity of Garpenny Street are more to my liking, I don't have to tell either of you that.

"And, incidentally, Julia, I have been having some exciting ideas in the area of utilizing your enhanced senses to make incredibly small mechanical devices. Devices, that in turn, could produce even smaller devices still.

"We have discussed this often before, and I believe we can move along with it now. As soon as we can head for home, of course. I don't feel there's much use in exchanging scientific thoughts here—"

As if in answer, as if real life were a playlet or a mime, a familiar actor appeared to speak his lines.

"Ah, Master Finn, Miss, and lizard as well," Dostagio said, standing alarmingly close to the edge of the dining pad, "I have spoken with Eighth Tallest Chancellor Heffik-Lor, who has carried my message to Fifth Heaviest Councilor Cletz, who—

"Well, to the point, sir, which is that your presence, your mission, has reached the ears of the King, and His Grace wishes to say he does not desire your gift, and he would like you out of his presence at once."

"What? What's that?" Finn found it hard to comprehend what the fellow had to say.

"Not immediately, sir, for there is quite a storm rushing at us from the south, and His Grace is a kindly man, in his way. It will not be possible to launch any craft of the aerial persuasion, and he would not be responsible for your demise, your, ah—death, as it were. Not that there's anything wrong with that, you understand. . . ."

Wแผ่HAT IT IS," FINN SAID, FEELING AS IF STEAM
might rise from his collar, might, indeed, whistle from his
ears, "what it is is plain arrogance, scorn, outright contempt. That's a royal for you, no sense of decency, no feeling for anyone except their own bloody selves!"

"I suppose that's so," Letitia said, glancing about, lay-
ing a restraining hand on his. "But I believe this is what
you were *asking* for, only moments ago. Just leave that infernal clock on the table, in the hall, *any*where, and let's be
gone from here."

"Of course, that's exactly what I'll do. Goes without
saying. That doesn't excuse the fellow's bad manners,
though. There's no way he can make up for that."

"Most likely, he won't even try," Julia said. "He's a
king, you know."

"I beg your pardon?"

"She was just clearing her throat, dear. Getting the rust
out. Are you going to finish your parsley pie?"

"Yes, if you don't mind?"

"What you do about this mess is your concern, love, but
don't you take it out on us, you understand? Julia's of the
mechanical persuasion, and I'm just a Newlie. We are not
responsible for big mental decisions, we are only here to
serve humankind—"

"If I have said something to offend . . ."

"Why, whatever made you think so, dear?"

"If I may interrupt," said Julia Jessica Slagg, making her way up Finn's back, iron claws digging at his cape, "those men are looking at us again."

"I can't be responsible for that. They can look if they like."

Finn squeezed the arms of his chair. His feet had gone to sleep, and he wanted to stomp.

"I don't see anyone leaving. Do you suppose we all have to sit here till the King's finished his lunch? Maybe he'll toss more fruit at the common folk to let us know."

"Finn . . . Those two men, they aren't looking at us. They're looking at him."

Finn twisted halfway around. The stranger was coming toward them over the fragile bridge that linked their dining pad to the outer wall. The bridge swung perilously as the fellow crossed, until the wooden slats began to clatter and roll in dizzy oscillation, like waves upon a beach.

The being coming at them clearly didn't care. He was a short, stumpy creature, but every muscle, every limb, spoke of great power and strength. His body, clothed beneath a dark green robe and chain mail, was totally at ease.

It looked as if he paid little heed to the busy world about, yet anyone but a fool knew a Badgie was ever alert, that any rude encounter with this sleepy-eyed fellow would be over and done, scarcely before it had begun.

As Letitia had guessed, this stout creature, one of the Newlie Nine, was the reason the villains across the way had grown cautious and aware.

"Forgive the disturbance," the newcomer said, in a voice somewhere between a hiss and a growl, "I would simply like a word, if you will. My name is Koodigern, colonel/sergeant of the King's Third Sentient Guards."

"A pleasure," Finn said. "It's nice to run into someone of the sentient bent around here. Most everyone seems to be dead."

If the Badgie saw a jest in this, he didn't let it show. His dark, bearded lips didn't move. His eyes seemed nearly as black and fluid as Letitia's, but any resemblance ended there.

There was kindness and love in Letitia's eyes, while those of Colonel/Sergeant Koodigern absorbed, swallowed, every beam of light that came their way. Everything went in, and nothing came out.

"I mean no offense of a personal nature, you understand. But I have been informed by Dostagio that His Grace commands that you leave Heldessia as soon as conditions allow. He is, in spite of the fact that he springs from humankind, prone to an indulgent nature from time to time."

"Tales of his compassion are legend," Finn said, "and we will be pleased to follow his desires. I expect Dostagio has told you that as well. Have you some idea when this great storm will arrive, and when it might pass?"

"I am not a student of weather, myself. I would have no knowledge of that. I should add, in case it's not clear, that you are to take this gift you speak of when you leave."

The Badgie looked curiously at Julia Jessica Slagg. "Is that it? Your present to the King?"

"No, it is not, I am not anyone's *gift*, sir, have no doubt of that." Julia shook her claws and snapped her silver snout, motions that startled even the wily Badgie himself.

"Amazing. I imagine that's the pizzard Dostagio's been talking about. I have never seen one before."

"Lizard," Finn corrected, "and I cannot imagine why everyone has such trouble with the name."

Still, he was pleased to be off the subject of the damnable present, which lay in its bundle at his feet, an object he was determined to leave behind, in spite of what anyone said.

The Badgie let his gaze rest briefly upon Letitia, a look that showed only idle interest and no expression at all. His head was rather broad, and his face was somewhat flat. His bristly hair was black, centered with a streak of white, the whole coming to his point above his brow. Features, in all, Finn noted, ill suited for more than the slightest emotion of any kind.

Letitia showed no alarm at the Badgie's gaze. Before the Change, when Newlies were in their animal form, Koodigern's kind had been the hunters and Letitia's the prey. Bowsers, Yowlies, and the leathery Vampies were former foes as well, but Mycers feared only the Yowlies now, for these fierce creatures with pumpkin-seed eyes had not lost their ancestors' hatred, though they were close, now, to humankind.

"Those fellows over there have no more liking for you than for me," Finn said, "though I never saw the pair before."

"They are Diggers, Rooters. They follow the charnel arts." The Badgie leaned in to Finn. "You won't be in Heldessia long, but while you're here do not make friends with anyone dressing in garish colors, unfamiliar wear of any sort."

Finn was taken aback. "What do they want with me? I'm not dead and don't intend to be."

"Not yet, you're not. These fellows plan ahead, and competition's fierce. Let 'em get close and they'll mark you with their sign. Can't rub it off. Anything happens, that's it."

"That's what?"

"The marker's got call on your carcass. Bones, organs, whatever they can sell, whatever's left intact."

Finn looked at Letitia, and was grateful she was distracted by the storm clouds darkening the skies above the dome. Lightning sizzled, and distant thunder rattled the leaded glass.

"Is that why they're watching you, then?" Finn asked. "They, ah—want your remains as well?"

"No, sir. If they ever get close enough to me, I'll mark them with this."

Koodigern held his cloak aside to show Finn a short, wicked blade, gracefully curved in the fashion of the East.

"That's why they're watching me. I got two of their kind last week. They're sly fellows, but not too bright."

The Badgie paused, then, as if gathering his words, to be certain they'd come out right.

"Will you think it improper if I ask if you have a weapon, friend? I cannot help but notice your belt seems rather bare."

"I had one, yes. A Bowser blade, but I fear I lost it somewhere."

"Lost your weapon. Truly so?" His tone said he'd never heard of such a thing before.

"You had best take mine, then. No—do not protest, please. I can get another. I have to see you safely out of Heldessia. I would be remiss if I allowed you to come to harm in any way. I would never be promoted again."

Once more, the Badgie paused in thought. "I have already been remiss in another fashion. I know what you are doing here, but Dostagio failed to tell me your name."

"Finn. Finn of Ulster-East in Fyxedia. Our countries have been at war for some seven hundred years, though I couldn't tell you why. I am a Master Lizard-Maker. Such as the one you see here. I make them, for various purpose. And I am pleased to get the chance to meet you, sir."

Then, as Finn thrust his hand across the table, the Badgie shrank back in alarm.

"The Badgie kind don't do that, Finn. Someone should have told you. It is an obscenity to touch another male's hand. It means, in our tongue, 'Your private parts are infinitely small.' "

"Sorry," Finn said. "Of course I didn't know. I really feel it is much too difficult to travel. It's best to stay at home."

"I cannot answer, as I have no experience in that. I was born here, and I have never—"

Koodigern's words were cut short as a deafening sound ripped through the dome, a clatter, a shudder, followed by shrieks and shouts of pain. A shower of glass rained down upon the diners below. A body plummeted from the heights.

At first, Finn thought lightning had hit the top of the dome and shattered the panes of glass. Then, staring in disbelief, he saw a thin rope drop from the jagged hole above, then another, and a dozen after that.

"Bowsers! By damn, it's those yappers again!"

A great horde of the bow-tied louts slid down from the dizzy heights, armed to the teeth with muskets, blades, and weapons of every sort.

"What is this," Finn shouted above the din. "I thought these rogues came on Tuesdays and Thursdays, what are they doing here now?"

"Bowsers drink, quite heavily, are you not aware of that? These dunderheads don't know one day from the next."

With that, Koodigern was off, waddling across the treacherous bridge, his green robe flapping at his heels. . . .

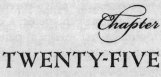

F ROM FINN'S PERCH BELOW, THE BATTLE RAGING
in the heights seemed a blur of great confusion, chaos,
awesome disarray. There was no way to sort intruder from
defender, no way to gain true dimension of the dying and
the dead. From this poor perspective, there was only a
flat, muddied canvas of devastation, a clatter, a frenzy, a
horrid bloody stew.

And, to further distort this grisly quarrel, much of the
action was lost in the blinding sheets of rain that lashed
through the cratered dome of glass.

Still, after a moment, after the shock of this bold
invasion had passed, he could see there was indeed a kind
of pattern and intent, that the Bowser attack had some
sort of structure after all. It was clear that more than
one set of lines descended to the royal dining pad. After
an initial assault to the right, which drew the defenders
to the fray, another horde of yappers slid down from the
left.

The Badgies saw this danger at once and rushed troopers into the seething mass, determined to upset the
Bowser plan.

"Amazing, if you think about it," Finn shouted over
the din, guiding Letitia quickly under the table, away
from flying debris.

"Bowsers, as a rule, have little use for method or direction. Disorder is usually the manner of the day. A two-pronged offense is something to see."

"Who cares, Finn? I'm going to *die* down here when one of those idiots falls on me!"

"I'd say the odds are against it," Finn said, though a Bowser's boater and his musket had just tumbled by, followed by a liveried servant of the King. "Really, these tables seem extremely sturdy to me."

It wasn't the answer Letitia cared to hear, and she let Finn know it with a look that said "that's two, dear, don't try for three."

Though this was not at all the time to show it, Finn was entranced, delighted by the careless, disheveled appearance of Letitia Louise. Huddled so close, pressed against her now, he was keenly aware of the blush of pink flesh beneath her fine, downy features, by her tiny lips and pointy nose, by her dark, enormous eyes, now deeper, larger still.

This rush of desire, he knew, was born of fear and apprehension, but no less real for all of that, and he longed to repeat these feelings in calmer times.

Just at that moment, something shattered against the alabaster column that held their dining pad aloft, something large enough to shake the table and rattle the dishes overhead.

Letitia covered her mouth and stared. Julia bounced once and turned over on her side.

"Now this isn't good," Finn said. "This may not be the safest place to be."

"You always go right to the heart of things," Julia said, flipping herself aright again. "I admire that in you, Finn."

Finn didn't answer. Instead, he lifted the white tablecloth in time to see that the King's Third Sentient Guards were still driving fiercely into the yapper foes, steadily pushing them back, away from the lofty royal pad.

Colonel/Sergeant Koodigern was likely in the midst of the battle, though Finn couldn't possibly single him out this far away.

"Our best bet's the bridge," Finn told Letitia, clutching her hand in his. "Julia, up on my back. No use taking chances out there."

"If you fall, you'd like to be certain that I go too . . ."

"Exactly. No need for you to survive without me. Stop gabbing and do as you're told."

"I don't like it," Letitia said. "It's narrow, and it's *swinging*, Finn."

"It always swings. That's the nature of the thing, it's supposed to do—Watch it, stay back!"

A cart of desserts tumbled by, trailing curds, compotes, pastries and puffs. Tarts, tortes, crullers and pies, puddings of every sort. And, still clasping his enormous cook's hat to his head, the hapless chef himself. For an instant, as he passed, he caught Finn's eye, and seemed to say he understood his plight, that it came as no surprise.

"I'm going to be sick, Finn."

"Don't *watch* him, Letitia. Don't look at anything, stay close to me!"

A veil of rain whispered by, diluted by the fall. Finn made his way to the edge of the pad, Letitia in tow, his package secure beneath his arm. Julia's claws dug into his flesh, but there was little he could do about it now.

The bridge swayed and trembled, somewhat worse than ever, it seemed. Finn took a cautious step forward, placed one boot on the thing, and turned to Letitia Louise.

"Easy now, go very slowly. This may look flimsy, but everything in this dome was carefully engineered by masters of their trade. I expect these suspensions have been in service for quite some time. Once we get to the outer wall, we'll be fine, secure as a—"

Finn's words were lost as the bridge literally exploded in the very center of the span. Two bodies, hurtling from different angles, met, like ill-fated comets, with a most revolting sound, then tumbled like a single horror toward the ground. There was nothing left of the bridge, not a plank, not a strand.

"The odds of two masses, meeting precisely like that, are not all that great," Finn said, unable to take his eyes from the sight.

"I think I could work it out if I had the math," Julia said.

"It would take some time."

"Indeed it would."

"Finn . . ."

"What, love?"

"If you two would cease your chatter, you'd notice it has grown quite still in here. It's over, I believe. They're done. Will you excuse me, please?"

Letitia turned away, knelt under the table and retched.

For once, Finn wisely pretended nothing had happened at all.

"It didn't slow down," he said when she returned, "didn't grind to a halt. It simply—stopped."

"I believe I mentioned that."

"Yes, indeed you did."

In a sense, he felt that the sudden silence was a sound unto itself. A ghostly echo, a distant refrain that rose up out of the clamor and the din, out of the babble and the clash of only moments before.

He reached out then, to bring Letitia close. She didn't hesitate, but came into his arms.

"I hope we won," she said. "I hope it came out all right."

"Yes, for everyone except those damned yappers in their awful straw hats. I can have no feeling for them. I regret my suggestion, Letitia. I don't like to think how close we came to crossing that bridge."

"We didn't though. Don't think about it, dear."

"I could work out the math," Julia muttered to herself, "but I doubt you'd care to hear . . ."

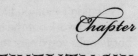

Chapter

TWENTY-SIX

T HE STORM, DESPITE ALL ITS FURY, MOVED SWIFTLY past Heldessia and on to northern climes. The people of the steppes, fierce Jihaulers and apathetic Roons, would get a soaking soon. Weary, then, the tempest would rend itself on the ragged peaks of Krak-Balu.

Perhaps, Finn thought, the mighty Grizz, the largest, and most elusive of all the Newlie kind, would look up from their fires and listen to the thunder roll by.

"I should like to see a Grizz sometime," Finn said. "Sit down with some burly fellow, have a cup of ale, and learn what they're all about."

"I don't think a Grizz likes to sit and talk with strangers," Letitia said. "I think they like to keep to themselves."

"I know that, but they could if they wanted to. They have, sometimes. Lord Gherick talked to one."

"Gherick did?"

"Oh, yes. On a mission for his brother, Prince Aghen Aghenfleck. A Grizz came out of the woods at Port Agony and looked up at Gherick, who was leaning on the rail of his ship. The Grizz said he wanted to trade. He had some nice carvings done in wood. He wanted to trade for hats."

"Hats?"

"He said they needed hats. Gherick told him they

didn't have any to spare. Apparently, the Grizz looked quite dismayed, then turned and walked away."

"I would have found a hat. It would be quite nice to have one of those carvings."

"I think I would have, too. Gherick said they smelled awfully strong. The wind was from the shore, and Gherick said it was rather bad."

"Well, it might have been," Letitia said, running her fingers through her hair, wishing she had a brush. "I expect if that Grizz had smelled a bunch of royals, he'd take offense, too."

Finn didn't doubt that. For some peculiar reason, those of noble birth thought silk, satin, ruffles and lace served as well as a tub of hot suds. Court, on a very warm day, could take your breath away.

FINN FELT THAT THE RESCUE TEAMS, THE BADGIES, the black-clad crew of the Gracious Dead, and servants in the livery of the King, were moving at quite a swift, efficient pace, cleaning up the mess the battle had left behind.

He and Letitia were not the only diners marooned on their pads. Many of the swinging bridges that had linked the massive structures together had been destroyed by entrees, servants and soldiers falling from above.

Below, there were bodies and debris to cart away. Above, beneath a clean, azure sky, craftsmen were already replacing the leading and broken glass destroyed in the Bowser attack.

Finally, a team extended a makeshift bridge from a dining pad nearby, and Finn and Letitia were led safely to the broad walkway that spiraled the inner dome.

"I am most pleased that you have survived," Dostagio said, as they arrived. "You have had so little time to see the marvels of the King's palace. I would regret it if you had perished before you had the chance to leave."

"I may be wrong," Finn said, "but it did occur to me that since the King was—awakened unexpectedly, as it were, there might be some chance he'd change his mind . . ."

"None, Master Finn. I had hoped Colonel/Sergeant Koodigern had properly relayed that to you."

"Yes, as a fact, he did, I just—"

"Excellent, then. Although he is no longer among the fully aware, he was able to complete the task he was given. And that is our purpose on this plane, is it not? Are you quite well, sir?"

"No, no I'm not. Are you telling me something has happened to Koodigern? I pray that's not what you said."

"I thought I made it quite clear, sir."

"He didn't, Finn," Letitia said, gripping his hand in hers. "He can't speak without sticking some frill on the end, but that's what he means."

"Sticks and Bricks. I admired that fellow. He was very polite, even when he told us we were not welcome here. He gave me his very own—"

Finn felt his stomach curl into a knot.

"—his own excellent Eastern dagger with the nicely curved blade. Damn me, if he'd had a weapon, he might have survived!"

"Those who serve in the King's guards expect this sort of thing, sir. Even if you were wholly responsible for his demise, there is so much more to be said for the deader side of life."

"I feel awful about this. Julia, if you dig any deeper, I'm going to bleed to death. What's the matter with you?"

"A minor malfunction of the rotator gears. Moisture was absorbed in the storm. Both my inner and outer workings are somewhat damp. I was splattered, not drenched. Sprayed, but soaked—"

"You're wet."

"The very word. Thank you, Finn."

"If you will come with me, sir and Miss, and lizard as well, I will take you to quarters where you may rest and change—I fear we will have to find you proper clothing again. You have soiled yourselves with food. Luncheon will be served in Mortuary Memorial Hall, at precisely two. Obviously, it will take some time before repairs are completed here. . . ."

"Dostagio, wait. A moment, if you will." Finn felt as if he'd missed a vital instant somewhere. As if the world had inched ahead and left him standing there.

"We're leaving, at once. The storm has passed. You're booting us out of here, but first we have to change for lunch. Help me out, if you will."

"I see no confusion, sir. You *are* leaving, there is no question of that. Your departure will be only slightly delayed. It is possible some of the Bowser intruders have eluded our troops. Until they are routed out, no one may leave the grounds."

"Why not?"

"A Bowser might manage to sneak through as well, sir."

Disguised as what? Finn thought. *A yapper's going to look like a Bowser, there's nothing he can do about that. . . .*

"What's for lunch?" Letitia asked. "I don't suppose you have a menu anywhere . . ."

TWENTY-SEVEN

BEFORE FINN COULD OBJECT, DOSTAGIO ASsured him they would not be staying in the suite of Celestial Bliss, as the storm had caused some flooding down below.

Instead, they were to be quartered in the Merchants, Second Class Envoys and Craftsman's wing, directly across from Brewers & Butchers' Hall.

"It is not a sanctified area," Dostagio said, "but I think you'll be comfortable there."

"We'll try," Finn said, with a glance at Letitia, for he knew, at once, what was on her mind. If the room wasn't holy, if you didn't have to be dead, then it might have an ordinary bed.

IF FINN THOUGHT HE'D SEEN EVERY ODD AND EXtraordinary sight, every strange and unnatural event since they'd come to Heldessia Land, now he would have to think again.

As they made their way from the dome, down a wide passageway with the usual dread decor, Dostagio stopped of a sudden and drew them into a small, open anteroom off the main hall.

Before Finn could question this action, Letitia made a breathless little sound, an "oh!" and an "oh dear me!" or something of the sort.

Following her glance, he saw the procession just as it appeared in the passageway. One did not need a quick mind, a keen intellect, to recognize a royal train. Every beggar, every thrall, even those of little wit in every land, had seen such a caravan before.

There is little, Finn thought, *that a royal likes to do more, unless it be nothing at all.* Even here, in the palace itself, where no one could watch, except those who saw it every day, the stately march went on. A royal couldn't go to supper, or see to his bodily needs, without a cortege of some degree.

Still, he noted, this indeed was no ordinary flock of noble birds. The strut, the color and the plumage were there, but this court had a definite image of its own.

The usual cast was there. He had seen them all, in one guise or another, at Prince Aghenfleck's Great Hall: Lords, ladies, chancellors and counts. Puffy ministers and knobby diplomats. Elders, councilors, generals and fools.

All in order of their rank, according to their place, each in proper attire. The code of dress among the titled and the toadies, and those who scamper in between, is rigid, fixed and not to be denied. Every pleat, every tuck, every doublet, robe, buskin or sash, reveals your true station. Or, if you dare, who you'd *like* to be.

The gaudy, the vulgar, the garish and the crude commit no sin at all in their attire. Often, they simply set the trend. This day, Finn noted, fashion favored the harness, the cassock and a splendid excess of lace. And every soul from the highborn to the Master of the Sewer wore some shade of purple, pansy, plum, orchid, lilac or mulberry hue.

All, that is, except King Llowenkeef-Grymm. He was dressed in tatters, rags and shreds. Torn, ripped, shabby bits of clothing that dragged along behind him in a long and dreary train. The royal colors were soot, smoke, bone and a maggoty tone of gray. The King's face was coated in ash, and his eyes were circled in black. And, though there were surely other members of the Royal Family about, only the King himself appeared to be here.

It struck Finn, then, that fashion in Heldessia's palace was precisely opposed to that of Aghen Aghenfleck's court. There, the Prince wore a bright array of colors, and his court was allowed only black. One ruler adored every shallow path of life, while the other celebrated death.

"Which of the two is more witless than the other," Finn muttered to himself, "is a mystery to me."

No one could have heard these words, for they were faint as spider breath. Yet, someone did, indeed. Finn had scarcely spoken before he felt the presence, saw its piercing eyes, felt it clutch his heart in a chill and alien hand.

Finn staggered, reached out in blind desperation for something, anything to keep him from falling weakly to the floor.

"Finn, love, what is it, what's wrong!?"

Letitia caught him and eased him gently to the floor.

"Don't know . . . *hurts*, Letitia. It hurts awfully bad . . ."

Letitia's voice was fraught with alarm. Dostagio, though, showed no concern at all.

"He is quite all right, Miss. Truly. There is nothing you can do."

"What do you mean he's all right? *Look* at him. He's white as he can be!"

"The fellow is right," Julia put in. "I can hear his pulse. It's normal. Or as normal as a pulse can get with Finn."

"You're a lot of help. He doesn't look normal to me."

"I'm—all right. Just back off a little. Going to be—sick right here."

"I wish you wouldn't, sir. Not until His Grace's party passes by. It's not the proper thing to do."

Finn didn't hear, surely didn't care. He crawled to the rear of the small alcove and rid himself of breakfast, lunch and dinner in the air the day before, and, it seemed, a great deal more.

Still, through the agony and the pain that wracked his bodily parts, the image of those cold and penetrating eyes refused to go away. He saw them, clearly, saw where they belonged, saw the gaunt features and the cruel and pitiless mouth.

And, for an instant, the image expanded, and Finn saw beyond the creature itself. Saw that it walked directly in the shadow of the King . . .

Chapter

TWENTY-EIGHT

"ARE YOU *SERIOUS,* DEAR? TRULY?"

Letitia covered her mouth and stared at Finn, her eyes as black as barley mead. "Oh, I hope you're wrong, I hope you're mistaken, Finn."

"I am not, though, Letitia. There is nothing wrong with my heart. I must confess I thought for a moment I would soon be a Coldie, but that will have to wait a while.

"I was hexed, my dear, there's nothing else for it. I suppose the fellow could have killed me with his spell if he'd wanted to. I'm sure he could do it still."

He told her, then, how he'd seen the man's image in his mind, quite clearly, and how he walked very close to the King.

"I didn't see him as he passed, but I am certain he was there. He's a sorcerer, and a good one. Better than that poor fellow they did in at Aghenfleck's court. You won't find this one hawking cheap charms in the street."

"Well, as you say, he could have slain you right there, and he didn't. I think that's a good sign, dear."

"I suppose one could look at it that way," Finn said, somewhat irritated at Letitia's sudden composure in the matter. She had certainly been quite alarmed only moments before.

He still felt shaky, drained of any strength, though he'd slept through the day. He had been struck just after break-

fast, and now it was late afternoon. He had no memory of
Letitia and Dostagio helping him to this room, or falling
into bed. The First Servant had brought Letitia soup,
marigold tea and fatcakes for lunch. There was soup left
over, but Finn had no appetite at all.

At least, he thought, the simple quarters had a bed and
other facilities common to civilized life. No stone floors,
no burial vaults in the wall. And, as Dostagio had promised, there were places to wash, and clean and comfortable
clothes.

Still, he was shaken by his experience in the hall. *Why?*
he wondered now. Why had the magician treated him so
cruelly, why punish him at all, unless he simply enjoyed
that sort of thing?

True, he had had a passing thought in which the word
witless had come into play associated with Kings . . .

*Cabbages and Kale, if that rogue can pluck tidbits from
everyone's head, he'd have to knock out everyone in
Heldessia twice a day!*

"Why me?" he said aloud. "Just because I'm from out
of town?"

"What, Finn? I thought you fell asleep again."

"Well, I'm not. I'm quite awake now. I'll be just fine in
a while."

"Would you like some soup now?"

"No. I'm not as fine as that. Thank you all the same."

It TOOK SEVERAL TRIES, BUT FINALLY HE GOT HIS
feet on the floor, paused for a moment, then stood, keeping one hand on the bed.

"As I said, I'm fine now, truly I am. A trifle dizzy, but
that will go away."

He made it to a bench across the room, wrapping his
cloak about him on the way. He was quite aware Letitia
followed him anxiously with her eyes.

The room seemed a little cool, or maybe that was the residue of the spell. At any rate, it lacked the funereal chill of the suite of Celestial Bliss down below.

"Did you feel anything, Julia, anything in the grand parade that seemed—unusual to you? Did you sense the presence of that seer?"

"I didn't, no," Julia said, in a voice like a rasp on tin, a sure sign she needed oil. "And that in itself is of some concern, Finn. I am able to hear a weevil's breath, the flatulence of fleas. I know when a beetle sneezes, when an ant begins to cry—"

"All right, you didn't get a thing when that sorcerer passed us by, when he knocked me for a loop."

"No, I did not."

"Well say that, then. I don't want to hear about your sensitivity to bugs."

"Bugs make quite a racket. You're lucky to be of humankind. Your perception is somewhat keener than the average rock, and that saves you a lot of pain.

"What that sorcerer did was block me out. It's simply as if he wasn't there. If he can do that to me, small wonder you didn't see him passing by."

"That's quite frightening," Letitia said.

"It is. And it's still a mystery why he picked me."

Letitia stood and paced about, hands clasped tightly to her breasts, clearly lost in thought.

"Dostagio . . . you won't recall, of course. He said . . . he said, 'he's quite all right, Miss. There is nothing you can do.' "

"He did?"

"That tells me he knew what had happened to you, though Julia and I had no idea. And one thing more. When he helped me bring you here, I asked him what had happened, and he said he had no idea. Which isn't true at all."

"No, it isn't. Dostagio is full of secrets about this place, there's nothing new in that. I don't suppose, Julia . . ."

"You asked me before. I don't know what he did, I don't know what he is."

"Is there anything you *do* perceive, anything at all?"

"Finn . . ." Letitia shook her head, a gentle reprimand.

"I am accustomed to abuse," Julia said. "It's part of what I do. And you forgot one point, Letitia. The bell . . ."

"Yes. The *Millennial* Bell. I asked Dostagio about it when he brought us lunch. There's still soup, you know, and a bit of bread . . . I asked him, and he pretended he didn't hear."

"No great surprise there."

"No, I fear not. Except, Finn, this time there was just the slightest moment of hesitation, scarcely a breath, but it was there. I could see through that sober mask of his. He lied to me, I'm quite sure of that.

"We Mycer folk are quite sensitive too, you know. In many respects, we see more than you, Julia, in a very different way. I doubt if anything of the mechanical persuasion can even approach your abilities. And much of that credit goes to you, of course, Finn."

"*Much?* You're too kind, love. All I did was invent this thing. So—the First Servant lied when you asked about the bell."

"No question of that."

"It's good to know. Though I'm not sure what it tells us, are you?"

Letitia shrugged. "I'm merely telling you what I sensed."

"Yes, and that's all you can do. I feel we must make every effort to leave this place as quickly as we're allowed. As soon as they've rooted all those Bowsers out. Since it's evening now, I guess it will be morning before we can go.

"Bottles and Cans, you'd think something would be easy now and then. Some plain, everyday act with a simple resolution. No chaos, no alarm, no Bowsers or balloons. Letitia, Julia—if we ever get back to Garpenny Street in one piece, and I pray that we will—please remind me not to go anywhere again, no matter what some google-eyed, whey-faced Prince says he *might* do if I don't produce a lizard that spins, ticks, stands on its head, or sings tenor in the choir.

"If I ever even show signs that I might waver in this resolve, I—"

"Finn."

"If I—I believe I was speaking, Julia."

"No one would argue that. But you should know that company is about to arrive. In roughly two seconds and a half. And it is not Dostagio, as one might guess . . ."

Before Finn could answer, the door burst open with no warning at all. An action so quick, so rudely done, that the heavy panel slammed against the wall, raining dust to the floor.

"Your pardon, I suppose. Though manners are not required in a mission such as mine. I owe you no courtesy at all."

Finn stared, unable to believe his eyes.

Koodigern! The squat, heavily muscled Badgie, chain mail under his heavy green cloak, flat features and bristly hair with a bright streak of white.

Only Koodigern couldn't be there, the Badgie warrior was dead. Dostagio had told them so. . . .

No, no it isn't, Finn saw at second glance. Newlies of any sort tend to look alike if you don't know them well. Newlies make the same mistake with humans. This was almost Koodigern, but not the same fellow at all.

"I can read you, human," the Badgie said, "and you *don't* know me, as you have guessed. I am Maddigern,

Second from the Last Brother to Koodigern, who gave his life because he gave his weapon to you."

"I deeply regret that," Finn said. "I would give anything if I had not accepted his offer. If I could bring your brother back—"

"If you had rejected his gift, he would have been deeply offended. You know nothing of our kind."

"No, I confess I do not. I would consider it an honor, though, if I could return Koodigern's blade to you. I'm sure he would want his brother to have it if he—"

Maddigern's eyes went dark. No other emotions played across his features, but the eyes told Finn enough. The Badgie drew back, and it was clear that he was plainly repulsed.

"Do you think I could handle that thing, after it has been tainted by your hand? My brother has served your kind too long. Don't confuse his careless ways with that of other Badgies, especially mine."

He paused, then, let his eyes touch Letitia a moment, then moved on to Julia Jessica Slagg. Finn sensed his curiosity was aroused, but he kept such thoughts to himself.

"I am wasting time here. I have duties to perform, only one of which concerns you. With the passing of Fifth from the First Brother Koodigern, his loathsome charge falls upon me. While you remain on royal grounds, I am responsible for your well-being.

"I would rather disembowel myself twice than ever look upon you again. Nevertheless, I am sworn to do what I get paid for, and, more than that, uphold my honor to the King's Third Sentient Guards."

Maddigern snapped to attention, looked at Finn, then bowed stiffly at Letitia Louise.

"I mean no disrespect, but you do yourself no honor, Mycer person, taking company with him."

"Damn you, I'll not take that," Finn said, feeling the

color rise to his face. He stepped toward the Badgie, drawing Koodigern's blade from his belt.

"Finn, no . . ."

Letitia placed herself firmly in his path. "Please. Let it be."

"If you'll stand aside, Letitia. This does not concern you."

"Oh, but it does, does it not? It very much concerns me. And I say let it *be*."

Finn looked over Letitia's shoulder. The Badgie stood his ground, showing no emotion at all. Then, turning away, he closed the door behind him.

Letitia looked at Finn, but he could do nothing but turn away.

"I had every right. You should not have interfered."

"I had every right as well."

"I didn't fear him. I'm sure he's quite practiced, but I feel I can handle myself."

"I have never doubted your courage," she said, reaching up to touch his chest. "Look at me, Finn. Don't turn away."

Finn faced her as she asked. In spite of his displeasure, he found it hard not to look into her eyes.

"It is not your courage at issue. Must I tell you that again?"

"There are times . . ."

"There are, indeed. And I hope you see that this was surely not one of those, my dear."

"I can't help but wonder," said Julia Jessica Slagg, "if it's possible to disembowel oneself twice. The first time, it seems, would strongly discourage attempting the act again . . ."

T HOUGH HIS RAGE, HIS ANGER, HIS WOUNDED pride, were somewhat abated by suppertime, an ember still smoldered here and there, and he was more than ready to pounce on Dostagio when he arrived—ready to impale the fellow with a quiver of questions on Badgies, bells, Bowsers and seers.

Especially seers, the kind that stunned perfect strangers with a spell, damn near knocked them dead.

But, in spite of this fervent intent, Finn had drifted back into restful sleep by the time Dostagio arrived. He woke, somewhat later, grumbled for a while, then fell onto the feast of thorncake, clutter soup, peppered kale, and a jug of nutty dark ale.

"Did he say anything?" Finn asked at last, dabbing his mouth with a linen napkin, bearing the arms of the King. "I wish I could have talked to the fellow. There's plenty these people have to answer for."

"He didn't say a thing, dear. Only that the Bowser scare is likely over, and the palace is secure."

"That's something, then. If it's so, we can get out of here early. I think I can find Bucerius. He knows that shopkeeper, what's-his-name, the one that sells greens. If he's not there, I expect he's at the balloon grounds. They surely have one here . . .

"Letitia, I don't mean to be rude, but that seer's chicanery has left me weak as a child. I cannot seem to stay awake, I'm shamed to say. I'm not at all certain what I was talking about before I dropped off. Was it anything I ought to recall?"

"Nothing that won't wait till the morrow, Finn. I'm sure you'll feel stronger by then."

"Yes, well, if you think so, tomorrow's fine with me."

Iᴛ ᴍᴜsᴛ ʙᴇ ᴀ ᴍᴏsᴛ ᴅᴇʟɪᴄɪᴏᴜs ᴅʀᴇᴀᴍ, ʜᴇ ᴅᴇᴄɪᴅᴇᴅ, one granted to the weary and oppressed, the anxious and the stressed, those who deserve a lovely treat in the deep, deep hours of the night.

The room was dark, except for the dim, pleasant glow of a candle against the far wall. There, the light flickered on golden scales, shimmered in ruby-red eyes, as Julia practiced her imitation of a nap.

That image vanished in a blur, as a finer, far more dazzling vision took its place.

There was, to say the least, passion in this dream, wild and joyous moments that took his breath away, swept him up to dizzy, incredible heights. And, just as quickly, took him gently into sweet and lazy bliss.

A thousand sensations assaulted his body, burned into his soul. There were tantalizing scents, elegant caresses, and secret delights. There were hollows, hills, slender limbs and iridescent eyes. There was love remembered, and whispers in the night.

"That was most elegant and fine," Finn muttered to himself, "truly the loveliest dream I ever had."

"Call it what you like." Letitia smiled. "Now go to sleep, dear . . ."

Fɪɴɴ ᴡᴀs ᴡᴏᴋᴇɴ ʙʏ ᴛʜᴇ sᴏᴜɴᴅ ᴏғ ᴀ ɢᴇɴᴛʟᴇ, but quite persistent tap, the kind you know simply won't go away. He pulled on his breeches, grabbed up his Eastern blade, in case it was the Badgie again, and stumbled to the door.

"I do hate to bother you, sir," said Dostiago, "I know it's not a decent hour, but I must ask you to dress and come with me."

"Where and what for? What new foolery is this? I have followed you before, and it always leads to trickery and deceit, lunch on a battleground, a cardiac attack."

"I am appalled that you would think I do not hold you in the highest regard, Master Finn. I am deeply pained, sir."

"I strongly doubt that." Finn peered around the fellow, checking to see if any rogues or rascals were about.

"I don't believe I've ever seen you pained, Dostagio. Or, for that matter, delighted, saddened, concerned with anything at all."

"Yes, sir. The King would like your presence at once. You are to bring your gift to His Grace, and the device you call your lizard. Do hurry, sir. The King is anxious to get to sleep. . . ."

FTER THE AWESOME SIGHT OF THE HOLY
Place of Emperors, Tyrants and Kings, the splendor of the
Great Dining Hall, Finn was prepared for anything that
might lie beyond the great oaken door. The portal was
fully nine feet tall, and nearly twice as wide, intricately
carved with legend and myth from Heldessia's ancient
times.

He would have liked to study this fine example of tal-
ented artisans' work, but there was clearly no time for that.
Moreover, the door was guarded by seven green-robed
Badgies, stout and grim-faced fellows at rigid attention,
gripping enormous pikes. And, to Finn, they all looked
closely related to the fiery, wild-eyed, Maddigern himself.

"Just go in, sir," Dostagio said. "His Grace is expecting you."

"So I do what? Bow, grovel, fall on my face? They always have rules about this sort of thing."

"Oh, nothing like that tonight. Enjoy your visit, sir."

"I'll do that," Finn said, certain that would not be
likely at all.

CAKES AND SNAKES," HE SAID ALOUD, SOMEWHAT
rooted in his tracks—certain, now, Dostagio for some
bizarre reason had led him to the wrong door.

Instead of a great and vaulted chamber, a stately columned hall, he was facing a small, unimpressive room with bare, chiseled stone walls. The monarch himself was a spindly, ruddy-faced fellow in a pink-and-orange nightshirt that came to his knobby knees. Perched on his head was a tasseled cap to match.

So why am I surprised? Finn wondered. The only time he'd seen King Llowenkeef-Grymm he was wearing tatters and rags, his features cold as the grave. If he was alive at the moment, why not look cheery and bright?

"Please," said the King, in quite a pleasant tone, "sit, Master Finn, and pour yourself a cup of ale."

"Why, thank you, sire, I will. And let me say I am grateful to be in your presence. It's an honor to meet Heldessia's King. I shall treasure this moment for the rest of my life."

The King waved him off, for he heard this a hundred times a day.

The ale was very nice, much like the nutty brew Dostagio had brought to his room. He was greatly relieved to find there were comfortable, cushioned chairs in the King's small chamber, as well as a sturdy table and several frosty pewters, in case they ran low.

No grim, funereal vaults here, only the homey surroundings of a middle-aged fellow who liked a comfy chair instead of a miserable throne. And, wonder of wonders, Finn and the King were alone. There were no guards or toadies about, unless they were hiding somewhere.

"You're the fellow who brought me a present from that scoundrel, Aghen Aghenfleck. Would I be right in that?"

"Yes, sire, you would indeed."

"Nasty, witless boob is what he is. Nitwit, soft in the head. Useless lout. Scatterbrain. Dull, shallow, mean-spirited wretch. A scalawag, a sneak. Worthless, sniveling beggar, not fit to call himself a prince. Ought to be working in a sewer, you ask me. I expect you'd agree, Master Finn."

"Ah, well, sire . . ."

"Loyalty, that's the thing, boy." The King shook a finger at Finn. "Never speak evil of your master, even if he's unworthy scum, which Aghenfleck surely is. That bundle there, that's for me?"

"Yes, Your Grace. It's a birthday present, I believe."

"Don't believe in birthdays. Everyone's got one, what's the fun in that? I do not want the fellow's present, don't want to see it at all. Put it somewhere. That thing thrashing about beneath your cloak. That's this mechanical device you carry about. Let's have a look at that."

At once, before the King's command was scarcely out of his mouth, Julia Jessica Slagg scrambled out of Finn's cloak, onto the floor, and up onto the table in front of Llowenkeef-Grymm.

"Well now, if that's not a splendid thing to see!"

The King leaned forward, hands on his knees, devouring every inch of Julia with his dark and penetrating eyes, taking her in from her spiny tail to her golden scales, iron teeth and shiny silver jaws.

He made no effort to hide his great delight. He clasped his hands together, and his face creased in a joyous smile.

"Amazing, I say. Astonishing device! Truly a work of art, something we appreciate here in Heldessia's halls, which I can't say for that uncultured, illiterate collection of louts in Aghenfleck's court. No offense, of course."

"None taken, sire."

"Yes, well. Ah, what is it?"

"It's a lizard, Your Grace."

"A lizard."

"Yes, sire."

"And how did you come to call it that?"

"No reason I can name, sire. While I was working on it,

it simply seemed to fit. I liked the sound of it, and it stuck. I called them lizards from that day on."

"Them?" The King raised a brow. "So you have crafted more than the one?"

"Oh, indeed, sire. It's my invention, and mine alone. I own and operate The Lizard Shoppe in Ulster-East. Lizards are my trade.

"I don't mind saying, in all modesty, sire, I come from good craftsman stock. My father worked in metals as well, and made a number of contributions to the common good. It was he who was responsible for the all-brass lice hammer used in households around the world today. He also did significant work at the Royal Fish Works, though he got little credit for that.

"Proud though I was of his accomplishments, I yearned to go out on my own. I began with a lizard that picks up debris about the house. I followed that with the lizard bellows, which works quite well, though small children are frightened by the noise.

"Then, there is the lizard cleaning rod for muskets of any bore. The special tongue gets in there and sucks out powder and soot that might cause a weapon to explode, resulting in bodily harm. And then—"

"Yes, fine," said the King, who had little interest in bellows, lice or soot.

"And this model here, what does *it* do? Dostagio says it talks, but I can scarcely credit that."

"It does, sire. Entirely too much, I'm bound to say."

"What Master Finn means, Your Grace, is that my vocabulary is easily twice as extensive as his . . ."

"Ha! Wonderful!" The King slapped his knees twice. "Impertinent, too. I wouldn't stand for that, but apparently you do. So. How do you do it? How do you make it *think*? I find that most unique in a mechanical device."

"It's really not as difficult as you'd imagine, sire.

Double wiring of futanic preen, a pair of copper doffits on the major boskin gear. Triple pankers, of course."

"Of course, yes . . ."

The King looked thoughtful, and tapped the side of his nose. Finn took a care to show no expression at all. A bit of prattle on doffits and preens always did the trick. There was no way to ask any questions after that, for it all came out of Finn's head. The one thing he dared not discuss, of course, was the fact that Julia had a ferret's brain within her silver skull.

Tampering with life in any fashion was something one simply didn't do. No one had forgotten the sin of Shar and Dankermain, the seers who had brought about the Change. It had been three hundred years since Newlies appeared, but the fears and hatreds that awesome event had brought to bear were still very much alive.

And, if they didn't hang him for Julia, Finn knew, there was always Letitia Louise. Intimate relations with nonhuman creatures was not unknown, and most people looked the other way. Still, it was against the laws of every land . . .

"May I say," Finn said, for he knew his host had noticed his attention had strayed for a moment, which was not the thing to do with a king, "may I say this is the finest ale I have ever had the pleasure to drink. Such fullness, such exquisite taste."

"Of course it is," the King said, ruffled, peeved, slightly annoyed, "it damn well better be. Now, that infernal present you brought—which I will not accept, by the way—what is it, boy, what did you bring?"

"It's ah, a clock, Your Grace. It is known far and wide that King Llowenkeef-Grymm is the world's foremost collector of rare and unusual clocks. Prince Aghen Aghenfleck has—"

"Lummox! Blockhead!" The King slammed his mug on the table with such a fury, the creamy ale flew this way and that.

"Exactly what that fool would do. Send *me* a clock. As if he had the foggiest notion what a fine timepiece even looks like, what it—what it—"

The King stood abruptly, unfolding like a broken spring.

"This way, Finn. Hurry along, I can't stand a sluggard or a slouch. Get moving, boy!"

Without a word, Finn followed the King through a back door of his quarters, a door that led to a hall exactly like the halls he'd seen before.

"Stay here," he told Julia. "I don't have any idea what this is all about."

"Tell him *you* made the clock. See what he says about that."

"Stay put and keep your snout shut, Julia. That's all I need from you."

He pretended not to hear a rusty cackle as he bounded after the knobby-kneed fellow in gaudy nightshirt with tasseled cap to match. . . .

THE CORRIDOR WAS DARK, EXCEPT FOR A TORCH now and then on a bracket in the wall. The walls, the ceiling and the floor, were standard Heldessia decor—great slabs of granite in colorful black.

Finn, young and strongly built, could scarcely keep up with the King, who bounded ahead like a boy on his way to the fair.

It took little thought to guess that the King was leading Finn to clocks. Finn didn't care about clocks, he could take them or leave them alone. The works, the cogs, the little gears and springs were of interest, of course, but he had gone far beyond such simple devices as that. He had stopped taking clocks apart when he was no more than a child.

"Which is not the point here," he said to himself. "The point is that Julia, for once, is quite right. I made the clock the King despises, for it came from Aghenfleck, and what am I to do about that?"

Nothing, the answer came at once. If the King didn't look at that tasteless device, all would be well, and he and Letitia and Julia would soon be out of sight.

EVEN BEFORE THE KING OPENED THE NARROW IRON portal—with a key he kept under his tasseled cap—Finn could *feel* the might, feel the beat, that lay just beyond that door. And, when it opened, when the heavy panel swung away, the shock, the power of the place nearly knocked him off his feet, nearly drove him back into the hall.

The strength, the energy behind this force was a thousand, ten times, twenty-, thirtyfold, a chaos, a din, an endless array of click-tick-clitter-clat clocks. Clocks that covered the walls and the ceiling, clocks that littered the floor. It was, as a matter, impossible to move, to take a step anywhere at all, without running into a hundred ticker-tocks.

They beggared description, these clocks of every sort. Great, enormous clocks, clocks big enough for a family, if, indeed, they could stand the horrid noise. Clocks so tiny you could scarcely see them at all. Clocks with rusty weights that swung ponderously about. Clocks that moved with such vigor they blurred before the eye. Clocks, Finn saw to his dismay, where little birds ran in and out. Clocks where woodsmen chased their wives, where their wives chased children dizzily around, then started all over again.

These horrors fueled the air with such heat, such a fierce, concussive beat, that Finn felt his body was under constant siege, that the very air conspired to punch and prod his head, his belly and his chest.

Before he turned and fled, with a hapless gesture to the King, he noticed that none of these mad, clamoring clocks seemed to tell the same time . . .

THERE'S A REASON FOR THAT," SAID LLOWENKEEF-Grymm, as they reached the King's door, and Finn's hearing began to return. "The Afterworld has its own sense of time. Those of us who follow the faith of the Deeply Entombed are in tune with the Great Eternal Hour, not the illusion of time we find reflected here."

Julia, waiting where Finn had left her, pretended to be immobile, as she sometimes liked to do. Finn ignored her and followed the King inside.

"Yes, I see, eternal hour, splendid idea," Finn said, who felt it was best to agree with a lunatic and let him have his say.

"Don't be absurd." The King smiled, for he felt it best to be polite to the hopelessly misinformed.

"You don't *see* anything, Master Finn. You couldn't possibly understand our beliefs. Why, I scarcely do myself. Besides, we wouldn't have you even if you did. You're not of noble birth, and if you were, I'm certain you're not kin to me. There are only eleven believers in the Church of the Deeply Entombed."

"Eleven, sire?"

"What, you think that's too many? I assure you, they are all sanctified. All blessed and approved by me."

Eleven? This whole funereal farce is for eleven rattlepates who like to take a nap?

"I have a great desire to learn about the many different spiritual paths one comes across in the world, Your Grace. It is most enlightening to understand more about yours. I—"

"Different? *Different* paths, you say?"

The King's demeanor, just this side of a frenzy or a fit, told Finn at once he might have put this remark another way.

"What I meant to say—"

"I quite understand what you meant," the King said, his anger quelled as quickly as it had come. "Ignorance, indeed, is a valid excuse. Even the sin of heresy comes into play."

He paused, then, to pour them both another mug of ale. "Do you imagine, Finn, the sorrow, the agony I must feel, the burden that weighs upon me, with the knowledge

there is no other true path but mine? That everyone outside my immediate family is doomed? Destined to walk
the earth as Coldies when they die? It is hard to live with
this, my friend."

Finn imagined a tear ran down the King's cheek, but
surely it was only a trick of the light.

"I—had not realized the great responsibility you bear
for us all, Your Grace. May I say that you handle it rather
well."

"No, no I don't. Nice of you to say, but I fear that I
don't. I should pray for those who will ever be awake, but
I seldom have the time.

"At any rate, nothing I can do about that, is there now?
I am pleased you were able to meet me, and show me that
marvelous machine as well. Where'd the damned thing
go?"

"My honor, sire."

"Yes, it certainly is."

"You have so many—truly unusual rites, sire. Anyone
aware of the Deeply Entombed, as I am now, can understand why it *is* the only true path."

"Very astute of you, boy," the King said, stifling yet
another yawn. "Now, if you'll excuse me, I have important functions to perform."

"I don't see how you handle the load, Your Grace. Your
eternal parades, your intense devotion to sleep, the
Millennial Bell. I must tell you I'm honored to have been
present here when that sonorous instrument struck again.
Would I be overstepping my bounds, sire, if I asked what
occasion you are commemorating now?"

"Which what?"

"The occasion, sire. The bell celebrates a, ah—theological moment of some sort. From the word, I would
guess, something a thousand years ago. That would have
been about—"

"Wendon's day."

"Sire?"

"Last time before this. About noon, I recall. I rose and ate three fowl hens. Two jugs of wine."

"Your Grace—"

"Time before that was the middle of Madge. Tootsday the fifty-third. I think I told you, Finn, I have a lot of things to do."

He stood, then, downed his ale, and ushered Finn to the door.

"Well, it's been a pleasure. Get out of here, I've had enough of you."

"Sire, if you don't mind—" Finn saw at once the King was nudging him toward the door where he'd first come in—away from the portal where Julia still waited outside.

"If I may suggest . . ."

With a somewhat rude gesture, the King gave him a push outside and closed the door.

Finn muttered to himself, nothing so loud that the rigid Badgie guards might hear. They might, every one, be Maddigern's cousins or brothers, as far as he knew.

Five minutes, then another ten. No sign of First Servant Dostagio at all, no way to find Julia without simply asking the King. That didn't seem like a good idea.

"Trees and Bees," Finn said, with no small touch of irritation. "I don't have the slightest idea where I am, or where I ought to be!"

Fine. One course is better than none, and far better than standing here . . .

With that, he walked confidently down the hall, turned left, followed the torches away, and turned right again. Lost, at once, but what did that matter? Every path was wrong in the House of the Perpetual Nap.

At least, he thought, his time had been fairly well

spent. He had learned a great deal about the spiritual life of King Llowenkeef-Grymm, even though none of it made a bit of sense.

The one point he hadn't dared touch upon was the one that concerned him the most. A sorcerer had knocked him senseless. That same seer belonged to the King, and what was His Grace's part in that? Did he know about it, or not? And, wasn't it even more disconcerting if he wasn't aware of it at all?

He was anxious to share this with Letitia, and even Julia, though he wouldn't admit to that.

"They are each, in their way, extremely good at puzzles such as this. They will toss a tricky question around until it gives up and rolls over and tells them what they want to know—"

"Talking to yourself, are you, sir? They say it's a sign that dark forces whisper in your soul . . ."

The voice came out of shadow, and Finn's heart nearly stopped, this time without the aid of a spell.

"Sacks and Tacks, you gave me quite a fright. Come out and show yourself now!"

She stepped into the half-light, then, no longer a phantom, but a person fully formed. Formed so nicely, in fact, she took Finn's breath away. A woman, though very lately a girl, slender and slight, with citron hair to her shoulders, a narrow face and wide-set eyes of the very palest blue.

The eyes of a girl who has drowned and lies beneath the sea . . .

Finn was stunned by this disturbing thought, and set it quickly aside.

"I'm sorry," the woman said, in a voice that brought vague, unwholesome thoughts to mind. "I like to walk in this hall, for there's scarcely ever anyone here."

"I don't suppose there is. I don't imagine anyone unfa-

miliar with the place could find it twice. I am quite lost
myself."

The woman gave him a lazy smile. "I'm DeFloraine-
Marie, and I'm the daughter of the King. You're the one
who makes lizards that talk, and you're not lost now,
Master Finn. . . ."

FINN RESISTED, POLITELY DECLINED, SAID HE WAS certain it wasn't the thing to do. The woman, the girl, the sprite insisted, wouldn't take no, and, she made it clear, she was a princess, and people did what she told them to do.

Her quarters weren't far. When they arrived, she slid past the door and he followed her through, certain, now, he was somewhere he shouldn't ever be.

He had seen her only as a dim and hazy vision as she hurried him through the shadowed hall. Even then he'd been dazzled by her beauty, by the lightness of her being, by her effortless grace.

Now, she stood before him in the glow of a hundred candles of crimson, tangerine and gold, clad in some pale and vaporous gown, something more a whisper or a mist that circled round her than a garment of any kind.

Finn felt as if his knees would give way. As if, in her presence, he would simply come apart. And, in a corner of his mind, there came a growing specter of shame, guilt, remorse and deep regret. How, he wondered, could he ever make up for the things he hadn't even done? For, in truth, when he faced Letitia again, he would surely stand condemned for his wicked thoughts alone, for the visions that heated his soul when he gazed on DeFloraine-Marie in this candle-scented room.

"Please, Master Finn, you mustn't stare. That is not the proper thing to do."

"I surely didn't mean to," he said. "Coming in from the dark, into the light, you see . . ."

"Yes, I expect that's so. I hope you don't have a fever. I keep it rather warm in here."

"No, truly, it's very nice, just right for me. Some people like it cooler, I like it—warmer than others do. Not overly warm, you understand, sort of, what it is now . . ."

"Make yourself at ease, Master Finn. I'll see to some hot spice tea."

Just what I need, some hot spice tea . . .

Finn watched her vanish past a veil of fabric fine as spider silk, watched her disappear past another cloudy weave, and another after that, each no more substantial than a lance of morning light.

Watched, and wondered if creatures of the female persuasion were endowed with some fine hydraulic parts, some wondrous gears than made them move like that.

Finn sat.

There were colorful pillows spread about the room. No table, no chairs. Only a sea of soft cushions and walls of airy veils. Some sweet aroma of the East lingered upon the air.

Candles, pillows, rare exotic scents, and a very leggy nymph. What happened, Letitia, is I got lost from Julia, I can explain all this . . .

TELL ME ABOUT YOURSELF, MASTER FINN. I AM SO pleased you're here. We never have guests. Father doesn't like anyone, you know."

She was there, close beside him, before he could blink. She might have drifted in on a breeze. *A gnat could sneeze,* he thought, *and make more noise than DeFloraine-Marie.*

"There's not much to tell, truly. I'm just—you know, me. I make lizards, that's about it. Lizards that pick up about the house, lizards that—"

"Tell me about Letitia Louise."

That threw him off guard, and the smile at the corner of her mouth told him this was clearly her intent.

"I have no idea what it is you want to know. Whatever it is, I feel you should ask her yourself."

The girl threw back her head and laughed.

"There's no need for that. You've told it all, you see."

"And what might that be?"

"That she is more than your Mycer servant girl. Not that I'm greatly surprised."

Finn took a breath. "And if that were so, is it some concern of yours?"

"It might be, Master Finn." She leaned in close, so close he could breathe the fresh scent of her hair.

"I hope you don't hold human ladies in disdain. Do you find some fault, some blemish in me?"

"Of course I don't. I think you look fine."

"Indeed?" She slid one hand across her bare shoulder, across her shapely arm. "I fear I don't have any *down*, any pink and pointy ears . . ."

Finn felt the color rise to his cheeks and quickly looked away to hide his anger. Here was another, then, one of the great horde who lashed out at others to hide the emptiness in themselves.

"I'm afraid I must pass on the hot spice tea," Finn said, coming to his feet, "thank you all the same."

"Doesn't matter, I'm all out of tea."

"Ah, well then."

DeFloraine-Marie looked up and held him with her startling blue eyes.

"I hope you don't take me for a fool. You have looked me up and down, you have scarcely missed an inch, and there's little more to see. You find me sweet, you find me fair. I know your desires, yet you dare not loose them, for you know where they would lead."

She smiled, then, a smile that tantalized, teased, tempted and promised, and all the while was only a mask for her contempt.

"What are you waiting for?" she said, as if she was startled to find him there. "You really must go."

"As you said, I do find you fair, lady, I am certain that any man would. But you are right, there is nothing for me here."

He stopped at the door. She was already somewhere a thousand miles away. He turned, and vowed he would not look back at her again . . .

I SEE YOU FOUND YOUR WAY BACK," JULIA SAID. "YOU might have let me know you weren't coming, Finn."

"The King let me out the wrong door, all right? What are you complaining about? You got here by yourself."

"Interesting scent," Julia said, lifting her silver snout. "My, a veritable garden of new aromas. Silk. Satin. Candles. A great deal of skin . . ."

"Go sit somewhere and turn yourself off. It's nearly dawn, I've got to get some sleep."

"How were the clocks?"

"Loud. Irritating. That's the nature of a mechanical device."

"I'm sure you don't intend to hurt others with your barbs. I suppose I'll let it pass."

Finn shed his clothes and sank wearily into bed. Letitia was sound asleep, and he was grateful for that.

Not that I've done anything. Not that I have a thing to regret . . .

He knew, of course, the truth of the matter was you didn't *have* to do anything with DeFloraine-Marie to earn a sackful of guilt. Before he'd found true and lasting love with Letitia Louise, Finn had encountered a number of human females of every shape and size, from the loving and the kindly to the outright nasty and mean.

And, within this gender, he had learned there were some who were a race, a tribe, a breed unto themselves. These were females born to haunt men, to drive them to despair—elegant, sloe-eyed creatures who moved with a careless, lazy grace, women and girls with secret smiles and eyes the color of rain. DeFloraine-Marie was such a one as this, and all they had to do was look at a man to cast their deadly spell.

Finn had known a woman once who told him this was not a matter of gender at all. That there was a male of that same cunning species who was the ruination of womankind.

And if he'd been such a man himself? Would he, indeed, have been able to gain such a prize as Letitia Louise?

"Not a chance," he muttered to himself, just before he fell asleep. "She would have struck me with something heavy, and that would have been the end of that . . ."

THIRTY-THREE

I SHOULD LIKE TO HAVE BREAKFAST, AT LEAST," SAID Letitia Louise, yawning for the second time in a minute and a half. "They do serve a very fine breakfast here, Finn. I don't see why we can't wait for that."

"Because, love, I have done what I came to do here, and that was to deliver a clock. He doesn't want it, fine. He can toss the bundle out. In truth, I'm rather pleased it turned out the way it did. That wasn't my greatest work, you know. I made it under extreme duress."

"I thought it really wasn't all that bad, as a fact."

"As a fact," Julia said, "it really wasn't all that good. What it was was a piece of—"

"No one asked you, Julia. Letitia, are you sure you have everything, dear?"

"No, Finn, I don't. I had that red valise you gave me for Winter's Day, but it burned up in that balloon. I really don't have anything at all."

"Yes, well, we'll get you another bag quite soon."

He looked about the room, though he couldn't guess why. He had nothing himself except Koodigern's dagger, and the clothes he had on, which seemed to be smelling rather stale.

He supposed he should be grateful for that. Letitia's senses weren't as keen as Julia's, but good enough to catch a hint of candles, say, or scents from across the Misty Sea.

The hallway was empty, as it ever seemed to be. And, as ever, the faint, slightly chill odor of the underworld was in the air.

Letitia had suggested they wait for Dostagio or Maddigern to help them find the proper way out. Finn said a definite "no" to that. He'd had enough of them both, especially the bad-tempered Badgie. They could find their own way, even if it took a little time.

And, once they did, he would find a proper breakfast at an inn and purchase a bath as well. That, and some new, fresh clothing would have their spirits up again.

"I believe we turn left here," Letitia said. "I recall this corner quite well."

"I have to disagree. We go straight ahead for some time."

"We go left," Julia said.

"Absolutely not."

"Who has the compass in their belly, you or me, Finn?"

"I don't feel your senses are working right."

"They were working right last night."

"What?" Letitia looked puzzled. "What's all this about?"

"I haven't the slightest idea," Finn said. "Julia says whatever comes into her head."

"I don't think she *always* does, Finn."

"All right, most of the time. Which has nothing to do with whether we should—"

Finn stopped. He saw them, from the corner of his eye, both of them, coming from the corridor ahead.

Dostagio and—to Finn's great chagrin—the odious Maddigern himself. He wondered, again, how the kindly Koodigern could be so totally different from his Badgie brother. Still, families were ever at odds, among Newlies and human folk alike.

"How nice of you to take your precious time to see us

out," Finn spoke to Maddigern. "Did you fear we'd try to stay, that we might miss your ever-cheerful ways?"

"I would be pleased to gut you right here," the Badgie said, with a wary glance at Julia, perched on Finn's shoulder, watching with her bright ruby eyes. "If that'd be convenient, Master Finn."

"It would be my pleasure, a fine way to start this lovely day."

"Finn—!" Letitia's look was dark enough to bring rain.

"Maiming and such will not be possible," Dostagio said, "as you are well aware, Captain/Major Maddigern. Plans have been altered, modified, changed, as it were, by the wishes of His Grace, King Llowenkeef-Grymm. He would have your presence, sir and Miss, in the Great Hall of Tedious Favors and Petitions, which is in endless session right now."

Finn shook his head. "I'm sure there's some mistake. We're supposed to be out of here. I doubt if the King has changed his mind about that."

Finn hesitated, turning on the Badgie with a curious eye.

"This is some doing of yours, isn't it, Maddigern? It has nothing to do with the King."

"I assure you it does, sir," Dostagio said. "We must not dawdle any longer. The King is most frugal about his time."

"As I understand it, the Afterworld has its own sense of time. One should be in tune with the Eternal Hour, not the illusion of time as we find reflected here."

Maddigern, ever in control of his rigid, sullen appearance, was clearly aghast. Even Dostagio's sober mask appeared to twitch.

"He quoted scripture," Maddigern said. "I heard him. He said it aloud."

"I'm afraid he did."

"We're not supposed to hear this. Damn the fellow, Dostagio, I have to kill us all."

"Wait, hold it there," Finn said.

"I suppose you do, Captain/Major, but I wonder if the rule applies if we have prior orders from the King. Might not such an order take precedence over Shameful Heresy and Disrespect for the Dead?"

"You have a point, First Servant."

"Well, then. I suggest I take it up with the Forty-Third Elder and get back to you on this."

"Good. That's that. Now, Master Finn and Miss, get on to the hall like you're told. And no more foul desecration or such as that. We're religious people here."

"Why?" Finn asked. "You're not even allowed to join."

"Of course we're not, sir. What kind of church do you think this is . . . ?"

Chapter

THIRTY-FOUR

I F FINN EXPECTED THE COMFY SURROUNDINGS OF the King's private chamber, he had clearly forgotten the awesome Holy Place of Emperors, Tyrants and Kings, with its fossilized rulers of the past, or the grandeur of the Great Dining Hall, and its magnificent dome of leaded glass.

The Great Hall of Tedious Favors and Petitions followed the theme of Heldessian splendor in all respects. The floor was a sparkling mosaic picturing myth and legend from ancient times. The columns that lined the hall were as massive as the trees of northern climes, where the mighty Grizz sat about their fires.

The vaulted stone ceiling rose to dizzying heights, nearly beyond the reach of the hanging crystal lights.

"Better than Prince Aghen Aghenfleck's hall, I'll say that," Finn whispered to Letitia Louise.

"Well, it's higher, all right. But Aghenfleck does have very nice balconies that let in the light."

"Those balconies are there so he can stand and watch his cousins go under the Grapnel and the Snip," Finn told her. "Or see how they fare beneath the Mush . . ."

"Hah! There you are, my boy. Good! Good! Nice of you to come!"

King Llowenkeef-Grymm suddenly burst forth through a small crowd of courtiers gathered at the far end of the hall.

Finn noticed everyone was dressed in red today, instead of purple hues. There were counselors in madder, cherry and pink. Chamberlains in ruby, cardinal and wine. Lords, ladies, toadies and fools in every shade of rust, amber, coral and rose.

The King was again attired in pious tatters and rags of soot and gray, with a face of ghoulish white, and large black circles about his eyes.

"You haven't missed a thing," the King said. "All the miserable wretches are gone, be thankful for that. Why is it the poor all *want* something? Is it that way in your country as well? I never grant more than three favors at a time, they *know* that, but they won't go away.

"Ah, lizard is with you as well. Fine, fine. And this is the charming Miss Letitia Louise. I'm sorry we haven't met. You're most welcome here. I have always said, if I were to take a female of the animal persuasion to my bed, it would be a Mycer girl. Oh, now, I hope I haven't embarrassed you in any way, my dear. You can say anything you like if you're the King, and sometimes I do."

"Yes. Thank you, Your Grace . . ." Letitia was appalled, but no longer greatly surprised at what a human might say.

"I shall introduce you to the court," the King told the two, "or as many as I can recall. First, though, I've prepared a little surprise. I hope you'll be impressed, Finn, it's all about you."

"Me, sire? I can't imagine what you mean."

Finn's throat went suddenly dry. He looked all about, to see if there was anything to drink.

"You're much too modest, boy, a quality I find abhorrent in a person. I do hope you'll work on that. Oh, we're starting. Just wait right here, if you will."

The King trotted off, leaving a string, a tatter, a bit of his shroud here and there.

"I have a very bad feeling about this," Finn said. "I

can't imagine what the old fool is going to do. Maybe I'm to be fossilized and put on display somewhere."

"Oh no, Finn. You're not a king or anything. They wouldn't do that."

"It was a jest, Letitia. A poor one, I admit, but I'm not in the best of form today."

"If it's anything fatal," Julia said from her perch, "explain that Letitia and I had nothing to do with whatever it is. That's the least you can do."

"I hope it's not that blasphemy thing," Letitia said. "You likely should have kept that to yourself, dear."

"I'm sure you're right. Unfortunately, it's too late to— Rocks and Socks, what's *that*?"

A terrible sound shook the hall, a squeal, a din, a flat and nasal blare, as if a flock of geese had some disorder of the bill.

A horde of courtiers, chattering, tittering, bobbing about, suddenly filled the Great Hall, a gaudy circus of crimson tones. And, as Finn noticed, one poor fellow in green, clearly blind to the color red.

The clamor, the blast, the most unmusical sounds, came from a dozen young boys in lurid salmon hues. They blew on enormous horns of brass until they were flushed, and someone made them stop.

"Even I cannot make more horrid sounds than that," Julia said.

"No, but on occasion you have tried."

The crowd began to cheer. Some waved and hopped about. Some tossed their hats in the air, and some kicked off their shoes. Finn was next to certain no one knew what they were cheering about. If the King cheered or booed, or cut off his ear, then they would do it too.

"Finn, would you tell me what's happening, please? It's awfully noisy, and I don't like it here."

Finn didn't like it either. It came on a golden cart with wobbly wheels. Whatever it was, it was hidden by a color-

ful kingly drape. The item, the thing, the burden on the
cart, poked itself up in sharp, pointy little peaks. It could
be a pot of eels, it could be a rocking chair. The King had a
fine sense of humor, and it could indeed be a Badgie with
an axe.

Whatever it was, it came with jolly trumpeters, who
couldn't find the key, plus a herd, a covey, a flight of
happy nobles, peers, and those about the palace with
nothing else to do.

"Here, now, gather round, all," shouted King Llowenkeef-Grymm. "This is something special, and I wish to
share it with my nobles, and even those of you who are nothing at all."

More cheers, more huzzahs. Courtiers far from the
center of things escaped to find a mug of ale.

"I want you to move in closer, Master Finn, and you
too, Miss. Right in front, if you please."

"Yes, thank you, sire," Finn said, and, in a quick aside
to Letitia Louise, "whatever happens, stay close to me. I
still have Koodigern's dagger, and I'll take as many with
us as I can."

"Finn, it's just some churchy thing, I'm sure. I don't
see why they'd harm us."

"You've much to learn about the treachery of kings, my
dear, but I've no time to tell you now."

And though he had no wish to alarm Letitia, Finn
could see that a company of Badgies had slipped in behind
them with no sound at all.

"I can take out eight or nine," Julia said, "possibly
ten."

"Don't. Not unless I do, you hear?"

"Striking first is the basic rule of strategy, set down by
Hephades the Sly."

"Staying alive is the basic rule of Finn the coward. Shut
it down, Julia, now."

"What's this all about?" Letitia wanted to know.

"Julia. I need to get her in the shop."

"Oh. What for?"

"Master Finn, up here, if you please."

The King reached out and entangled Finn in a clutter of grim, funereal gear, sooty snips of this and that.

"We have here," the King announced, "one Finn of Fyxedia, craftsman of lizards, a device he thought up by himself.

"With him is one of the very lizards he's produced, along with Miss Letitia Louise, a Mycer girl in his service, and, in my eye, as attractive as any human girl you'll find around here."

What is this royal rascal up to? What does he think he's going to do?

". . . now, as a treat to all my subjects, a treat which few of you deserve, for you never do anything for me, I would show you something you have never seen before. And, I daresay, will never see anything like it again. Thus, with a touch of my royal hand . . ."

The King pulled a cord, the drape slipped away and the thing was revealed.

The crowd was wary of whatever was to be. They muttered, mumbled, chattered in a voice of indecision, whispered in clear uncertain terms, waited on the edge, waited with no idea what the King would have them do.

Finn's heart nearly stopped. *The clock. That damnable, tasteless lizard with a clock in its belly, was mounted on the golden cart, for all the court to see. . . .*

Chapter
THIRTY-FIVE

T HE TRUTH OF THIS SCAM, THIS TRICKERY OF THE King, struck Finn like a blow, near took his breath away. Here was the clever monarch's cunning, his sly and hateful deceit. Here was the reason Llowenkeef-Grymm had stopped him, moments before he was free of the place for good.

The King had *not* tossed his present aside, as Finn had prayed he'd do. This mad collector of clocks had torn into the bundle and found the ugly item inside. And, in a fit of fury, in a moment of rage, he had planned this moment of dread disclosure for the man who had dared bring this artless, base, vulgar piece of rubbish into his land . . .

"We're in for it now," Julia said. "I would like to say, our acquaintance has been a partial delight."

"He's not going to kill us. He just wants to flog us a bit. Just keep your snout shut, I'll handle this."

"Master Finn . . ." The King looked at him with a grave, thoughtful look in his noble eyes.

"You have said this gift comes to me from Aghen Aghenfleck the Fourth?"

"Sire . . ."

"And, though you've not said it, I'd guess you made this artifact yourself?"

"I did, Your Grace. And if I might say a word here . . ."

"No, you may not! It is bad manners, Finn, and blasphemy second class, to interrupt me."

"Yes, sire."

"Come here. Do it now."

"Oh, Finn," Letitia said beneath her breath.

Finn stood straight, though he feared his legs might collapse.

"In all fairness, Finn, you should know I have taken into consideration the fact that your, ah—Prince, ordered you to craft this piece."

"I appreciate that, sir."

"It is magnificent, Finn."

"I regret, sire, that—what?"

"A masterpiece, a thing of wonder, glorious in its artifice and design. I have seen clocks without number, clocks from the immortal crafters of the East, clocks from the tiny folk who are said to live beneath the sea, and have fins instead of knees. Frankly, I have my doubts about that.

"At any rate, none of these, Finn, are worthy of an artist such as you."

"He *likes* this piece of crap?"

"Hush, Julia," Letitia whispered. "The man's a connoisseur."

"I would deem it a favor to a grateful king, if you would show me how it works."

"Now, sire?"

"What did I say, boy? Now, indeed."

The King clapped his hands in pleasure, a signal to the watchful crowd that they should openly admire, with speech and gesture, this man who pleased the King.

"It's really quite simple, sire."

Finn moved to the golden cart, a bold new note of confidence in his voice.

"The timepiece itself is embedded in the belly of the lizard. Rampant, as it were, upon its hind legs, its forelegs raised in what I like to call a, ah—whimsical salute."

"Whimsical, yes. The very word, I feel."

"The tail, which is gilded with golden scales, serves as the pendulum of the clock. I release this small locking device and—so, the tail begins to swing."

"I am beside myself, Finn. I never expected as much. Who would have dreamed of having the tail itself swing?"

"He did," Julia muttered to herself, "not me."

"Now, sire, there is another function here. I release another switch . . ."

The King gave such a shrill cry of delight, Finn feared he might have shed his mortal form.

"The eyes—the eyes move back and forth as well!"

"It's a small thing, sire."

"Small? *Genius*, I should say, for it has never been done before in the history of clocks."

He turned to Finn, and Finn was near certain there were tears in the fellow's eyes.

"The honor of creation is yours. The honor of owning this wonder is mine. You have made yourself immortal in clockdom, Finn."

"Well, hardly, sire."

"Did I say immortal, boy?"

"Sire, I believe you did."

"To say otherwise is to contradict the King."

"I know he didn't mean that," Letitia said. "He's good with his hands, but he's not real proficient with the spoken word, sire."

"He's not," Julia said. "I can vouch for that."

"Indeed?" The King raised a curious brow. "Never taken a lizard's vouch before. I suppose it's all right. At any rate—You"—he waved at anyone at all—"you will proceed with this now."

Two servants, plainly clad in the drab uniform of the Gracious Dead, came quickly and offered the King a velvet box. The box was clearly quite heavy, for it took the pair to set it down.

"Now, both of you, get the thing out here, what do you think I hire you for?"

The two servants lifted. And, it was indeed weighty, for they breathed hard, and the veins stood out upon their brows.

"Your Grace!" Finn was astonished, truly speechless for a time. Letitia muttered something in the Mycer tongue, which she rarely did at all.

The thing that arose from the box was a chain, a golden chain, with links Finn was sure would anchor a ship of good size. Each of these monstrous links was encrusted with gems of every sort—rubies, sapphires, diamonds and such—many gems that Finn couldn't name.

At the end of this chain was a resplendent circle of gold. A large green stone lay at its center, and small diamonds cluttered about the edge.

"Seems a bit heavy," said the King. "I expect these fellows would be grateful if you bent for just a moment, to allow them to get it on."

Finn did as he was told. With a great deal of heavy breathing, and fussing about, the men wrested the loop over Finn's broad shoulders. Julia leaped into Letitia's lap not a moment too soon.

Finn gasped, and caught himself before he fell to his knees. The King began to clap again, and the crowd began to cheer. Finn tried not to stagger, made a great effort not to sag. The thing surely weighed a good eighty pounds, and came down to his knees.

"Looks good on you, Finn." The King stepped back and grinned.

"I am overwhelmed, sire."

"I shouldn't wonder. That's a Ninety-Fifth Degree decoration you're wearing there. We only go to ninety-six. Here. You need to read it. It's hand engraved, you know."

With some degree of effort, Finn lifted the great pendant that hung below his knees. It read, in florid script, enameled in lilac and blue:

. THE HUMAN PERSON NAMED FINN
IS HEREBY GRANTED THE TITLE OF
GRAND MASTER OF MECHANICAL OBJECTS,
GEARS AND VARIOUS PARTS, AN HONOR OF
THE NINETY-FIFTH ORDER, BY COMMAND
OF MYSELF, LLOWENKEEF-GRYMM,
KING OF HELDESSIA LAND

✧ ✧ ✧ ✧ ✧

"I am honored," Finn said. "I scarcely know what to say."

"Words won't suffice, I shouldn't think," the King said, rising from his gilded chair. "Here, come with me. You too, Miss, and lizard, as well."

Without another word, Llowenkeef-Grymm stalked across the Great Hall, scattering courtiers aside.

Finn looked at Letitia, and Letitia looked back. Neither, with the slightest idea of what might be coming next.

Finn gathered the loops of his fine decoration and kept up as well as he could. The King didn't pause until he reached a small, arched door, set neatly within the wall.

"The family doesn't take part in these events. Isn't good for those louts to see too many royals at a time. A lot of them faint. We had a fellow die."

"I can see that," Finn said.

"You keep saying that, you'll stir up my ire, Finn. You couldn't possibly comprehend even half of what I'm saying, don't pretend you can."

"I certainly won't, sire."

Llowenkeef-Grymm waved him off, clearly annoyed, a mood which seemed to strike him at any given time.

"At any rate, you'll get to meet the royals. We'll all be dead again soon, so there isn't much time."

Finn started to speak, but Letitia shook her head in warning.

The King threw open the door, then, and Finn suddenly understood. He didn't have to count. He knew there'd be ten, plus the King himself. Eleven. Minus one, and he was thankful for that. Still, nearly the entire congregation of the Deeply Entombed. The only true believers in the world, and they were all gathered here. Each and every one in the rags, snags, tatters and snips, bound, wrapped, happily trapped in the drear and dusty shrouds of the fashionable dead.

Huddled together, they appeared to be a great dust bunny, swept from under a giant's untidy bed. Finn met them all, overweight uncles and undersized aunts, nieces, nephews, beady-eyed cousins, and two old men who shared the same shroud. Finn hoped they weren't joined in some horrid manner, and didn't want to ask.

Then, when all was done, Finn breathed a great sigh of relief, grateful again that the one royal member he dreaded to see had failed to appear. He could clearly see every smudgy feature, every sooty nose, and she clearly wasn't there. Count all you like and there were still only ten—

"You must forgive me, Father dear, for I had a hundred tiresome little chores. There's no rest for a princess of the realm, I cannot call my life my own . . ."

She stopped, halfway from the door across the room, paused, hesitated, tarried in a manner, then realigned her bodily parts in a posture that was likely illegal somewhere, bit her saucy lip and blinked at Finn.

"Finn, you sweet man, what a marvelous surprise, I had no idea we'd be together again so soon!"

Finn's prayer to die failed. The earth didn't part and swallow him up. Indeed, nothing seemed to work at all. Instead, Fate flung DeFloraine-Marie into his arms, where she pressed herself against him in a most indecent manner, kissed him on the mouth, pushed him away, and smiled at Letitia Louise.

"I'm glad we could finally meet. Finn has said so much about you. I think Mycer girls are prettier than any of your kind. I'm DeFloraine-Marie, Princess of Heldessia Land. My mother's in the Afterworld, but Father's such a dear. Do make Finn take off that terrible chain before he holds you again. I expect it left bruises everywhere on me."

"Finn. I need to talk to you."

He didn't look at Letitia, he didn't have to. "You really don't, my dear. It only seems like you do, and I quite understand how things might appear when they're actually not as they seem at all."

"I'm relieved to hear that, Finn."

"Well, then," said the King, somewhat puzzled by this display. "So you and Master Finn have met, my dear?"

"Oh, we have, Father."

How can she possibly look so lovely in a garment made of lint?

"We'll be having refreshments, now," said the King. "Black ale and sogcake, you know. We shall all be returning to the dead persuasion after this, and we usually have a little snack."

"Thank you, sire, but I feel Letitia and I—"

"Oh, no, *you* can't have any, boy. This stuff's sanctified. Just thought you'd like to watch."

"Do stay, Finn." DeFloraine hung on her father's arm, looking limp and lazy-eyed. "And the Newlie too. She would enjoy it as well."

"How very kind," Letitia said. "I feel it would be too exciting for me. Finn? I'm leaving. Do as you please."

She turned and was gone, Julia rattling in her wake.

Finn was sure he heard thunder in her path. "If I may, sire. I'll leave you and your family to your personal rites. I trust you will all have a, ah—most enjoyable burial, pass-

ing, confinement, whatever you desire, and I trust I am
not committing any breach of manners if I wish you a
pleasant demise."

"Your intentions are likely good, but your sentiments
are disgusting, Finn. Blasphemy, desecration, it's downhill from there.

"You make a damn fine clock, sir, I have to say that.
Why, I could watch those little eyes go back and forth all
day. You didn't molest, abuse, debase or defile my daughter in any way, did you, Finn? Any nonsense like that?"

"Sire, certainly not! Who could imagine such a thing?"

"Just about anyone, I'd say. Don't ever do it. I won't
put up with that."

"No, sire."

Though Finn betrayed no emotion, he feared he was
not out of danger yet. One lie from DeFloraine-Marie and
his head would be on a pike atop the palace walls. Royals
could turn on you, just like that. A king and a prince
didn't have to think twice.

AFTER THE SOMBER CELEBRATION OF THE DEAD,
the party in the Great Hall of Tedious Favors and
Petitions seemed riotous at best.

Try as he could, he couldn't spot Letitia in the crowd.
If she was there, she was caught in a dizzy swirl of crimson, flush, blush and maroon.

Working his way through the colorful crowd, he was
hit several times by a flailing arm or an errant foot. At
first, he thought this horde of counselors, lords, ladies and
loons had been struck by some collective fit. Some seizure
or violent distress.

Then, upon reflection, he began to see the cause. The
agonized limbs, the cruelly twisted joints, were essential
parts of a local dance. All these contortions were in and
out of step with an octet in the corner, the same young

lads who couldn't play trumpets were now playing other instruments they couldn't play as well.

She's angry, for sure, no doubt about that. But so irate she would flee into a bedlam like this?

"No," he said aloud, "not Letitia Louise. Noise, chaos, total disarray, turns her keen Mycer senses into mush. She would never linger in a place like this.

"But where is she now? Could she find her way through the halls alone?"

"She's quite safe and sound," Julia said, guessing Finn's thoughts, suddenly appearing out of nowhere at all.

"Dostagio took her to our quarters. The ones we vacated on our way out of here."

"We're still vacating, Julia. I'm sorry she's angry, but I am not at fault in this matter, and this is not the time to let personal matters stand in our way."

"I hope you can relay all this as easily to her, Finn. She got a good look at DeFloraine-Marie."

"The princess is quite attractive, you don't have to tell me that."

"Attractive, you say?" Julia laughed, a sharp and rusty chuckle like iron filings with the flu.

"The creature's not attractive, Finn. She's a snare, she's a trap. She has the power to cloud men's minds, to bend them to her will . . ."

"All right, that's enough."

"That's scarcely the start. Though any list of her witcherly charms would likely be sorely incomplete. I expect Letita could add to the—"

Of a sudden, Julia stopped and went rigid on the spot. Her golden scales quivered, her ruby eyes blinked.

"Something coming, Finn. Something—over there. Get back, quick!"

Finn needed no further warning. Julia had a sense for such things, knew when trouble was about an instant before it began. Before her words were scarcely done, Finn heard the tortured sound of splintered wood, and the great oaken doors at the end of the hall burst open and tumbled to the floor.

They spilled into the hall then, a veritable plague of Bowsers, yipping, yapping, waving their muskets, clashing their swords, tossing their tasteless boaters in the air. They snapped at their comrades, growled at their foes.

And, before the startled courtiers could gather their wits, before the fierce Badgies could resist, the second wave was howling through the broken doors . . .

IF IT HADN'T BEEN FOR THE LORDS, THE STRUMPETS, the cowards in colorful array, Finn was near certain the Bowsers would have quickly won the day. As it was, this frantic herd of flunkies, stooges, leeches and fools, fled in such mad disorder, they upended friend and foe alike.

The Badgies, then, won a moment of respite, a moment to bring their ranks to order, to form the famous Badgie Square. The Bowsers threw themselves at the solid block of the King's Third Sentient Guards, and found themselves in trouble from the start.

In spite of his contempt for the sullen Maddigern, Finn found himself cheering for the Badgie and his brave cohorts. Every time the yappers assaulted the green-cloaked warriors, they came up against an unyielding wall.

Some, wiser than their fellows, chose to save their necks, avoid the killer square, and go after easy game— counselors, servants and such, running about like witless barnyard fowl.

A portly duke stumbled by, a lass of lesser rank clinging to his back. Merchants, pages and varied parasites fought each other to escape the barking foes.

"I fear there's no way I can stay out of this," Finn muttered, "unless it be in shame. Damn it all, Julia, don't any of these louts know how to fight back?"

"They hire people for that. It gives the poor something to do. I suppose you could say there's some good in that."

"I'm afraid I don't agree at all. You there, stop that, get away from him!"

A stout Bowser halted in his tracks, startled to find Finn in his path. A chamberlain in crimson cowered beneath the Bowser's blade.

"You be mezzin' mit me, hooman perzon. Don' be doin' zhat."

"I think your burgundy vest is ugly. It doesn't go with the tie. Those straws you fellows wear went out of style thirty years ago."

The Bowser wrinkled his puggy nose. Without another glance at his victim, he came at Finn, swinging his blade in both hands.

Finn reached for his own blade, and recalled with some dismay that he only had Koodigern's dagger, a weapon considerably shorter than a sword.

The Bowser's eyes gleamed. Fun was only seconds away.

"Julia," Finn said, as calmly as the moment would allow, "I could use some help here."

"You're always polite when cornered," Julia said. "Don't think I haven't noticed that."

The Bowser hesitated, looked down and stared, astonished to see something gold and scaly streaking right at him, something awful, something *talking*, words coming out its silver snout.

The Bowser shrieked, shouted, scrambled away as the thing crawled swiftly up his leg, digging with its claws, snapping with its teeth, leaving bloody tears along the way.

The frightened raider dropped his blade, stumbled back, slapped at his trousers as if he'd been ravaged by ants. Julia leaped free, a blue bow tie entangled in her teeth.

The Bowser sprawled on his back, cursed, came to his feet, bent to grab his blade, then rushed at Finn with a will. From the corner of his eye, he saw a shiny blur coming at him with a whisper and a whine. He ducked, too late, and the thing struck him hard across the chest, spilling him to the ground.

He came to his knees, not so quickly this time. Once more, Finn swung the King's deadly decoration in a wide, whistling loop, once above his head, and then again. The gold-chained, gem-encrusted Ninety-Fifth Order struck the Bowser a solid, bone-crunching blow, a blow that would have felled a large tree.

"I only meant to put him down," Finn said, shaking his head with some regret. "I wasn't looking for a terminal effect."

"*He* was, Finn. You might recall from another encounter, these rogues enjoy their work. He'd gladly do the same to you."

"True enough. And there's no reason we shouldn't bring ourselves down to their level, if they intend to act like this . . ."

Finn had no time to finish. Two Bowsers broke from the fray and came at him on the run. One was a big, heavyset fellow with a shaggy face and sad, droopy eyes. The other was short and intense. Of all the Bowser folk, Finn disliked the wiry, nervous yappers most of all.

"All right," he muttered under his breath, "have at it if you must."

The larger raider stomped in with no finesse at all. He raised his blade and hacked at Finn with all his might. Finn took a quick step back. The Bowser's blade struck the hard granite floor and shattered like glass. The sad-eyed fellow blinked in surprise, then howled as his arms went numb.

Finn swung the lethal decoration over his shoulder, but his foe turned and fled.

"Wake up," Julia said. "On your right!"

The smaller warrior was circling Finn, baring his teeth, cursing in the raspy, irritating tongue the Bowsers called their own. Julia tried to head the wretch off, but Bowsers of this type were quite hard to catch.

Finn whipped his heavy chain at the snapper, much like an angler after a wily trout. The Bowser hopped lightly aside, went to his knees, and hurled his dagger at Finn.

Finn nearly moved too late. The Bowser was quick, and the weapon whined past Finn's head only inches away. Determined not to quit, the Bowser drew another blade, intent on hurling it on its way.

Finn didn't have to duck. Julia Jessica Slagg sank her teeth into the fellow's ankle, slamming him to the floor. The Bowser yapped in pain. Julia munched, Julia crunched, then flung her head back and let her prey go. The Bowser wasted no time, hopping off as quickly as he could.

Finn waited, holding his heavy weapon at the ready, determined he would not be taken unawares again. Though he'd scarcely noticed, the Great Hall had gone suddenly quiet. Courtiers were huddled together in tight, terrified knots of henna, crimson, and blush. Two appeared to be dead. Finn counted eleven Bowsers as well, besides the pair he and Julia had downed themselves.

He didn't think it likely a single Bowser had gotten away, or that any the Badgies had taken were still alive. Mercy wasn't in these brutal fellows' style.

One Badgie had a limp, but the others had apparently come through the fight without a scratch.

"Over there," Julia said, and Finn followed the lizard's glance. The door to the Royal Family's anteroom was open, now, and Maddigern was there, in earnest conversation with the King. Other members of the family milled about, nervous and intent, disturbed by the recent events—

Finn's pulse quickened, for there was DeFloraine-Marie,

close to her father's side. And, as he watched, for he found it hard to look away, he saw the girl shift her glance from the King to Maddigern himself. It was only for an instant, and was likely of no import at all. Still, it was a moment that stuck in Finn's mind, though he couldn't say why.

He turned, then, as Dostagio entered the Great Hall, with eight more servants in the harsh black livery of the Gracious Dead. Dostagio noted the King and his family, but gave them no mind. In a moment, he had given terse directions to his crew, who quickly began to sweep the room with wide bristly brooms.

A squad of Badgies led the surviving courtiers past the ruins of the door where the Bowsers had burst in. Others emptied the room of bodies and marched away.

In the center of the room was a small pile of straw boater hats, some badly bent, very few intact. There were a number of monocles and varicolored bow ties among the litter that was soon scooped up and carried away.

The room was nearly empty, and Finn felt foolish watching Maddigern, the King, and the rest of the royals mill about. The princess had left, or had stepped out of sight.

To his great regret, he had lingered too long, for Maddigern seemed to notice he was there. With a bow to the King, he turned and marched in a soldierly manner toward Finn.

"Well, you survived, I see," the Badgie said, as if he'd swallowed something bad. "Took on a pair of the rascals yourself, I understand."

"We were here. We felt compelled to act in our defense."

"With that."

"I beg your pardon?"

"You used the King's decoration as a weapon. You assaulted these foul, dirty beasts with His Grace's award. You tainted the honor of Llowenkeef-Grymm."

"Well, I suppose I did," Finn said, too irritated with the sour-faced warrior to greatly care what he said.

"You want to stand there and scowl, fellow, it makes no matter to me. I don't think the King will hang me, and neither do you. Now, if you'll stop this nonsense and move aside, I'll get back to my room."

"To the Mycer girl, you mean."

Finn looked the Badgie straight in the eye. "Yes. That's who I mean. And we don't call Newlies beasts. That's not what they are anymore. And if they were, what are you?"

The Badgie smiled, though it was not the sort of smile that Finn took to heart. "I am not authorized to maim, cut or decimate your person in any manner now. But that could surely change."

"I am a Grand Master of the Ninety-Fifth Order. What are you?"

"The King's Third Sentient Guards work for honor. We don't need your filthy medals."

"Come along, Julia," Finn said. "Captain/Major Maddigern has better things to do. . . ."

THIRTY-SEVEN

ALL VERY NICELY PUT," JULIA SAID, ONCE THEY were down the corridor, past the Great Hall. "Not very prudent, however. Somewhat bold, clearly indiscreet."

"That fellow's a thug, a bully, Julia. A ruffian through and through. You have to stand up to his kind or they'll surely run you down."

"I hope your ruffian understands this as well."

Finn stopped. "We're *leaving*, remember? He doesn't have to put up with me much longer. Soon he can torment someone else."

Finn earnestly hoped his confidence was not misplaced, that he could soon put the Badgie out of mind. Hoped, also, that he could somehow make Letitia understand that he was not, in any way, involved with the King's desirable, somewhat leggy, breathtaking daughter. That he had no thoughts for anyone but his true lifemate, his only love, Letitia Louise.

LEFT, FINN. I DO HATE TO BRING THIS UP BUT YOU'VE turned the wrong way again."

"This is your compass talking, or just the urge to get the better of me? I'm inclined to believe the latter, for I'm sure we should forge straight ahead."

"What's the matter with you?"

"Nothing at all. I see no reason you should ask."

"Oh, well, your pardon then. Your testy temper and your loathsome attitude led me to believe you might be out of sorts. Disturbed, aroused by that vixen who was born to enslave men's souls, riven by torment and guilt . . ."

"That's quite enough, Julia. I am not *riven* in any way at all."

"Ah, that's good to hear."

"If I were to be riven, I doubt I'd need help from a mechanical device."

"I'm used to abuse, it matters little to me—Finn, down that passage, coming this way."

Finn stopped, backed off a pace and drew his small dagger, his gift from the hapless Koodigern.

"I perceive your presence, Master Finn," came a voice from beyond the bend in the corridor ahead. "I only wish to talk, I mean you no harm at all . . ."

A figure appeared, holding his hands out wide in a gesture of peace. The gesture, Finn thought, that everyone gave, whether they intended it or not.

The fellow was a young man, stout, and rather short of stature, with a round, chubby face, thinning hair and an open smile, a smile Finn distrusted at once.

Then, a step closer, Finn could clearly see the stranger's eyes, and knew his suspicions were more than justified. The fellow's eyes fairly glowed with a hint of trickery and guile, a real sense of power, cunning and deceit, set in this kind and friendly face. A quick glance at Julia told Finn she had sensed all this as well.

The stranger shook his head and smiled. "It is the curse of my life, Master Finn. I can seldom hide from fools, and never from beings as keenly aware as you two. This is your delightful lizard, yes? You must demonstrate it to me sometime.

"I'm Obern Oberbyght, the King's seer. I'm sorry I caused you such pain, sir, I truly meant no harm at all."

"No *harm*?" Finn backed off, his hand around the hilt of his weapon. "You damn near fried my head, and you meant no harm in that!"

"Well, I suppose I *did*" said the seer, "but I didn't know you at the time. I assure you the King has given me what-for about that. May I congratulate you on your honor, sir? It's really quite an elegant piece. I've never even seen a Ninety-Fifth before."

"Yes, indeed. It's very heavy, too."

Finn was more than wary of this seer with the winning smile and penetrating eyes. He understood, now, why the fellow projected such an evil, frightening image when he cast his spells. For, in spite of the menace in his eyes, he could easily pass for a junior clerk or a crafter's errand boy.

Even his dress seemed designed to belittle his power and win a stranger's trust. His robe was plain, a modest shade of blue, with no adornment of any kind, not a pendant or a broach, no amulet or magic charm of any sort.

"Allow me to answer the questions I'm sure you wish to ask," said Oberbyght the seer. "It is my job to protect the King. Someone tries to kill him every day or so. This place is full of shadowy halls and dark hidey-holes, and there's always some rogue with a blade or a bludgeon lurking about. I fear I took you for one of those. I hope you won't fault me for that."

"I suppose it was—a mistake," Finn said with a certain restraint, "but I'm not likely to forget it, sir."

"Nor would I ask you to. Only that you understand that persons of the magic persuasion are imperfect like everyone else."

"This—happens all the time, you say? Someone popping out to murder the King?"

"Oh, indeed. You have no idea."

Finn gave some thought to this. He glanced at Julia Jessica Slagg. She hadn't moved since the seer came on the scene. The lizard, he knew, sensed the magician's power on a level he could not comprehend. She was watching, alert to any cunning move the fellow might make.

"I'd ask a question," Finn said. "It may seem foolish to you, but it seems damned odd to me. If you possess such powers, and I can attest that you do, perhaps you'll tell me why you allow these frightening attacks on the King by this maniac band of Bowsers? I should think it would be a good idea to cast some of your spells on them. Socks and Shoes, those louts try to kill the King every other day!"

For a moment, Oberbyght looked genuinely perplexed.

"Why, I couldn't do that," he said at last. "It wouldn't be proper at all."

"Might I learn why not?"

"There is much confusion among the uninformed about that. The Bowsers are licensed to *assault* the King and the royal house. They are not allowed to kill him. That's entirely against the law. I can't interfere in a contractual act. I would be breaking the rules as well."

"What—what contract are we talking about here? You clearly lost me somewhere."

The seer patiently folded his arms. "The Bowsers are adjoined by a contract on the King. This gives them the right to assault, annoy, maim, injure or slay any human or Newlie folk under the aegis, or in the pay, of King Llowenkeef-Grymm.

"I strongly doubt the contract will be renewed, however, as it specifically calls for attacks on Tuesdays and Thursdays alone, and the King is quite upset about that."

Finn shook his head. "And the King allows this sort of thing? That makes no sense at all."

"I agree it doesn't now, since the Bowsers have broken the Tuesday-Thursday clause. But of course he allows it,

Master Finn. Why, if he didn't have a sound agreement with some responsible party, *everyone* would be charging in here and we'd have chaos on our hands."

"I hadn't thought of that. . . ."

"You see? This way, anyone who loathes the King can pay their part, and the Bowsers get work."

"Some of them seem to have outside jobs," Finn said. "When we arrived here, they were running loose in the streets."

"Those fellows are not under contract at all. They have no right to that, and they'll be dealt with severely. It's just that we have a war on our hands with your despicable nation at the moment, and we can't spare the troops to clean up things here. No offense intended, of course. I don't, in any way, mean to imply that you yourself are despicable, Master Finn."

"None taken, of course. Though I must tell you that in Fyxedia we feel much the same about your disgusting, odious ways as you do about ours."

"Well said, my friend." The seer's pudgy features colored with delight. "I was just leaving the royal grounds, by the way, for a mug at the Fractured Foot, which is not far from here. It would give me pleasure to treat you to the hospitality of Heldessia, Master Finn."

"Any other time, I would be delighted," Finn said. "But we have been asked to leave your country at once, and we'd be on our way now if the King hadn't thoughtfully delayed me with this weighty decoration. I hope you won't take it amiss if I get on my way."

Seer Oberbyght looked somewhat puzzled. He placed a finger on one side of his nose, closed his eyes a moment, then gazed thoughtfully at Finn.

"The King, though well intentioned, is not always clear about things. He has a great deal on his mind."

"Yes, I suppose. And what exactly does that have to do with me?"

"This fine decoration you've received. An award of the Ninety-Fifth degree . . ."

"I understand it is, but—"

"It is a very *high* honor, sir. You may be of foreign birth, but you are officially an esteemed citizen of Heldessia now. There can be no question of going home, I fear. You *are* home, Master Finn. . . ."

THIRTY-EIGHT

F INN, MASTER LIZARD-MAKER, LATE OF GARPENNY Street, Ulster-East, was stunned, stupefied, shaken to the core. Even three mugs of dark, syrupy ale at the Fractured Foot did little to ease the pain. The words that came to mind were madness, disaster, the end of the line.

"You simply mustn't let it get you down," said Obern Oberbyght, signaling the young lad for another plate of fried kale. "One country is much like another, you know. There are kings, princes, merchants and thieves. Some folk are rich, and some are quite poor. Some are living, and many are dead. I expect every nation has a great many taverns much like the one we are drinking in now."

"How many countries have you been to, seer, would you care to tell me that?"

"Only the one I'm in now. Why do you ask, Master Finn?"

Finn was doing the best he could to hold himself together. He simply could not let himself go to pieces, break, shatter, come apart at the seams. None of that would do. He had to find a way out of this, to stay at least partially intact for Letitia, Julia, and the future of them all. If he didn't keep his own wits together, he would be of no use to anyone else.

The answer, of course, was Bucerius. The Bullie had gotten him into Heldessia, and could surely get them all out. All he had to do was *find* the hefty fellow. And that, at the moment, seemed a near-hopeless task.

Finn gave an uneasy sigh and covered the action with a swallow of ale.

Y OU'RE A CITIZEN OF HELDESSIA NOW," THE SEER had told him. "You're free to go anywhere you like. Come and share a mug, and I'll tell you some of the delights you'll discover in your exciting new life . . ."

Fine, Finn thought, *and how do I get rid of them?*

There were two of them, sitting at a table across the narrow, timbered room. They weren't wearing long green cloaks or chain mail, but Finn had little doubt they were soldiers of the King's Third Sentient Guard, and they were there to watch *him*.

He could lose them, he was sure, and unless Obern Oberbyght knocked him senseless with a spell, he could outrun the stocky seer as well.

For an instant, he was sorry he'd sent Julia back to let Letitia know what had happened and what he intended to do. Once he got free, Finn was sure he'd simply get lost again in the unfamiliar streets of Heldessia Town. Julia could have likely sniffed her way back to the grocer friend of the Bullie, or at least to the proper part of town. . . .

"I know you're distressed, friend, it does not take a person of magic to see that."

The seer took a bite of the heavily battered kale, smacked his lips and let the crumbs fall in his lap.

"What I would say, and this comes from me, by the way, and not from a loyal servant of the King—which, of course, I remain—what I would say is I strongly suggest you free your mind from any path that might lead to tragedy or bodily harm. Think, instead, of a bright new life ahead—and not the one that you *cannot* ever live again. . . ."

"That's easy to say, and not that simple to do, sir. I'm not certain I—"

Finn stopped. Something gripped his chest in a vise. He felt as if someone were driving nails in his head.

He took a deep breath, felt tiny beads of sweat sting his brow.

Rocks and Stones, does the fellow know *he's doing that? Does he hold the power, or does it hold him?*

When he looked up again, he met the seer's broad, open smile, the smile full of goodwill and cheer, devoid of any malice at all.

At that moment, Finn decided Obern Oberbyght was one of the most frightening creatures he'd ever met, and surely the nicest person in all Heldessia Town.

"I'm grateful for your sound advice," Finn said, "and I'll surely take it to heart. You must understand, though, I'm deeply troubled by this. I have no doubt Heldessian folk are as good as any you can find, but I would never feel I was not a prisoner here."

"Oh, my friend!" Oberbyght looked terribly pained. He nearly reached out for Finn's hand, then drew his back again.

"I hope this feeling will pass. Surely you will change your mind and find happiness here."

"I think, if the King truly understands that though I'm grateful for his honor, I don't belong here. . . ."

The seer shook his head. "Do not pursue this, sir. There is no chance that he will change his mind."

"Why, though? He could at least listen to me."

"He likes you. He holds you in high regard."

"He doesn't *like* me. He scarcely knows who I am."

A glance from the seer told Finn he might wish to guard his tongue when speaking of the King.

"You won his respect with that clock of yours. He's quite delighted with that. The way the eyes and the tail go back and forth. I find it most amusing myself."

Oberbyght was good at guessing another's thoughts, and Finn didn't wish to reveal his own opinion of clocks. Instead, he turned his attention to the corner of the inn, where the two Badgie snoops were pretending they had no interest in him at all.

Past them, closer to the door, a table of hefty Snouters were having the time of their lives. There were seven of them, farmers in red overalls and tattered felt hats. All had the tiny, tar-colored eyes of their kind, bristly faces, ugly noses that seemed wet all the time, and scarcely a trace of any chin.

The more dark ale they consumed, the harder they laughed. No chortles or chuckles, no snickers and such— these fellows roared, and shook all over with unabashed glee.

"You will find Heldessia is more than tolerant of Newlie folk," the seer said, following Finn's glance across the room. "There are many Snouters and Bullies about. And Mycer folk, I believe. Your companion would find friends here."

"And Bowsers," Finn added, for he felt he had to toss that in. "Plenty of them around."

"You might wish to open a shop," the seer went on, as if Finn hadn't spoken at all. "No one makes lizards here."

"No one makes lizards anywhere," Finn said, making no effort to hide his irritation. "No one but me."

"I meant no offense, Master Finn."

"No, I'm sure." Finn paused, as if he'd given this matter careful thought. "And if, I say *if*, now, the King will not allow me to return to my home, would you be kind enough to suggest that we return to Fyxedia, close things up there, and bring our tools and goods here? This is not a choice I would favor, as you know. Still . . ."

The seer looked at Finn with no expression at all.

"And you would, of course, agree to come back."

"Why, you would have my vow, sir."

The seer took a healthy swallow of his ale. "That, of course, is something you would have to take up with the King."

"I would be glad to do that. May I ask when you think he'll be, ah—up, again? How long is it, as a rule, from one demise to the next?"

Oberbyght didn't answer, and Finn was sure he didn't imagine the slight, oppressive pain in his head, as if a band of iron had been wrapped about his skull.

Why, he wondered, was he wasting his time, crossing swords with this man? No one in this land of lunatics would ever let them go. If he and his loved ones were ever to see Garpenny Street again, they would somehow have to break free on their own.

"I wonder if we might have another ale," Finn said. "You have been so generous, sir, I should like to buy the next round myself."

"I wouldn't hear of it, Master Finn," said Oberbyght with a cheerful smile. "You're my guest here. When you get settled, and begin your new life, then you may treat me, my friend."

The seer's pleasant manner, his insidious grin, filled Finn with such rage and desperation, he could scarcely keep himself from strangling the fellow on the spot.

Instead, he gripped the edge of his chair and studied the damp circles of ale on the table, lest he give himself away before the seer's penetrating eyes.

"Are you all right, Master Finn? I hope you're not ill?"

"A little dizzy, is all, I'm shamed to admit. I am not used to the strength of fine Heldessian ale."

Oberbyght laughed. "We'll get you used to it, sir. I'll personally see to that."

Finn glanced up, then, as the table of Snouters broke into another boisterous round of good cheer. Some of the stout farmers had indeed consumed more than their share of the dark and heavy ale. A bench overturned. One fellow stumbled and nearly fell. Then all began to gather up their cloaks, say their farewells, and converge upon the door.

Seven hefty Newlies and only one door. One didn't have to be a master of odds to bet on this event. It was, Finn thought, much like squeezing potatoes into the neck of a pickle jar. . . .

"Friend Oberbyght," Finn said, rising rather quickly from his chair, "I fear I must relieve myself before we start back. I doubt I could make it that far."

The seer raised a brow. "Well, then you must. That way, out the back."

"My thanks," Finn said, and forced a painful smile.

He was next to certain that the seer's eyes shifted for an instant to the pair of Badgies in the corner, but the motion was too swift to truly tell.

Finn made his way through the tables toward the door at the rear of the inn, walking quickly like a man who dared not hesitate.

From the corner of his eye, he saw the two Badgies rise from their chairs. Slowly, though, only as a caution, as Finn had prayed they would. Dealing with Maddigern had taught him the Badgies had rigid restraints concerning their conduct with humankind. Neither wished to follow him on such an appalling errand as this.

And, in that instant, the moment he saw them pause, Finn turned on his heels and raced for the tavern's front door.

He heard a Badgie curse, heard the other shout. Finn didn't pause to look. He lowered his head, braced his shoulders, and plowed into the brawny pack of Snouters fighting for the narrow front door.

He hit the bunch low, plunging into a thicket of ponderous legs. The Snouters howled, roared, squealed in dismay. They tumbled, fell, tripped like a brace of nine pens, or seven as the case might be.

Finn caught a boot in the belly, another to the jaw. A weighty fellow landed on his back, driving his breath away. For a painful moment, he was trapped, crushed beneath this furious mass.

Then, of a sudden, he was scrambling free, on his feet again, darting through the crowded streets of Heldessia Town. Free, quit of his watchers, on the loose again—with no idea what he ought to do next. . . .

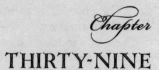

THIRTY-NINE

OR A MOMENT OF PANIC, SHEER DESPERATION AND outright fear, Finn darted through wagons, carts, humans and Newlies of every sort, leaving angry strollers in his wake.

"This won't cut it," he muttered to himself. "I'm leaving a trail for those louts, clear as whale doo!"

Turning at once into an alleyway, he left the busy boulevard behind. Taking a breath and releasing it again, he leaned against the damp brick wall, letting his heart slow down, willing the tension away.

He was safer, there, at least for the moment, especially with night coming on. Had they really lingered that long? He chided himself for not keeping a better account of the time. He remembered, too, that the last time he'd been on these streets at night, the Bowsers had been on a tear, and every door and window was shut against the yapper horde.

Moving down the alley, farther from the lights, he paused, waiting for any sign the Badgie pair was on his trail. By now, they could have sounded the alarm, and raised a whole swarm of the King's cloaked guards. Maddigern would be at the head of this band, furious that his fellows had let his hated foe slip away.

—Or maybe not. Maybe the two rascals would try to do the job themselves instead of admitting they'd let their prey get away.

THE TREACHERY OF KINGS 213

And what of Obern Oberbyght, what would the wily seer do? Somehow, Finn thought, he might do nothing at all. Oberbyght was such a cocksure, irritating fellow, he'd surely imagine his drinking partner had no chance to get away.

Finn nearly laughed aloud, for there was surely one cheering thought in this game. The King's weighty honor still rested where Finn had left it at the inn. The seer would have to find some lackey to carry the thing back to the palace, or drag it there himself.

THE NIGHT SEEMED TO COME ON SWIFTLY AS HE made his way past one pile of garbage and another in the odorous alleyways.

And, while he was greatly concerned, Finn had no regrets for his actions. He had known that his dash for freedom was risky at best. Even if he found Bucerius in the maze of Heldessia Town, even if the Bullie could somehow help him get away, Letitia and Julia were still in the palace, and doubtless under double watch now.

Yet, it was a thing he had to do, for he could not, would not, lose his freedom, could not doom himself and his love to a life in the service of a man who cared only for death, colorless clothing, and a thousand tasteless clocks.

ONCE MORE, HE WISHED FOR THE PRESENCE OF Julia Jessica Slagg and her uncanny sense of recalling everywhere she'd been.

"What a marvel she is," he said aloud, "what a wonder I've performed!" Sometimes, he was even amazed at himself—that such a cunning thing had been born in his head and brought to life with his hands. That golden gears and a ferret's brain had become such a clever, if somewhat conceited, device.

. . .

TWICE, HE THOUGHT HE'D SIGHTED HIS PURSUERS in the maze of alleyways. Twice, he had been mistaken. Once, the pair had been humans, the other, heavyset Bowsers, lurking about on some illegal enterprise.

The street where he stood was quite narrow. The crowded stone houses sometimes arched together overhead. Candlelight flickered in a single grimy window above. The neighborhood seemed familiar, but so had the one he'd passed through moments before.

He was cautious, here, for though the hour was late, there were beings still about. Even in the near darkness, he recognized them at once. They were Newlies, Dobbin folk, hard to mistake for any other creature, for they were quite distinct in both their bearing and their size.

If any of the Newlies could wear the mantle of the noble and the proud, Finn believed it would have to be the Dobbin kind. Theirs was not a vain and arrogant pride, but a pride of dignity and grace. They were tall, elegant creatures, with broad shoulders, flaring crops of stiffened hair, and warm and caring eyes.

Perhaps their most distinctive feature was the thick and lengthy nose, which dominated every other feature of the face. Finn had several Dobbin friends back in Ulster-East. Many of their kind seemed to favor the retail trade, for they were known as purveyors of expensive clothing— jackets, trousers and vests of satin and silk, in colorful checks and spots. They favored such garments themselves, and looked quite dapper as they strolled through the parks on pleasant days.

Finn didn't wish to reveal himself, to be remembered as a stranger roaming about in the dark. Still, he reasoned, he was hopelessly lost, and felt he could put his trust in the kindly nature of Dobbin folk.

Finn waited. In a moment, two stately fellows appeared from a doorway across the street. The light from the single window showed him one wore a broad-striped jacket, while the other had chosen a pattern in spots. Both wore fine derby hats. They chattered as they walked, and wouldn't have noticed Finn at all if he hadn't managed a prudent cough.

"Your pardon, sirs," he said, "I am a stranger lost, and would ask you directions if I may."

The pair stopped. They made no move to come closer, or back away, and one very subtly took a better grip on his cane.

"What address y'be seekin', sar?" asked the fellow in spots. His voice was deep and mellow, though somewhat nasal, due to the prodigious size of his nose.

"I am even more lost than that," Finn confessed. "I'm looking for a friend named Bucerius. He told me his address, but it totally slipped my mind."

"Bucerius."

"Yes."

The Dobbin in spots looked at his comrade in stripes. "Are we familiar a'tall, ye think, with such a name, Flynn?"

"Why no, I cannot say we are."

"My friend is of the Bullie folk. Very large fellow. Well, aren't they all? He owns his own balloon. That is, he did, until a Bowser band shot it down."

"Oh, dear, Bowsers, is it, then?" The Dobbin named Flynn seemed quite alarmed.

"They don't come down here," the other said. "We're peaceful folk indeed, but we don't put up with such foolishness as that."

He nodded, slightly to his left. "The yappers know better, I'm thinkin', than to be comin' here."

Finn, following the fellow's eyes to the arch overhead, saw six fine nooses, hanging ready in a row.

"A most excellent idea," Finn said. "I'm sure it makes for a quieter neighborhood."

"Aye, it does indeed. Sorry we canno' be of help. If I might suggest . . ."

"Yes, please."

"Don't be a-walkin' about Heldessia Town at night. Our folk are quite—tolerant, of other kind. But I won't be sayin' that fer everyone. And a pleasant good night."

The pair tipped their derbies and turned away.

"I'm grateful for the advice," Finn said, "and one thing more, if you please. Which way is the proper direction toward town?"

Finn's words were lost, for the Dobbins were no longer there. . . .

Chapter

FORTY

WHICHEVER WAY WAS RIGHT, HE WAS SURE
this wasn't it at all. Not far from the neat, well-kept houses
of the Dobbins, the neighborhood began to go downhill.
Crumbling structures and boarded windows appeared.
Shops had been plundered and burned. Vagrants had taken
up residence in the empty buildings, and the foul evidence
of their presence was everywhere.

It seemed to Finn that every town he'd seen in his trav-
els—including, he had to say, his own—had its sections of
grim desolation. And, strangely enough, poverty and ruin
often bordered the streets of the well-to-do. A reminder,
each to the other, of what might have been, and what
might surely be.

*Our folk are quite tolerant of other kind, but I won't be
saying that fer everyone. . . .*

Finn understood the Dobbin's words well. If many humans still resented Newlie folk, the feeling worked two
ways. Even now, three hundred years after the Change,
the undercurrents of hatred and suspicion were very
much present everywhere.

And would it ever be the same? Finn wished he had a
more hopeful answer, but in his heart, he could not be
sure such a day would ever be.

·   ·   ·

THE BLEAK, SHABBY STREETS REMAINED THE SAME, but there was a difference now, one Finn recognized at once, for he had encountered it many times before. Ahead, a mist, a pall, a faint luminescence hugged the earth, rose and curled away, then sank to ground again. Standing amidst this dark, unwholesome veil were figures, vague and indistinct, specters, phantoms, wan and haggard shades, ragged, wispy apparitions, dank and ghastly things long devoid of mortal life.

Finn breathed a sigh of relief, for nothing here could do him harm. Whatever good or evil these Coldies had done in living form, none of it mattered now.

Several of the wraiths watched him closely, then one began to drift his way. A swirl, a flux, a vapor ill defined, yet a pale reflection of human form.

"What brings you among the dead tonight, sir? Searching for an old friend, a mother, perhaps, some dear departed kin?"

The Coldie's voice was a chill and awful thing, like dead bones a'rattle in a can, but Finn was used to that, for all the dead sounded much alike.

"No, but I thank you for asking. I'm not from around here, I'm from out of town. I was looking for an, ah—acquaintance of the living persuasion, as a fact. I fear, though, I've become quite lost."

"Hah!" the Coldie laughed, a sound close akin to strangulation, a final deadly gasp. "You've come to the right place, sir. We're *all* lost here."

Some of the Coldie's friends overheard him, cackled at his jest, and came near. Some were mere wisps, faint scintillations, fireflies lost in a mist. Others were ghostly shapes, foggy and obscure, but still of mortal cast.

The worst of these were the recently dead, for they had yet to shed the husks of their remains. Thus, they carried tatters, scraps, chill reflections of the horrors of the grave.

One, he thought he might know, but only for an instant, before it flickered away.

The specter that faced him now was better off than some, but scarcely a pretty sight to see.

"I was Artuzio Bliek, by the way," the phantom said. "A seaman by trade, though I can't recall just where or when. The memory fades with the bodily form, you know. It's likely just as well. Who can say what foul deeds a fellow leaves behind?

"A lass named Idis, I do remember that. Or was it Peribee? I don't suppose you'd know her, sir?"

"Sorry, friend. I fear I can be of little help at all."

"Well, perhaps it'll come to you again. . . ."

Then, as if an errant wind had passed, former seaman Bliek shuddered in brief agitation, then vanished in a wink.

"I hope you'll recall some very fine moments of the past," Finn said, in case some whisper of the fellow remained. "There's good in every life, I can vouch for that."

"Not that poor beggar, not our Bliek. I doubt he's got a pinch of anything much worth bringing up again. . . ."

Finn turned, startled for a moment, to find a grisly figure there. The specter was illusive as smoke, thin as spider breath. Yet, it was clear he had suffered greatly in life, for all that remained was a twisted limb, a bony chest, and half a hazy head.

"A rather gruesome sight," the thing said, "but I can't help that. You might come over worse than me someday, you can't tell."

"If I reacted rudely, I apologize," said Finn. "I meant no disrespect at all."

"No offense taken, friend. I'd say you've spent some time with the dead before. I've had many a fellow jump right out of his skin at the sight of me."

"As you say, no fault of yours."

The awful apparition seemed to pause, as if to gather what little was left of itself.

"I'm Prawn-Wallis the Second, by the way. King of this begotten land at one time, though I doubt you'd know that. I know you, though, Finn, Master Lizard-Maker, the one with the winsome Mycer lass."

"Scones and Bones!" Finn glanced over his shoulder, to see if some living foe were there. "How could you possibly be aware of that?"

The specter laughed, a most disturbing sound. "Those of the croaked, the stiff, the perished, so to speak, know a great deal—unless you're as dumb as Artuzio Bliek, who might as well not be dead at all."

"It's true, then, you were really a king in this land?"

"Why would I lie about a thing like that? Yes, of course I was the King."

"And when exactly was that?"

"*When* is not a big thing with the insubstantial crowd. You've spoken to the dead, you ought to know that. I don't have the foggiest idea *when*. Some time ago, all right? I'm in that fossilized museum somewhere, go find me yourself."

"The Holy Place of Emperors, Tyrants and Kings."

"Whatever they're calling it now, that's where I am."

"I'll certainly take a look. That's if I get back there, again." Finn paused for an instant, wishing he had a mug of the Fractured Foot's ale.

"May I ask you a question, sir? Would you take offense at that?"

"I'm dead. How can you get more offensive than that?"

"I'd ask if you followed the rites of the Deeply Entombed in your time? I'm curious to know if religious napping is truly beneficial, after you've, ah—passed on?"

"The what?"

"The Church. The Church of the Deeply Entombed. I wondered if—"

"You've lost me, sir. What are you talking about?"

Finn, puzzled by the phantom's reaction, explained the beliefs of the Deeply Entombed, how sleep was quite helpful in picking up points for later on.

The ghostly image of the King seemed to twitch and waver about. Finn felt certain he was really quite annoyed.

"Ridiculous. Never heard of such a thing."

"Possibly you forgot. It may have been a long time."

"No. There's much I don't recall. I doubt I'd forget something as foolish as that."

Finn sighed. "Then I guess there's no use asking about the bell."

"And what bell is that?"

Naps and tacky shrouds and crypts without a blanket or a sheet. Bells that ring every thousand years, and sometimes on a Tuesday afternoon . . .

"I haven't been comfortable with much of the royal beliefs since we arrived," Finn said. "I've felt all along that the Grymm family church is not all it's said to be."

He frowned at the gruesome dead King. "This Afterworld they talk about. I've pondered on that myself for some time. What do you know about that?"

The wraith gave a nasty laugh. "I've heard this one once or twice."

"You're saying it isn't true. There isn't anywhere else."

"I'm saying I'm *standing* in it, friend."

"I've heard both sides of this, most of my life. My uncle was in the Church of Unrequited Lust. Mother wouldn't let him in the house. His wife was Tabernacle of the Frequently Annoyed. She believed we came back as bees."

"There's a lot to be said for that. I'd be willing to come back any way I could."

"Is it really that bad over there?"

"There's nothing to *do*, boy. No recreation of any sort,

no place to go where you aren't dead, too. What's the damn point? I used to be one who frequently said, 'Hey, I might as well be dead.' I suggest you think twice before you give any credence to that."

"Yes, I see what you're saying. I don't believe I've heard it put that way, I appreciate that—"

Finn stopped, taken aback, for the phantom Prawn-Wallis the Second seemed to blur, dissipate and scatter here and there.

"Wait," Finn said, "I hoped you'd stay, sir. There are quite a few things I'd like to know."

"That's the living for you. Everybody wants to know something, and there's nothing you know that'll keep you from ending up here. The thing *you* need to know, Master Finn," came the hideous whisper, the rattle and the moan, "is some are sayin' you might be joinin' us soon. I'd take a care if I was you . . . !"

A shiver, a gust of air sharp as an icy blade, struck Finn to the bone. Truly, no one likes to hear news of his demise, especially from the dead. . . .

Chapter

FORTY-ONE

NOT QUITE STIFF AND NOT QUITE COLD, AND not beyond the pale. Still, he felt as if he'd spent the whole night in a burrow or a well, somewhere as comfy as a grave.

And, if they didn't stop pounding at him, jerking him apart, shouting in his ear, he'd rise from the dead and show them what-for . . .

"Get up, you damn fool, on your feet, boy. I be gettin' some annoyed with you!"

"Whuka-whoo," Finn said, or words to that effect, "wudda-wudda-boo."

A pummel, a yank, a slap hard enough to bring him back from wherever he might have been.

"Ah, it be about time you gettin' your wits about you, Finn. No one be sleepin' here but the dead."

"You mean I'm not?"

"If you be deceased, then I be too, and I'm fair warmer than that."

The head, the knobs above the brow, the ring in the nose, the massive shoulders that blocked out the sky.

"Bucerius?" Finn sat up so quickly his head began to spin. "Hooks and Crooks, what are you doing here?"

"I be askin' you the same. You lost your fool mind, or what? Wouldn't nap in Coldtown was I you. It irritates the dead. They be entitled to whatever peace they's got."

Finn's back gave him fits. His feet were frozen bricks.

"I'd challenge that. I feel those who've passed away miss talking to folks more than anything else. Besides food and ale, that is.

"I chatted with a fellow who'd been to sea. Bliek was his name, as I recall. Then I met a former king. Gruesome chap, but he set me straight on a number of things, and I'm grateful for that."

"I'm right pleased to hear it. Now you don't mind, I don't be feelin' real easy standing 'round here."

"You, Bucerius? Why, I can't believe you're afraid of the dead."

"*Afraid!*" Bucerius seemed to swell to half his size again. "There's not a thing on earth I be a'fearing, human person, and you'll not be sayin' such again. What I be somewhat *uneasy* 'bout is the day comin' on real soon, an' half a hundred Badgies out there sniffing after one Master Finn. I'd not care to be standin' real close when those rascals lop off your head. . . ."

THE BULLIE'S WORDS WERE DISTURBING ENOUGH to shake Finn fully to his senses again. It was, as Bucerius said, getting close to dawn, light enough to see the stark shadows of houses and shops against the lowing sky.

Bucerius was puzzled that Finn was surprised to see him there. His presence did not seem at all peculiar to him.

"Have you no sense at all, then? There scarcely be a soul in Heldessia Town don't know you're wanderin' about. Me, I'm getting a fair night's sleep, and there's a pair of stuck-up Dobbins be rapping on my door. Two dandies in their gaudy jackets and such."

"I talked to those two," Finn said, astonished to hear this news. "They said they'd never heard of you."

"And best they be a'sayin' it, too. They got their big noses in the air, but they'd not be pleased if their neighbors was to know what kind of goods from foreign lands they be buyin' off of me.

"Now, if I might be askin', what kind of mischief you be up to at the palace, friend? And don't be makin' up lies and fancy tales, for I'll know for certain if you do."

Finn stopped and scraped something awful from his shoe. "Why, I haven't done any sort of *mischief*, as you put it, none at all. In fact, I was given quite a large decoration from the King. I did encounter several problems at the palace, but I shouldn't call it mischief at all."

With that, Finn gave the Bullie a brief account of events that had occurred since they'd seen each other last. The Bowsers' two assaults, his visit to the hall of irritating clocks, his encounter with the seer, and the fact that he didn't get along too well with Maddigern.

Lastly, he explained that Oberbyght had given him the staggering news that he, Finn, was stuck in this country for life—which is why he'd plowed through a pack of Snouters and made his getaway, determined to find Bucerius—who, luckily, had managed to find *him*.

"That's about it," Finn said, "except for minor incidents, which I won't bore you with now. And, I'm sorry I didn't ask, how have you been, friend?"

Bucerius pressed an enormous hand on Finn's chest, and though this gesture was gentle enough, it nearly knocked Finn to the ground.

"You need not tell me more, Master Finn, for I be quite aware of most of them deeds, and some you was reluctant to tell."

"Indeed? Then why do you bother to ask?"

"Don't get your blood up, friend. I'm not surprised you're keepin' the worst part to yourself. For worst indeed is what it be, if you're dallyin' about with that sly and cunning spawn of the King."

Finn felt the color rise to his face, and was thankful for the morning's pale light.

"I chanced to meet this person, through no fault of my own. What I have to do with her is nothing at all. And since you and I haven't spoken since I entered the palace, how would you know who I came across in there, and what I've seen? Perhaps you have a nest of *spies* inside, friend?"

This last was meant in jest, but it was clear the Bullie saw no humor in Finn's words at all. Instead, he grabbed Finn's shoulders in his two immense hands and lifted him off the ground.

"*Never* even be thinkin' such thoughts, you hear me plain? If you had your wits about you, you'd see it's in a trader's favor to know what be goin' on in that damp and dreary place.

"And what I be knowin' is there's danger and peril afoot in there, things you couldn't guess, things a crafter of lizards don't *want* to know, if he values his skin and the safety of his Miss."

"Put me down, Bucerius. Right now."

The Bullie lowered him to the ground, muttered to himself and ran a hand across his face. Finn had seen Bucerius in a simple huff before, but this was something else. The Bullie was anxious, clearly out of sorts. His face was dark and somber, like the onset of a storm.

"Listen to me, Master Finn," Bucerius said, "and listen clear. I can't answer none of the questions be whirlin' about in your head, for there be danger enough in knowin' what you do. Might be I can get you out of this mess if our luck'll hold a bit, but there isn't no chance if you be goin' back in there."

Finn started to protest, but Bucerius raised a restraining hand. "Don't have to say it. I know you'll not be leavin' without the Mycer and that damn device of yours.

"I be telling you what you knows yourself. You knew the risk you'd be takin' when you took off runnin' through Heldessia Town."

The Bullie sniffed the air and looked solemnly at Finn. "I'll show you a safe way in and out. I doubt it'll help, but it's all I can do. Don't be trustin' no one in there. And 'specially that brazen witch you be pantin' after."

"Will you quit saying that? I *looked*, all right? Anyone would."

Bucerius gave a throaty laugh. "Any fool *human* person would. By damn, I can't see why. One of you's as ugly as the next. For the life of me, I don't know how you tell each other apart.

"Do like I say, and you might get out of here in one piece. Though I be havin' grave doubts about that. . . ."

Chapter

FORTY-TWO

GRAVE DOUBTS, INDEED . . ."

If Finn wasn't certain the Bullie had no place for
whimsy in his life, he'd accuse the fellow of a play upon
words, and a meaningful play at that.

The air was chill with the damp scent of raw, unfin-
ished stone, for this passageway bore no kin to the King's
polished granite halls. The twisting corridor was hewn
from the earth itself, a course so narrow and close it was all
Finn could do to hold back the panic that threatened to
crush him, choke him in its grip.

Would it be better, or worse, he wondered, if he could
see, instead of feeling his way in the dark?

"No torch, no light at all," Bucerius had warned him in
no uncertain terms.

Why? Finn had wanted to know. If this was a secret
way, who would guess that he was there?

"Didn't say that *no* one knew, now did I, Master
Finn?"

Thus, another chill to add to his growing list of fears,
things to remember, things to brood about as he made his
way through the smothering dark. For Bucerius had given
him a map, a map he couldn't see, a map he must carry in
his head:

Twenty-seven steps, then right . . .
One hundred nine, then left, and left again . . .

Finn had a good head for cogs, gears, springs and silver wheels, minuscule wires that wandered this way and that. He could keep a dizzying array of lizard devices in his head, but he wasn't fond of numbers at all.

And why, he asked himself, *if Bucerius has my interests at heart, why not share the dire secrets he knows about Llowenkeef's court? Why not give me a better chance to get out of here alive, with Letitia and Julia Jessica Slagg?*

He had no answer to that. It did occur to him, however, that a good way to get rid of meddlers was to dump them in a tunnel where they'd never get out, and bid them fond farewell. He shook his head and cast the thought aside. That sort of dark speculation made little sense at all.

FOR A FACT, IT WAS NO GREAT SURPRISE TO FINN that the Bullie knew a lot more than he liked to tell. He had known about this secret way all along, and had never said a word when he'd ushered him into the palace with the "help" of Devius Lux.

When Finn had confronted him with that, the Bullie had merely laughed. "An' why would I be tellin' you 'bout that? You don't be sneakin' in a place when you can go politely in the door."

"That's not what I was asking," Finn said.

"No, you be askin' why I don't be tellin' you everything I know. . . ."

DID THE TUNNEL SEEM SOMEWHAT WIDER THAN before? Was it slanting deeper now?

"Pikes and Spikes, how am I supposed to keep all this in my head. There's enough churning about in there as it is!"

There was much he had to tell Letitia Louise. He wished he could recall all the amazing things the Coldie king had told him before he disappeared. Letitia would surely have a great deal to say about Prawn-Wallis' revelations, for she firmly believed there *was* an afterlife. All the Mycer folk did, and many other Newlies as well.

And, though he wanted very much to share Letitia's beliefs, he had grown up among his own kind. Most everyone of the human persuasion believed what they could see: You became a Coldie when you shed the mortal coil. Period. That's what you did.

"This is all there is, right here!" as the specter king Prawn-Wallis had said.

So why were there no Newlie Coldies about, no wispy Bullies and Snouters gathered in the night? Letitia had an answer to that: "Why, because they pass on to a greater Being when they die."

"Nonsense," most any human would say. "You're not going to see no Newlie specters, 'cause they're not the same as us. They're *animals*, still. They don't go anywhere at all. . . ."

THIS WAY OR THAT? LEFT, HE WAS NEARLY CERTAIN, though it could be right as well. The breeze from the left seemed more intense, as if the inner winds, the earthen streams of air, were coming from a source closer to this labyrinth's end.

And, scarcely a moment after that, the wind brought a sound, a sound so faint Finn could not be certain it was more than a deviation of the current itself. . . .

He stopped, listened for a moment, heard nothing more and moved on, his fingers feeling the way ahead. Almost at once he paused again, certain that a pale luminescence had appeared past the tunnel's subtle bend. That, or the constant darkness was playing tricks on his eyes.

"It's not in my head, it's a light, and it's damn well there . . ."

He moved very slowly, counting each breath, determined to keep his wits about him now, for light meant danger as well as release from the dark.

That light, though faint and indistinct, was very real, he no longer doubted that. The sound was real as well, no trick of the wind, though he wished that were so, for it bore such sorrow, such deep and terrible loss, it filled him with a sadness he couldn't explain.

He was struck, then, by a chilling premonition, a feeling of such dread he could hardly bear to look past the corridor's end, for fear of what he might see. And when, at last, he made himself peer upon the scene, he could not begin to comprehend what lay before him there . . .

THEY WERE SILENT, STILL, IN THE FAINT AMBER light, amidst that awful sound of desolation and regret. Eleven, in all, the Royal Family of Llowenkeef-Grymm. Each solemn, naked form dozed in its carven stone vault, and each was attended by a robed attendant, one of the Gracious Dead.

Near each of the vaguely deceased was a low stone table, and upon each table sat an array of jars, bottles, salves and glass vials of liquid in varicolored hues. Some of these containers were fitted with coils of copper tube, and each tube ended in a small ellipse, much like one might see on a flute or a fife.

As he watched in horrid fascination, Finn saw what these bizarre devices were for. One of the Gracious Dead bent down and gently lifted the head of a royal cousin, niece or noble aunt, parted her lips and thrust his fingers in her mouth. Then, he inserted some instrument designed to keep this orifice agape.

When he was satisfied, he lifted one of the copper-tubed vials, and slowly fed some dark and turgid soup into the royal's mouth. Finally, the task done, he laid the woman's head gently down and moved along to the next naked form.

Farther along the row of vaults, another robed figure turned a heavyset man on his ample belly and carefully kneaded the fellow up his legs, his buttocks and his back. It might have been the King himself, for all Finn knew, and he was much relieved that it was too dark to tell.

He couldn't say how long he'd been staring at this incredible sight before he noticed the smell. He supposed it had been there all the while, but he had been so stunned and astonished by the horde of unclad nappers he had failed to notice the scent at all. It was a sweet, heavy scent, somehow familiar, though one he couldn't name.

The sound he had heard, even before the shadowy chamber came in sight, was still very present there. Now, though, as he came aware of the powerful scent, the source of this sound was clear. It was not an errant wind, but the solemn lament of the Gracious Dead, the song they sang for their masters, the royal sleepers of Heldessia Land, the Deeply—or somewhat deeply—Entombed. With the words of the Coldie fresh in his mind, Finn was unsure just what he was watching now. Whatever it was, it was surely an odd, disturbing scene.

On the other hand, it was really quite nice, peaceful and very satisfying. If one could simply rest for a while, breathe the sweet sedation and drift into long and pleasant dreams—

Finn caught himself, suddenly alarmed, and shook himself awake. He recognized that numbing scent before it dragged him under again. It was, for certain, a deadly drug of the East, the dark distillation of the poppy that enslaved men's minds!

This, then, was the source of the haze that hung in the air about these silent forms. It was not the sooty smoke of torches as Finn had perceived. The Gracious Dead kept those they served in a trance, in a deep and timeless sleep, until it was time to wake them again.

And why did these cowled servants not succumb to the paralyzing fumes themselves? Were they somehow immune to the drug's effects?

A dozen questions whirled about in Finn's head. And, most puzzling of all: *Who was behind all this?* Who was responsible for the feeding, kneading, cleaning and constant care of these royal lunatics?

"Someone knows when to start this flummery, and when to stop . . ."

He realized, with a start, that he had spoken his thoughts aloud, that he had nearly fallen under the spell of the poisonous stuff again.

He knew he must keep his wits about him, leave, get away from this place at once. A wrong turn had brought him to this damnable chamber, and now he must find another way.

And which way might that be? Finn hadn't the vaguest idea. It could be any turn he'd passed, to the left or to the right, anywhere along the way—

Finn started. Someone moved within the dimly lit room, and he knew at once it was not the slack, lethargic manner of the Gracious Dead. It was a figure who slipped from one vaulted hollow to the next with sure and agile steps, scarcely leaving a shadow on the wall.

He watched, never letting his eyes off this nimble form, who darted from one patch of darkness to the next.

Someone in this dreary place is not napping at all. Someone is extremely lively, very much awake. . . .

Even as the thought touched his mind, the figure stopped, paused in its flight, caught, for an instant, in the light of a flickering torch.

Finn drew a breath of the sweet and noxious air. The figure was a tall and slender beauty, lithe as a willow and endowed with a haunting, sensuous grace. She was only there for a moment, hardly long enough for a shaft of amber light to brush across her naked flesh.

Long enough for Finn to see another figure reach out and embrace DeFloraine-Marie, and draw her into shadow out of sight. . . .

Chapter

FORTY-THREE

FINN STUMBLED BLINDLY BACK THE WAY HE'D COME, desperately drawing breaths of clean air, fighting the cobwebs in his head. The raw, heavy scent of the Eastern drug was still with him, and, for a while, he was certain he saw pale aureoles of light, witching globes of fire bobbing in the dark. Then, as his head began to clear, the lights quickly faded away.

That other vision, though, would not go away, and, in truth, he made no effort to erase it from his mind. The image of DeFloraine-Marie had nothing to do with endearment and love, but only of lust and desire. To deny that he could have such feelings would be a pointless lie.

And the other figure there, the one she ran to, who might that be?

There was no question that she had, indeed, hurried to him and quickly accepted his embrace. He told himself he was merely curious, that it wasn't his concern. Still, he could not deny that he resented her actions, her willing consent. It was not a vision he could quickly forget.

FINDING THE PROPER PASSAGE SEEMED A NEAR-hopeless task. The Bullie's directions had long since scrambled in his head. All he could do was guess, sniff the flow of air at each dark entry, and imagine where it led.

"And where did that get me last time? To a roomful of bare-ass royals who imagine they're the sleeping dead."

Two of the tunnels he felt were most promising came to dead ends. Another led him back the way he'd been.

Tunnel Four . . .

Tunnel Five . . .

Tunnel Six . . .

Tunnel Seven was an open sewer, his nose was dead certain of that.

Tunnel Eight smelled fine. It sent a chill of expectation up his spine. It smelled of smoke—it smelled exactly like the torches that lit every palace hall.

In spite of his relief at possibly finding a way, Finn crawled forward with caution, and even paused to listen when he saw the first flicker of light through an opening ahead.

Moving an inch or so at a time, the light grew brighter, and he saw that it came from a narrow slit directly in his path. Directly in his path and—

His heart nearly stopped when the tunnel came abruptly to an end. Taking a calming breath, he peered through the small hole, and knew at once he had stumbled on one of the many small alcoves common to the long granite halls.

And, if the tunnel ends here, at one time or another it was open to the other side . . .

Bracing one hand on the wall, he bent forward and slid his fingers through the small niche, getting a firm grip lest the barrier give way and fall. Then, he raised his knees to his chin and pushed firmly against the stone.

Nothing.

Not a splinter, not a break, not a crack in the thing. It simply wouldn't give. And, if he pushed too much, if he really struck it hard . . .

And if you don't, Finn, you'll likely sit here and rot, and what good will that do?

He shut his eyes, pressed his palms against the wall, and kicked the rocky surface as hard as he could.

It broke, shattered, crumbled into fragments, shards, flying chips of stone. The great report of this event rolled like a clap of thunder down the hall.

Finn was up and out, on his feet and running, before the sound of his action echoed to a stop.

He hadn't the vaguest idea where he was, for the King's decorators had no imagination—every inch of the place looked exactly like the next.

"Letitia, I'll find you, love, I'll get you out of here!"

Proud, courageous words indeed. Just how did he intend to do that?

Once more he wished for Julia's uncanny sense of direction, instead of his own, which was feeble at best. How could a man create such a marvel and be such a stumble-foot himself?

Yet, it was often true that a craftsman's work outshone the craftsman himself. Finn knew a builder of ships, one Karpus Keel, who was terrified of the sea. Even a tub of water would make the fellow retch . . .

Finn stopped, numbed, taken a'fright by the sound that reached his ears. *Boot steps!* There could be no question of that. Two, three, and maybe more. Plenty, whatever the number, more than enough to run him down. Closer, and coming at a faster pace as well.

Reason this out. Panic is your greatest enemy, Finn. You can tell which way they're coming by the way sound bounces off the floor, off the polished stone walls.

Three bounces, one on the heels of the next. Divide by two, carry your four . . .

Taking a deep and heady breath, he darted to the left, took the next turn to the right. His pursuers were still behind him, but not much closer than before. Somewhere there'd be a door. Wherever it went, it would get him out of the hall. Nothing offered more peril than these damnable corridors. Take each problem as it comes. Some clever soul had said that.

Finn almost ran them down.

Badgies, four of them, mean-eyed fellows in green cloaks and mail. They weren't surprised to see him at all. They had heard him coming and had their swords drawn.

Now how could this be? He could still hear heavy boots pounding down the hall.

"Not my fault, really," he said aloud. "I couldn't hear this bunch, the fellows were standing still."

One of the Badgies, the broadest, hairiest of the lot, almost grinned, which was not a Badgie thing to do at all.

"If I don't get me a day off for this, I'll eat my socks and my shorties as well!"

"At least," Finn said, too weary, too wretched to even be scared, "I won't have to watch that . . ."

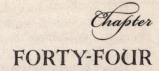

Chapter

FORTY-FOUR

HE COULDN'T SEE HER, BUT HE HEARD HER CRY out, heard the tremor, the fear in her voice, but he also heard the bold tenor of defiance, and he was proud of her for that.

"I'm all right," he shouted, his words nearly muffled in the thick, odorous sacking his captors had bound 'round his head. "I'm fine, I'm right here, my love!"

Not too reassuring, but the best I can do for now. . . .

The Badgies tossed him roughly to the floor. He tried to duck his head between his shoulders, protect himself from the fall. The brutes would have none of that—one tripped him up, while another buried a fist in Finn's gut. He went down hard, gasping against the pain. A soldier kicked him savagely in the head. Another sat on his back while his comrade straddled Finn's legs.

They were quick and thorough, and clearly enjoyed their work. His arms and legs tightly bound, they lifted him roughly and slammed him down on a stool. A noose was looped about his neck, the free end tied to some object in the wall.

No one had to explain this arrangement to Finn. If he moved his head forward or side to side, he'd quickly choke himself. If he struggled and upset the stool, he would strangle quicker still.

Someone jerked the sacking off his head. The Badgie

who'd pledged to eat his socks studied Finn for a moment, then turned and followed his comrades out the door.

"Finn . . . *Finn!*"

His heart nearly stopped at the sight, for she was bound to a stool across the room, in much the same manner as he himself.

"If they've harmed you in any way, by damn they'll answer for it," he said, "and they'll get no mercy from me!"

"No one has hurt me, Finn, no more than you can see. I suppose they will, though, for I've not been shown any kindness since they brought me here. I don't expect much from those who'd treat a being like this."

"Who was it, who did this?" he asked, though he was near certain that he knew.

"The same bunch that brought you here, I think, though they all dress the same. Maddigern, though, he was the only one I knew."

"Obern Oberbyght. Was he here as well, or only Maddigern?"

"I don't know any person with a name like that. Who's he?"

"Sorry, I forget. You don't know him, and that's no regret."

Though he tried not to show it, Finn was greatly alarmed by Letitia's appearance, by her sad demeanor. While Maddigern hadn't done her bodily harm, he had clearly broken her spirit, left her too weary, too shorn of all feeling to even be frightened anymore. The luster was gone from her eyes, the dark, iridescent Mycer eyes that brought Finn a love of living he had never known before.

"Don't, Finn, please," she said, with the weary shadow of a smile. "I can guess your thoughts as clearly as if they were printed in a book. You're bursting with anger, and that will do us no good at all."

"A chance will show itself, Letitia. And when it does,

anger may well prove a most effective weapon to set us free, for surely—

"Knaves and Staves, I've been so relieved to find you I haven't asked. Where's Julia, did she escape, did she get away?"

Letitia sighed. "They took her, dear. It breaks my heart to tell you, but she's gone."

"Gone? And where, do you know? Have they harmed her, could you tell?"

"They took her, that's all. She maimed two or three, but they overwhelmed her at last. I imagine the very worst, for they'd never seen the like of her before. I think the Badgie folk have a great fear of any mechanical device. At least, I've always understood this to be so."

Finn took a deep breath and fought to still his heart. Learning of Julia's loss, he had tightened the noose around his neck without thinking and nearly throttled himself.

"I don't know Maddigern's intentions," he said, "but you're quite correct in thinking he wishes us ill. I have learned there's a great deal amiss in this place, intrigue and deceit, dark manipulation of a kind I've yet to understand.

"Though you and I have no part in this, it appears we have landed in the midst of a very sticky mess. There is great danger here, Letitia, I'm certain of that."

"I don't guess you have to tell me, Finn. I'm not feeble-minded, you know."

"Of course not. I didn't mean that, I only meant to say . . ."

The words seemed to stick in his throat. He didn't know where to begin, didn't know what use it would be to waste words at a time like this when there might be little time left at all.

Maddigern wouldn't simply leave them here, he would see the business out. By now the Badgie would have discovered the spot where he'd broken through from the tunnels into the palace hall. And, if he guessed, if he imagined what he, Finn, had seen down there, if what Finn guessed about the Badgie was true . . .

He pushed the thought aside. That wouldn't happen, that couldn't be. The horrors a creature as cruel and demented as Maddigern might conjure in his head would make the simple act of dying seem a welcome reprieve.

"I don't know exactly what to say to you, Finn," Letitia said, suddenly breaking into his thoughts. "I was quite angry—more than that, I suppose—when I left you there with the King and that—I saw how she looked at you, a look of such raw, unfettered lust, yet a look of cunning, cold and uncaring contempt for every male who ever gazed at her with helpless desire.

"She quickly let me know you had met her before, and that pained me most of all, Finn, for you hadn't shared that with me.

"That's when I turned and left you there, for I was so hurt, so angry, to think I had been betrayed . . ."

"I have *not* betrayed you, Letitia," Finn said, cursing the deadly stricture of his bonds that kept him from going to her.

"I have wronged you, but only in a very slight manner. A passing weakness, a frailty of the moment, but never a betrayal of the heart. Never, certainly, a physical thing, an action beyond restraint—"

"Please, Finn, you'd best stop there and let it be, for you tend, in every matter, to go a mile farther than you need."

Her smile, then, reaching him even through the weight of her weariness and fear, brought him such relief his eyes stung with tears. And, when he blinked them away, he saw that she was crying, too.

"I was not thinking clearly at the time," she told him, "or I would have known you had truly done me no wrong.

Or surely not a *great* wrong, for such an exotic creature would turn any man's head. Even one as stalwart and strong as you, my dear."

"Yes, uh, well . . ."

Letitia's smile faded. "When Maddigern came, he told me that you had run, that you had left me here on my own."

"You did not believe that."

"No, not for a moment. It is what he told me next that all but shattered any hope for us all. He said you would be taken. That you would be brought here and—and that we would both pay the price for your acts against the King."

"That is not what happened at all, of course. There are no *acts* against the King. Pots and Pans, there is so much I have to tell you, and I don't know where to begin . . ."

"Then don't, all right?" She closed her eyes, as if she dared not look at him again. "I don't think we have time to waste on your ventures, or any matter that may have passed before. I think that all we have is now."

"It's not over, Letitia." He strained against his bonds again. "I promise you, though things really do look chancy now, that we will overcome this, that no harm will come to you again. This I vow, with all my will, my love!"

And, it was at that instant, that moment, that the door burst open with such power, such might, that it slammed against the wall and sent a rain of dust to the ground.

"Well, then," Maddigern said, his bristled face a piti-less mask, his eyes as hard as stone, "we are all here to-gether, at last. Now we can begin . . ."

Chapter

FORTY-FIVE

YOU GAVE US A CHASE, MASTER FINN. THAT was not a wise thing to do. Maybe you have no laws in that foul land of yours, but you cannot flout the King's justice here."

"And what law did I flout?" Finn asked. "I'm afraid I don't remember any crimes at all."

Maddigern studied him a long moment, as if he were giving the question deep and serious thought. Then, he bent down until his dark face was close to Finn's, so close that Finn flinched at the fellow's odorous breath.

"It is not going to be this way, human," the Badgie said, his voice a near-gentle reproval, as if Finn were a rebellious pupil who had broken the rules.

"There are things I need to know. You will tell me these things, and you will not waste my time with foolish jests."

The Badgie straightened, glanced at Letitia, then back to Finn.

"If I like your answers, things will go easier in the end. For the Mycer, I mean. There is nothing you can say that will be of help to you."

Letitia gasped. The Badgie had meant for her to hear his words, and Letitia reacted as he was certain that she would.

"I don't expect any decent behavior. Nothing would

surprise me, Maddigern. But you'll have to help me recall my misdeeds, or we'll be all day at this."

Only the Badgie's eyes betrayed his fury. "Do you think I won't do things to her? Here, in front of your eyes?"

"Of course I think you will. And when you do, I'll admit to anything you ask. I'll tell you whatever you wish to hear. You've done this before, you know that's so. And when you're done, you'll wonder if anything I've babbled is true.

"Now. Why don't you simply get to it? I know I have nothing to win for myself, but I'll do what I can to save her."

Though nothing I say will make the slightest difference in what you do, we both know this is true. . . .

"We understand each other, then. What would you like to know?"

The Badgie scratched his bristly chin. In the cell's faint light, the white thatch that streaked his dark hair gave him a fierce demeanor that matched his chill, uncaring eyes. Finn thought of Koodigern, who had given him a dagger to protect himself, then gone to his death unarmed. How such a fellow could be a brother to this wretched creature was something he would never understand.

"I know the features of the human face," Maddigern said. "Do not look at me in such a manner again. Now, you will tell me how you got back in the palace. Who told you there were passages beneath the grounds?"

"No one told me. I found the entry myself."

"That is not so."

"I said I would not play games with you. I won't risk her life to beat you."

"You did not find this entry yourself. Those tunnels have been abandoned for a hundred years."

"I said I found the way myself, and that is true. I must also tell you I gave a great many silver coins to a slightly drunken servant. Don't concern yourself, he was human, not a Badgie at all. Certainly not a courageous member of the King's Third Sentient Guards."

For a moment, he thought he had gone too far. He had to hide his anger from this creature, who had filled Letitia with dread, driven her to the edge with his dire promises, and threats of greater pain and humiliation to come.

Now, he sought to break Finn himself, make him lose his self-control in front of Letitia Louise. Finn knew his strengths, and his weaknesses as well. If he didn't stand up for himself, the Badgie would bring him down. And, though he knew there was little chance the brute would spare Letitia any pain, he had to walk the thin line and play the fellow's game. . . .

If Maddigern had learned to read a human's features, Finn was becoming adept at piercing the near-inscrutable Badgie's expressions as well. Finn was sure, now, it was Maddigern he had seen in the chamber below with DeFloraine-Marie. Maddigern knew he'd been in the tunnels, but he couldn't know for certain Finn had seen the lair of the Deeply Entombed.

This, then, was his quandary, for the knowledge of that place was a secret so deeply ingrained in all who were privy to it, that Finn was near certain the Badgie could scarcely bring himself to speak of it aloud, even if his prisoner was never meant to leave this cell alive.

"Let me begin at the beginning, Master Finn. Perhaps that will help bring your answers to mind."

The Badgie peered thoughtfully at the ceiling, at the hard stone floor, as if the thing he truly sought lay hidden there.

"You left the palace with our esteemed seer . . ."

"With his blessing, as it were. As a free citizen of Heldessia. You can find no fault in that."

". . . and then you escaped, through a mass of irate farmers at the inn."

"How could I escape? Escape from what? I hold one of the

highest honors in the land. Higher than a Captain/Major, though that is a worthy rank in itself."

Maddigern bent quickly to Finn's face. "If I kick that stool away from her, she'll strangle. Right here, right before your eyes."

"And I will answer your questions better then?"

Maddigern backed away, as if Finn hadn't spoken at all.

"You left with Obern Oberbyght. Some hours later you discovered a way back into the palace. I think you know the question I'm asking now, human? How did you get back into the palace the *first* time? After you left the seer, and before you came back through the corridors underground?"

Finn stared. "What first time? What on earth are you talking about? I left once, I came back once. You're already aware of that—"

Maddigern didn't answer. He turned so swiftly his long green cloak billowed in his path. He stalked out the open door, stopped, shouted orders to a pair of the King's Guards who stood rigid in the hall. The two turned and disappeared.

Moments later, the Badgies were back again. Between them they dragged a heavy bundle, wrapped in a dirt-stained cloth. With a nod from their leader, they tilted the burden and spilled its contents roughly to the floor.

Letitia cried out, a low moan of despair. Finn felt the bile rise up in his throat and prayed his stomach would behave, and not choke him to death.

Dostagio had been savagely cut across the throat, his head nearly severed from his body. In death, his face showed more emotion than Finn had ever seen him betray in life.

"This is the question you will answer," Maddigern said, his own features nearly reflecting his true feelings now.

"Why did you do this thing, Master Finn? By damn, you'll tell me why you murdered a loyal servant of the King or I'll skin that Mycer of yours alive!"

D*AMN ME, THIS ISN'T WHAT IT SEEMS TO BE,
it's some dark scheme, some deadly pursuit. And only
Maddigern knows its name!*

Finn felt strangely calm, somehow detached, as if he
played no part in this at all. He didn't look at Letitia, for
she would understand what had happened here as well.

"There's no point in telling you I had nothing to do
with this," he told the Badgie. "Whatever nasty business
you're about, it has nothing to do with me. You're well
aware of that."

"Don't talk to me of nasty business, Finn. There's little
worse than murder most foul."

"Yes, I quite agree with that. And this is what the King
will hear, no doubt. That Finn, maker of lizards, was discovered slitting this poor fellow's throat. Loyal guards
tried to take him alive, and had no choice but to cut the
maniac down."

"You've a way with words, human. I'll hand you that."

"And Letitia? She's a slasher as well?"

"I think she hangs herself in despair."

For all his efforts, there was no way Finn could hide his
fear, his apprehension now. The Badgie's words had
struck home, and Maddigern knew it well.

"I'd face you on even ground," Finn said, "if you had
the courage for it."

"That would be too easy, too quick. I'll need more than that."

Finn risked a look at Letitia. She returned his glance with a smile, her eyes bright, her chin raised in defiance. Finn gave her an encouraging smile in return.

The Badgie shook his head. "You so carelessly show your feelings to the world. I cannot imagine such a weakness as this. . . . Cadigar! Sigdin!"

The Badgie's words had scarcely left his lips before the two cloaked guardsmen came at a run through the open door. Both came to rigid attention, as Maddigern shouted orders in the harsh Badgie tongue.

At once, the first mailed warrior took up a position at his leader's side. The other moved to Letitia, stood with his stubby legs apart, his hands behind his back.

"Tell him to get away from her, Maddigern, now!"

"Don't concern yourself, please. I'll give you time to say your farewells before he takes the stool away. I have something else for you first. My kind are more efficient than humans, Finn. When we begin a task, we see it to completion. We do not leave a job undone."

He turned, then, facing the Badgie by his side. The Guardsman started to move, but Maddigern stopped him with a glance.

"Hold your post. I shall handle this myself."

Maddigern stalked to the door and disappeared.

"What do you think, Letitia? I'm guessing fatcake, sugar tarts. Squash pudding with a cherry on top."

"Thornberry pie," Letitia added. "That's the least I'd expect from such a caring fellow as this. Thornberry pie, dripping at the crust."

"I knew you'd say that. A thick red filling, bubbling at the—"

"Stop. No talk!"

The Badgie close by clutched the hilt of his sword.

"You know what we're saying, then? Fine. What would

you fellows think of a tub of gold coins? One each, of course, wouldn't ask you to split a single tub, why, you'd slaughter each other out of hand.

"No? How about two tubs, a place in the country, a vat of ale so big you can bathe in it if you like. Wouldn't hurt either of you fellows, no offense—"

"*Wassik! Jass dega!*"

Something in the Badgie tongue, Finn was sure, and no translation was required. The tip of a sword at Finn's throat said it all.

"Oh, I think I understand. One thing more if I may . . ."

"Finn!"

At Letitia's cry, Finn turned, startled, and stared in disbelief at the door. Maddigern held an iron cage in one hand, held it out stiffly well away from any bodily parts. Behind the thick, rusty bars, hung Julia Jessica Slagg. Her long tail was fastened securely to a chain attached to the inner dome of the cage. Julia swung free, flailing her wicked claws, snapping at the air with her jaws.

The two Badgies glared at the angry lizard and backed up a cautious step as Maddigern hung the cage from a hook in the ceiling of the cell.

Clearly, the two had faced Julia's wrath before and didn't care to get within her reach again.

"Julia, you're not looking your best," Finn said, "but it's good to see you again."

"*I'm* not looking well? That's the bush calling the grass green, I'd say. You're not one to talk, but it is, indeed, a pleasure to be back. Though I wish you would inform me before you leave on one of your exciting expeditions again.

"Letitia, I'm sure you know I did what I could to maim these brutes, but I fear I was foully undone."

"I know that, Julia. You did what you could."

"You never get that right," Finn said. "You do it every

time. That business of the bush. It's not a bush it's kettles and pots. And it's black and not green . . ."

"Enough," Maddigern said, and stepped between Finn and the lizard's cage.

"Sigdin, when I tell you, remove the Mycer person's stool. Do it slowly, for Master Finn will want to see the life go out of the creature's eyes. When he's finished, Finn, I'll personally slice this damnable machine into very small bits. Then we'll get to you."

"What do you want?" Finn said, straining at his bonds. "Did I kill poor Dostagio? Yes, of course, and anyone else you'd care to name. Let them go, they're no use to you at all."

Maddigern waved Finn's words away. "I'm done with you, Finn, there's nothing I want to hear. Look at her once more. In a moment, she won't be a pretty sight to see."

"*Letitia* . . ."

"Oh, Finn, look away, please. I don't want you to see."

"I love you, Letitia, and I will not turn away. Just keep your eyes on me. Look at me, love . . ."

"Do it, Sigdin. Do it now."

Finn shouted her name until his throat was raw, until the cords about his neck choked off his words.

Sigdin, the Badgie Guardsman, looked at his leader once, then did as he was told. . . .

SIGDIN DIDN'T CARE FOR HUMANS. THE PAY was good, but he was never comfortable around them. Humans didn't smell. They didn't smell bad, they just didn't smell at all. That was only one of the qualities he didn't like. Next to a Badgie, they had very little hair. Good, thick hair and a smell you could count on set a Badgie apart from humankind and most other Newlies, as well.

A Bowser, now, creatures that every Badgie loathed, a Bowser had a most unpleasant smell. Especially a Bowser that was wet. Now *that* was not a good smell.

The Mycer, she was something else again. The Mycer smelled nice. Musty, dusty and sweet. You wouldn't tell a Badgie female that, she'd tear you to bits. But it was true. The human tied up across the cell found the Mycer appealing, and Sigdin did as well. One kind of folk could find another attractive, it happened all the time.

Sigdin felt bad about doing away with the Mycer, but he knew he'd feel a lot worse if he didn't do what Maddigern said. Everyone in the King's Third Sentient Guards feared the Captain/Major, and well they should. It was common knowledge in the barracks that Maddigern was completely deranged. Touched, wiggy, whacked-out, nuts. Cross him, look at him crooked, and he'd have your head on a stick.

So, as much as he might regret it, Sigdin gave the Mycer's stool a little nudge, then another, and another after that. Slowly, the way the Captain/Major said. Soon, she began to make really awful noises in her throat, but the human male was screaming so loud, and the scaly thing was squawking, making such terrible sounds, that Sigdin could hardly hear her at all. . . .

FORTY-EIGHT

.... ̗I̗T SEEMED AS IF HIS SCREAMS WERE INSIDE HIS head as well, as if a horde of demons were in there, clawing, ripping, tearing at his skull. The pain tore like a fiery bolt from his head to his chest, exploded in his belly, cut, sliced through every tendon, every muscle, burst every vessel, snapped every bone.

He could feel himself flailing helplessly about, feel his body smashing against the stone wall, quaking, shaking, jerking this way and that.

The agony seemed to last forever, as if it had always been. Then, an eternity later, Sigdin was vaguely aware he was lying there, staring at the ceiling, wondering who he might be, and where he might have been. . . .

Ⓨou, WHATEVER YOUR FOUL NAME IS, GET OVER there *now*, cut the Mycer free or I'll boil your blood on the spot!"

The Guardsman's eyes went wide. Cadigar wasn't afraid of much, but he was terrified by the seer. Obern Oberbyght's chubby finger trembled before his face, and he could feel a great mass of spiders, flies, and pale wet worms squirming about inside his head.

He hesitated for scarcely a blink, then rushed to the Mycer, stumbling over his friend. Without even thinking of his knife, he snapped the cords from her throat with his hands, and set her straight on the stool.

Letitia gasped, filling her lungs with the precious air. Finn gave a joyous cry that ended in a strangle and a choke.

"Damn you, this is not your business, seer!"

Maddigern clutched his fists at his sides, scarcely able to contain his rage.

"It is, indeed my business, and you're the one damned, not I."

Oberbyght pushed Maddigern roughly aside, ran to Finn and sliced the cords about his throat with a small silver blade. Finn tried to mutter his thanks, but the words came out dry as dust.

In spite of his anger, and his greater strength, Maddigern made no effort to lay a hand on the seer. One of his Guardsmen lay jerking about on the floor. The other stood trembling, his back against the wall, staring at nothing at all.

"Both of your louts will be fine," said Obern Oberbyght, following Maddigern's wary glance. "If I intended them harm, you couldn't sweep them up with a broom by now.

"What is this about, Maddigern? You've committed torture here, dire affliction, and one step short of murder, it would seem. If I hadn't appeared—"

"Murder, is it?" The Badgie stepped back and thrust an accusing finger at the floor.

"Open your eyes, sorcerer. Murder's what brought me here!"

When the Badgie's shadow vanished from the wall, Oberbyght saw the body there, eyes glazed in death, the blood now a necklace of black about its throat.

"Dostagio?" The seer frowned at Finn for a moment, then turned his gaze on Maddigern again.

"He killed this poor fellow? Is that what you're saying?"

"No. I did not," Finn said. "He knows that as well."

"Would it be too much to ask," Julia said, flailing her body about, rattling golden scales against her cage, "for someone to get me *down* from here? This is a most improper position, and quite undignified."

"I think you will stay as you are for the moment," said the seer. "You look proper enough to me."

"I am unjustly confined!" Julia protested, snapping at the iron bars.

"Julia, you'll be all right," Letitia said from across the room. "Truly you will."

"My legs and arms are numb," Finn said. "I can't feel a thing. If you won't release me, at least see to her."

"No one's getting *released*," Maddigern said. "You are held under the King's law."

The seer, too, ignored Finn's plea. "You saw him kill Dostagio? He did this deed before your eyes?"

"No, he did not. What of it? You have no say in this. I don't need your spells."

"Tread easy, my friend. You are not on steady ground here."

Some understanding, some knowledge shared, passed between the two. Finn saw this happen, saw that though Maddigern would not back down, he would not, for the moment, push the magician too far. There was caution, distrust, even loathing between this pair, but there was something else there as well.

"You should not have taken him out of the palace. That was a fool thing to do."

"I have reasons for what I do, Captain/Major. I do not have to explain them to you."

"This trickster came back and killed Dostagio, First Servant To His Majesty, and Most Esteemed among the Gracious Dead. That should concern *you*, I cannot see how it would not!"

Too late, the Badgie knew he should not have spoken

these words. Finn could see him draw in a breath, run a hand across his mouth. He could see, as well, the seer's eyes, see his face go rigid, see the dire warning there.

"This is—a matter of the King's justice," Maddigern said, looking at the floor. "I will handle it myself."

"I have still not heard how this killing came about."

"He came back to the palace. Murdered Dostagio, and came back again. Through another way." With that, he briefly met Oberbyght's eyes.

"So I have been informed."

Maddigern looked somewhat surprised. "I say again, stay out of this. I'll see the matter quickly done. The King will be distressed, but that will be that. Dostagio will be discovered in an alleyway."

Oberbyght shook his head. "You are a foul and disgusting creature, Maddigern. You have a great liking for all of this."

"I only serve. As you do, seer."

Oberbyght stepped away, his mouth distended as if he tasted something vile.

"This time you will not serve. This time, it is you who will step aside."

"Be damned, Oberbyght!"

The bristles on the Badgie's chin began to quiver as if they had a life of their own.

The seer stood perfectly still. His eyes met Maddigern's, and the Badgie turned quickly away. "You dare not do your magic on me!"

"I did nothing to you. I am a mirror, my ignorant friend. If you saw something that made you squirm, that is your reflection, not mine.

"No, don't speak. Listen, and let your blood cool. You need say no more than you've said about this fellow's ventures, for if he's strayed somewhere he shouldn't be, it is I who must deal with him now. In my own way."

"I see no need for that."

"Yet I do. And if it is done, what does it matter how it is done? You want more wretches to meet your needs? They are not hard to find, you don't need these."

"And that one?"

Oberbyght frowned. "Dostagio is dead. What would I need him for? I shall take Master Finn with me now. Leave the girl where she is, but she need not be so tightly bound that she loses her limbs. Although I'm sure you are not concerned with that. Leave the mechanical fiend in its cage."

Oberbyght raised his voice so the Guardsmen could hear. "Post guards in the hall, but tell them they are not to come in. That goes for you as well. Until I think on this, consider that I shall leave a few—very small spells about."

Oberbyght paused. "Do leave them alone, Maddigern. Is that clear enough for you?"

"Do as you will. And don't think I'll forget. You have said things this day that cannot be so easily unsaid."

"Then I won't bother to try." The seer's face split in a warm and generous smile. "Loose the fellow, please. And bring Master Finn to me. We'll be having our little talk, up there . . ."

It was only a very small gesture, hardly a nod, barely a motion at all, but enough to raise the hairs on all the Badgies there, for none of them wanted to think about what might lie in Obern Oberbyght's lair. . . .

Chapter

FORTY-NINE

THERE WERE DOORS, LOCKS, LATCHES AND BLOCKS. Bolts, bars, narrow twisting stairs. Finn had been down in the dark and narrow maze beneath the palace; now he was learning there was also an up.

The seer, Obern Oberbyght, in the kindness of his heart—a kindness that cheered Finn not at all—had given Finn time to let the blood flow back into his limbs, which were cold to the touch after Maddigern had so fiercely bound them up.

And why not? For he never intended to loosen them again....

Thoughtful though he might be, the seer had given Finn no time at all to look to Letitia's care, only a glance between them before he was gone. Finn could only think of her still in torment, her flesh chilling cold beneath the tight, unyielding cords.

No guards at Finn's back, no warnings or threats. No one to stop him but the pleasant, stout, and clearly deadly seer. Finn made no effort to get away. He had seen what happened to the Badgie Guardsman in their cell. He had surely not forgotten what this happy sorcerer had done to him before. There would come a chance—he had to believe this was so—and when that chance came, he would take it, whatever risk that entailed.

· · ·

Though finn had heard very little of the talk between the Badgie and the seer, it was clear their meeting had been most intense. Maddigern, cruel, cunning, past the edge of madness, had nevertheless backed away from Oberbyght in the end.

There's hope in this, he told himself. *This pair cannot be done with one another, there is too much enmity for that* . . .

It seemed near forever before obern oberbyght came to a halt, took a silver key from his ring, and rattled it in a brass lock set in a heavy oaken door. Spiderwebs of cold, intense blue light danced along the silver key. The lock began to crackle, shiver and glow.

Oberbyght cursed beneath his breath, words in a tongue that made Finn's stomach turn.

The seer jerked out the key, frowned, gave it a sniff, polished it against the fabric of his robe.

"Damned thing's not a thousand years old. They don't make them like they did anymore."

The sorcerer tried again. This time the lock protested with only a sizzle or two, before the key slid into place.

"After you, Master Finn." The seer stood aside and waved a welcoming hand. "The place is a mess, but nobody comes here but me."

Oberbyght loosed a hearty laugh. "A whimsy, you see. The jest here being no one could *possibly* come here but me. Why, you'd find a patch of grease on the floor if they tried!"

Finn wasn't nearly as amused as the seer, but the point was quite clear.

Oberbyght was right. The place was, indeed, a terrible mess.

"It's home," said the seer. "It's not much, but it serves me quite well."

"It is—very nice, really," Finn said. "I expect there's an excellent view from up there."

"I suppose. Never been up there myself. Sit, Finn. I'll find us a jug of ale."

Finn sat, while the seer moved about, humming to himself.

As the sorcerer said, it was nothing much, but there was room to move around, if one was careful where he stepped. The room itself was perfectly round—no great surprise, as Finn had climbed the twisted stairways of lofty towers before.

A wooden ladder led to a trapdoor above, no doubt leading to the view the tower's owner didn't care to see. Past it, there would be a circular floor, a shoulder-high wall, and all one cared to see of Heldessia Town and beyond.

Inside the seer's quarters, covering nearly every wall, were high wooden shelves filled with books, tomes, ancient scrolls, yellowed piles of paper stacked precariously high. Finn was sure they'd been there long before he, himself, was born—or possibly his father's father sometime before that.

There were vials, pots, jars, a trail of gummy fluids hardened on the floor. Strange, unfamiliar smells, foul and aged odors that had long since eaten into the stony floor.

"Here, then," Oberbyght said, offering a mug of dark liquid in a most peculiar jar, with odd symbols on the side. Finn brought it to his nose and sniffed it, bringing another laugh from the seer.

"It's ale, boy. Won't turn you into a stone. There's an easier way than that.

"Now," he said, leaning forward on his stool, "we have

much to talk about. Or let me put it plainer than that. *You* have a lot to talk about, and I have much to hear."

In an instant, the cheery smile was gone, and the seer's heavy features turned merciless and grim. No matter how often this occurred, the abrupt change took Finn by surprise.

"Good," he said, tipping back his stool against the wall, as if he didn't have a care. "I do love a good talk. It's better than climbing those damnable stairs."

The seer was not amused. If anything, the room seemed to chill by several degrees.

"A bold and jaunty manner will get you nowhere with me. If you think your life's not at risk here, you're a fool. I didn't save you from Maddigern's wrath so we could share a mug of ale like old friends."

He paused to stare at Finn over the fold of his hands.

"Badgies can scarcely smell more than the food that cakes in their beards from one year to the next. Maddigern could not detect the drug on your skin and on your clothes, but I can. You *reek* of the stuff. I don't have to wonder, as Maddigern does, where you might have been.

"He knows you came in through the underways. He can only guess what you saw down there. He didn't have to know for sure. If he strangled you, it wouldn't matter what you saw. That's Badgie logic, and I can't say it doesn't have its points."

"I've no need to speak any more than the truth about this," Finn said, as calmly as he could, though the seer's words went right to his heart. "All I wanted to do was get back in to get Letitia and Julia out. I wasn't expecting to come upon something like—that."

"You did, though. And that is a problem. I expect you can see why that might be."

"I don't suppose you'd take my word . . ."

". . . that you would keep this all to yourself? Please, Master Finn."

"So I've traded Maddigern's justice for yours. I'm not making much progress here."

"You are in a rush to pass sentence on yourself, Master Finn?"

"Does it matter if I'm not? Whatever is to happen, it will happen. And I suppose it will happen to Letitia as well. You may take offense if you like, sir, but I see little difference between you and that brute downstairs. You *left* Letitia and Julia there. Under guard, perhaps, but the fact that you left them tells me you have no interest in their fate."

Obern Oberbyght showed Finn a weary sigh. "You're right, boy. I don't. Not a whit. It's a lack in my character, I suppose. I simply can't work up much sympathy for anyone but myself. Still, apart from that, I don't think the good Captain/Major will cross me on this."

Once more, Finn imagined the room had become even chillier still.

"What did you see down there? Exactly, now. Start with who let you in the secret way."

"A guard. I gave him some coins. I told this to Maddigern—"

It felt like a hot blade between his eyes. Finn gasped, grabbed his face and tumbled off his stool. The pain was there, then suddenly gone.

"All right," Oberbyght said, "let's try this once again."

Finn pulled himself up, found the stool and sat. Even the memory of the pain brought beads of sweat to his brow.

"Bucerius. A friend. But don't blame him."

Oberbyght almost smiled. "Ah, that old rogue. Why did I bother to ask?"

"You know him, then?"

"He is extremely large, and has an annoying habit of

sticking his Bullie nose anywhere a profit's to be made. How could I not know him?

"I also know he was the one who brought you here. Now, we're going astray. Exactly what you saw there below, I'd hear about that."

Finn began to tell him. Everything, from the start. The sweet, overpowering scent of the drug extracted from the blood-red poppy. The still figures of the Deeply Entombed, the sorrowful chant of the Gracious Dead as they went about their chores.

And, as he spoke, as he came ever closer to the part of his tale he hoped not to reveal, Finn allowed certain images to blur, fade, become vague and indistinct. Figures, colors, shapes began to run, as if a quickening rain had swept them away.

It was a thing he had simply come to through the discipline of his craft, a trick of the mind that let him put all other thoughts aside, except a complexity of minuscule parts—cogs, gears and golden wires as thin as gnat's breath, motes, flecks, particles and specks, the workings of a lizard one could hardly see without the aid of a glass.

Thus, Maddigern, and the bare, unmistakable vision of DeFloraine-Marie were, for but a moment, lost and unseen. And, if he was wrong, if this cunning magician could peer behind Finn's screen, he would find out quickly enough and pay for this deceit.

A moment, an eternity, passed. A slow and agonizing moment for Finn, who wandered in his thoughts through lovely vistas, dancing streams, and a near-insufferable parade of puffy clouds. At no time did he dare meet the seer's penetrating eyes. . . .

Oberbyght looked curiously at Finn, as if there was something he was trying very hard to see. Finally, he set down his mug and blew out a gentle breath.

"There is little need for me to tell you that near every turn you have taken since you graced us with your presence here has been a *wrong* turn, Finn. I swear I do not know how you do it. The odds are a man plays the fool only half of the time, but you have managed to overcome that.

"You have become, ah, *acquainted* with the King's wanton whelp, the Princess DeFloraine-Marie, though I've yet to learn how . . ."

"Now that was no fault of mine."

"Every fellow who trips on a woman's gown says the same. Don't bore me, Finn. You didn't trip very far, but I doubt it was because you didn't try.

"And good Dostagio . . . not a bright fellow, but none of his kind is. Still, he was useful to me."

"I didn't kill him, damn it all!" Finn came off his stool, sending it clattering to the stone floor. "Why would I do a thing like that?"

"Sit, Master Finn . . ."

The words barely brushed the edge of his mind, but Finn felt their fiery kiss. And, more frightening still, he knew the seer hadn't spoken at all.

Finn didn't bother to sit. He leaned wearily against the cold wall, getting his breath again.

"I know you didn't murder Dostagio. You haven't done *anything* but drop from your damned balloon and stumble about, causing chaos everywhere you go."

"I've done nothing of the kind—!"

Oberbyght raised a restraining hand. "Your presence is all that was needed, Finn. Why the Fates have done this thing, I cannot say. The point is, you have stirred up a pot that was already bubbling here. You have tossed in the peppers, and we don't like peppers in our stew. You have muddied the broth, you have soured the sauce . . ."

"Are we cooking something? I fear you lost me with the sauce."

"Do not try my patience. I have let your japes, your waggery, your wit, your foreign-tainted quips go by more than once without plucking out an eye or perhaps some manly part. Do not push. Merely listen, do I make myself clear?"

Finn didn't answer. His mouth was too dry for that.

"There are dark events here, deadly deeds, dreadful schemes and dangers undefined. It is not your business to know of these things. Still, I tell you that a dire drama unfolds in Heldessia Land. All this palace is a stage, and every creature an actor on it.

"You aren't even in the play, Finn, yet you've mucked about through every act, tossing in your own bloody lines, knocking over the sets.

"Before your innopportune arrival, the brew was only a'simmer, bubbling a bit, but no real threat. Now, the pot's boiling over, the curtain's going up, the game's afoot.

"Damn you, Finn. Why didn't you and your Mycer and your loathsome machine simply stay where you belonged? We don't need your kind here!"

Finn waited. Understanding at last, that even when this fellow was done, when all the sauce was finished, all the lines spoken, all the villains dead, he might simply start all over again.

"Well, do you intend to sit there, staring at me like a loon? You always have something to toss in the kettle, whether it's worthy or not."

Finn heard a peculiar sound, then looked past the seer to a bookshelf swelling with the weight of ancient tomes, tracts, royal acts and boring decrees. Even as he watched, a stack of homilies groaned, and tumbled to the floor.

"May I ask a question? You won't drill me with a spell?"

"Certainly not. What do you think I am?"

"You won't like me asking it again. Will Letitia be harmed?"

"I gave you the answer to that."

"Your pardon, but that's not so."

"All right. She *won't* be harmed. Next question, Finn."

"When I was at the Fractured Foot, you could have knocked me silly then. Why did you let me go?"

"I miss sometimes. Not often, but I do. If I had crisped one of those fat Snouters, every farmer in town would be screaming for my hide. I do a good business in agricultural spells. I don't *have* to, but it's expected if you're in the magic trade. What else?"

"I don't guess you mind if I ask, for you know what I've seen. I'd like to hear about the Deeply Entombed."

Obern Oberbyght grinned, a grin of such dimension that his chubby cheeks swelled and his eyes squeezed shut. His lips disappeared, and every tooth was on display.

"That, my foolish friend, is the question I've been waiting to hear. It isn't that I'm slow, or dense, or feeble in the head, for none of that is true. The question was ever there, and I could have pushed it some, but I have a sense of order, of the end, of the termination of events. I wanted you to come to it on your own."

Finn felt a sudden chill. "When the sauce is done. When it's time for Act Three."

"Exactly, you have it now!"

Obern Oberbyght sprang to his feet, quicker than Finn imagined the fellow to be. He thrust both his hands out wide, encompassing the invisible sky. The room began to tilt, waver, quiver and shake. Red veins of lightning scurried across the floor, scampering like frightened spiders, drunken centipedes.

Everything melted, everything oozed. Time ran down the walls like syrup, with the sound of sleepy bees.

Finn threw up or threw in, he couldn't tell which. He floated, bobbled, pitched dizzily about somewhere or somewhen . . .

And, when the world stopped spinning, he opened his eyes and stared at the sky, at the endless dome of golden light that stretched out longer than forever overhead . . .

Not exactly endless, Finn decided, and clearly not the sky. More like a great, colossal, impossible bell . . .

Chapter

FIFTY

ONE CAN BE JAILED, LOCKED UP, CLOSELY CONfined," said Julia Jessica Slagg. "I see how this might happen when one point of view simply clashes with another, no harm in that.

"Still, to shackle, fetter, bodily restrain one's adversary, that is improper to every extent. *That* is damned impolite!"

"It is," Letitia said. "I'd be the first to agree, for I am under severe restraint myself. At least I won't strangle now, for that poor fellow has freed my neck, but that will do little good if my arms and my legs fall off. I'm afraid Maddigern didn't fully follow the seer's advice. I am still quite tightly bound.

"Julia, I don't like to complain, but if you could possibly hurry over there . . ."

". . . and talk a great deal less, I know. Finn tells me this all the time. What no one seems to understand—including the learned Master Finn—is that I am a superbly functioning mechanical device with a quick and cunning brain. Unlike Newlie folk and humankind, I can perform a multitude of functions *and* speak at the same time."

"How is your eyesight, Julia? Can you see that my arms and legs are a ghastly shade of blue? Can you—Julia, are you listening to me?"

"Listening, but not talking, you'll note. That was your complaint, I believe."

Letitia sighed. Julia, she knew, was doing the best she could. Perhaps, if she had not severely bitten, slashed, maimed the Badgie guards who tried to catch her, they would not have hung her by her tail in a cage.

"Still," she muttered beneath her breath, "I can't fault her for that. She *was* trying to help me get away."

That was the thing about lizards, or at least such a unique and marvelous lizard as Julia Jessica Slagg. Other lizards Finn had made swept up debris, kept a musket clean, and stamped out perfect little biscuits at a very rapid pace.

None of these devices had a brain, so none was encumbered with the power of reason and speech, and an ego the size of—

". . . well, in truth, the size of Finn's, for I fear she mirrors him in a startling number of ways."

Oh, Finn, my dear, I am not complaining, for I love you just the way you are, and I pray you are well and I know we'll soon be together again. . . .

"I don't know that at all," she said, certain her flesh was turning from blue to a horrid shade of gray. "But I will not think of you in any other way!"

"Letitia. Letitia Louise."

"What?" Letitia looked up with a start. Julia's iron cage was swaying rapidly back and forth on its chain, drawing bizarre shadows on the wall.

"Julia, what are you *doing*? If you strike the wall with that thing, those louts will be in here on us in a minute!"

"I am not overly concerned about that. Those primitive brutes are certain that seer left a few horrid spells about, and I doubt they care to come in here and see.

"And I must tell you it is no great feat to calculate the force of the swing of this object with the motion of the body within—that body being me. I shame myself, Letitia, for not having thought of this before. The solution was right there behind me, and I simply didn't see it until now."

"Behind you? Whatever are you talking about?"

"My tail, Letitia. My own lovely *tail*. Those savages hung me securely by my tail. All I have to do is bite it off, you see. Even a Badgie should have thought of that."

"Oh, Julia, are you certain that's the right thing to do?"

"Are you certain you want to get out of this blasted cell?" Julia said, twisting, twirling madly within the iron enclosure, as the thing swung perilously close to the ceiling and the wall. "Are you still intent on keeping your limbs intact?"

"Yes, of course. They're very essential to me."

"Patience, then. Don't distract me anymore. Not that it's likely anyone could."

Letitia watched, holding her breath, refusing even to glance at her limbs. She was certain that Julia would careen into the wall at any time, and bring Maddigern or his minions rushing into the room, dreadful spells or no. Her very worst fear—next to hopping about on stumps—was ever encountering those creatures again. Even the promise of Oberbyght's wrath wouldn't keep them away if Julia smashed her cage against the wall. . . .

A sudden, peculiar noise brought her out of her thoughts. She stared at the swinging enclosure, at the silver snout and the bright ruby eyes, at the iron claws that struggled to wrench the bars apart.

Then, at once, the whole of Julia appeared, golden scales aglow as she slithered forth to freedom again.

Not entirely the whole of Julia, for a goodly portion of her tail still hung within the cage, a sad, long appendage, a rather ridiculous sight.

"I hope you'll forget what you saw here, Letitia," Julia muttered, in harsh and gravelly tones. "Symmetry, order, elegance and grace are properties essential to my being, to the purity that was meant to be. Without the integrity of the whole, I have no beauty, no balance, I am simply not *me*."

"Please, I won't look. Just come down from there now!"

"Only another moment. If I don't get this thing now, I never will."

Grasping the cage firmly in her foreclaws, her incomplete afterparts dangling in midair, the lizard used her strong iron teeth to slice the cords that held her tail captive within the cage.

Letitia heard the bonds snap and breathed a sigh of relief as Julia's nose appeared, the severed part hanging limply in her jaws.

"Hi god id," Julia muttered, or words to that effect.

LETITIA COULD NOT RECALL A MORE AGONIZING pain, as the blood flowed back into her limbs like a rush of liquid fire. And, when it was done, she felt as if all her strength had drained away with the pain, as if there was nothing left of her at all.

"I understand the concept of suffering," Julia said, "but only in a distant sort of way. If you don't mind me saying, we do not have a lot of time for you to experience this feeling, Letitia. You're going to have to put it aside and get on your way."

Letitia had an answer to that—several, as a matter of fact, but she kept them to herself.

Finn, ever the cunning craftsman, had constructed his greatest triumph in such a manner that every part of Julia, large or small, interlocked with strength and flexibility with the next. Once a part was rejoined with the others, the whole was as good as new. Julia could only vaguely comprehend that this system did not work as well on humans or Newlie folk.

Julia walked off her kinks, stretching her legs, whipping her tail about. Letitia took one cautious step after the next, swallowing the pain that lingered there, then started all over again.

To a spider on the wall, a curious fly, Julia and Letitia must have seemed a peculiar couple in a most bizarre dance.

And, when the dance was done, Letitia felt she might, in time, function once again. It was then that Julia Jessica Slagg waited in the shadow of the door, waited for Letitia to make very worrisome sounds within the room, sounds that might attract a Badgie in the hall.

When the door opened, the Badgie saw Letitia, apparently bound in a stool across the room. Then, he glanced at the cage where the fierce, mechanical horror ought to be, and wondered, for an instant, why it wasn't there.

Wondered, for a blink, and then ceased to wonder or worry at all. . . .

T HE OTHER ONE WILL LIKELY BE BACK," LETITIA said. "He'll expect to find his friend."

"And he will," Julia said, scrambling about, iron claws a'rattle on the hard stone floor. "He simply won't be where he was, and he won't be feeling too well."

"They'll go right to Maddigern, you can count on that. We don't have much of a start, Julia, and I'm a bit concerned about my legs.

"I hope you didn't hit him too hard, Julia. I know what he did, but I don't want anyone hurt. Not too badly, anyway. Unless you can't avoid it, of course. When it comes to that, I suppose those brutes have it coming, there's not much question of that. They weren't too gentle with us, you know. The Mycer folk have a saying: 'Strike me once and I'll strike you back. Strike me twice and they'll find your bones in a phlack.'"

"What's that?"

"Sorry. It's a Mycer word. Means a hole, a pit, a very

deep well. It also means if you're really feeling down, one could say you're in a blue phlack. It comes from the sound an egg makes when you drop it on the floor. *Phlack!* Like that. The Mycer tongue is very descriptive, you know. I could tell you a number of words that—"

"Letitia, you're rambling, raving, running off at the mouth. Believe me, I know. You're worried, concerned, completely strung out, and I don't blame you for that.

"I don't *know* where that seer took Finn. I'm trying to sniff him down. I cannot tell you how many creatures have walked these halls and left their foul scent. Well, I could, but there's no sense in that. Just stay close and let me try."

"I don't care for that seer," Letitia said, running a hand through her hair, glancing warily down the dim hall. "You can't tell what a sorcerer will do. They're as sly as they can be."

"I guess that's part of the trade. People don't want some simple, plain-speaking fellow they can trust. Not if he says he's a seer."

"That's so true. You couldn't depend on a magician like that. . . ."

THE TRAIL WAS SO THICK WITH THE SMELLS OF countless passersby, that more than once Julia was certain she would never find Finn's path. The sorcerer himself had passed this way a hundred times before, but not, it seemed, with Finn.

"You're lost, aren't you?" Letitia said, for the Mycer folk have keen insight into the emotions and fears of all creatures, even one of the mechanical persuasion with a shrewd ferret's brain.

"Not lost, really. I know where I am. We're not looking for me, we're looking for Finn."

"You know exactly what I mean. Don't play your silly lizard games with me."

"Actually, the lizard game is the only one I know. I should think you'd be aware of that."

Letitia glared. "Stop it, right now. When you get like this you drive me out of my mind. Find Finn. That's all you have to do!"

"Ah, well, of course. Beings with wheels and springs inside instead of gooey things should keep silent and out of the way unless they're called upon to—*Get down, Letitia, now. Not that way—over here!*"

Letitia scurried quickly after the lizard, her heart in her throat. Crouching down in shadow, pressed against the cold wall, she could hear them now herself. Badgies, more of them than two, jabbering at one another in the harsh, clacking tones of their native tongue.

"They don't have to be quiet, they know we're here. Do something Julia, please!"

"They know where we *might* be, that's not the same as knowing where we are. Left, I should say. The odds are quite good they'll follow the hallway to the right."

"Wrong," a voice whispered from the dark. "That's exactly what they won't do. They must be total idiots where you come from, Mycer, to listen to an ugly hunk of scrap. This way, and don't ask me any stupid questions; we don't have time for that!"

For a moment, Letitia was too startled to move. Then, getting her wits about her, she knew she had very little choice than to do what she was told. Thus, she followed the slender figure of the King's daughter into shadow, and didn't look back. . . .

Chapter

FIFTY-ONE

HE HAD TO TOUCH IT, THEN TOUCH IT AGAIN.
And even then he could scarcely believe it was real.

*Wait, think, use your head, Finn. Just because you see
something, just because you can touch it, doesn't make it
real. . . .*

He closed his eyes, opened them again, lay perfectly
still. Not much help. The thing was still there, still chill to
the touch. It loomed above him, impossibly far, impossibly high, there was no end to it at all. Only that couldn't
be, nothing could be as big as that, certainly not a bell.
Where would you cast the damned thing, how could you
haul it up here . . .

Finn squeezed his eyes shut again, took a deep breath.
When he let it out, it turned to frost. It was cold, chilling
cold, still and cold as a midwinter's eve.

"What am I thinking? Haul it up here, haul it up
where? Where is here supposed to be?"

Logic, reason, ordinary common sense. That was the
only way to approach this thing. It was all a sorcerer's
trick, of course, none of it was real. An illusion could seem
real, though. That was the point. That's what a trick, a
fake, a fancy was all about.

Somehow, Obern Oberbyght had woven a spell around
him, made him imagine he was a gnat, a speck, a mite inside a vast, enormous, inconceivable bell. A Millennial

Bell, no less. One of those famous, thousand-year, every Wednesday and Friday sorts of bells.

Finn laughed aloud at the thought, but the sound that came out was empty, hollow and dead, a sound that left him full of fright.

And why not? It was all an illusion. Why should a sound be real when everything else is a sham?

Finn came to his feet, taking it slow and easy, watching every step. What if the magic didn't work unless you were flat on your back? What if you just stepped off into nothing at all?

He shook that thought aside. Magic had its rules, like everything else. Why go to all this trouble if you didn't do it right?

"There's a greater, more frightening question than that," he said aloud. "What am I doing in here? Why did that fat-faced trickster put me here at all?"

Such a question should have raised the hackles on his neck, set every hair a'tingle, shivered his flesh and all of that. Here, though, on this unearthly plane, those were the ordinary, everyday conditions of life. Aches, shakes, chafing of the skin, distress of every sort, and every breath like a bite of polar ice.

"If I were in the magic trade, what I would do is summer, with some nice trees about, and a comfy place to sit. I surely wouldn't do a place like this."

He learned, after one or two tries, that looking at the awesome heights above made him terribly sick. Looking down wasn't bad, and that is how he learned there was one way out of the bell.

He had walked nearly halfway around, staying well away from the golden, frost-covered surface of the thing, when he spotted the hole. Not so much a hole as a dip, a cant, a crawlway in the surface of what was really no surface at all, but a piece of imaginary ground, somewhat more solid than the rest of the illusion thereabouts.

He didn't hesitate more than a second and a half. Wherever this hollow, this crawly-hole went, it would take him somewhere else, out of the alarming presence of the bell, and, with any luck at all, out of the illusion as well.

He went headfirst into the hole, sliding on his back, pulling himself along. In an instant he was clear, and peering out the other side . . .

"Bones and Stones," Finn gasped, drawing in a breath, "I've gone mad, wiggy, off the deep end. At the very least, I've completely lost my wits!"

Still, though he was shaken, stunned, stupefied at the sight, he could scarcely contain his elation at the wonder, the marvel taking place before his eyes.

The Millennial Bell was a vague and distant blur on the far horizon now, a golden mountain lost in purple deception, hidden in a lavender veil. The sky was not a sky at all, but a lucent, ever-moving machine, a clutter, a mass, a tangle of such complexity that he had to look away before his mind rebelled.

Yet, when he dared to look at the thing again, he saw within this churning, whirling miracle, a *simplicity* beyond belief, a pure and irreducible sense of order, as if this great device might mirror the intricate works of the cosmos itself.

It struck him, then, that *works* was indeed the word for this perfection, for here, in their ultimate incarnation, were the cogs, gears, ratchets, pins, springs and wheels—wheels within wheels within wheels—of Mechanics itself, the foundation of the art.

Here was the concept of clocks, grinders, binders, of simple devices such as gut trimmers, lint cutters and pie machines.

And, if he could allow himself the praise, the esteem—and indeed he could—his invention of the lizard was a prime example, in a most sophisticated form.

With this thought came a vision within a visionary world. For a dazzling moment, he saw himself as a single mote of dust, a being on a tiny world in the midst of the vast, incredible workings of Julia Jessica Slagg. He laughed with joy as he saw a mirror of what he had created himself, in a manner he had only dreamed of before. And, for a moment, he listened to the clatter and the rattle and the hammer and the tick, sounds that came together like the hum and the thrum of a bright silver heart. . . .

That small moment, scarcely a blink, vanished abruptly as a sudden motion startled him out of his thoughts. As he peered at the marvel overhead, he sensed there was something different in this great convolution, something he hadn't seen before.

A shadow, at first indistinct, had appeared on the far horizon of the cosmic machine. As it neared, it took a more definite form, a bar of darkness stretching from right to left.

Closer, Finn discerned its motion as a shudder, a jolt, a hesitation as it reached one position, then moved on to the next.

Jerk, pause . . .

Move on again . . .

Ordered and steady with a pace of its own . . .

One, two . . .

One, two . . .

And then Finn *knew* . . .

. . . knew this enormous illusion was clipping off snippets of time, its shadowy hand measuring out the unthinkable minutes, counting impossible years, here in a place that knew no time, that wasn't even there . . .

It's a spell, a trick, a great hallucination, what do I care? I'm still in Obern Oberbyght's tower with a bunch of dusty tomes. All this nonsense is only in my head . . .

The hand, the shadow, moved again, *one, two . . . one, two . . .* and now this motion was more than a quiver, more than a jerk, now it moved with a creak and a groan, with a deep and ponderous moan.

And, as it thundered to a stop, paused, trembled and rumbled on again, Finn felt the great, illusory machine shake as well. Under his boots, the imaginary ground began to shudder and a veil of fanciful dust began to drift down from above.

The deadly shaft moved one eternal moment then the next, its mindless cogs and gears marking off another afternoon, ticking off another thousand years.

This is why Oberbyght saved me from the wrath of Maddigern . . . this is why I'm here. I pray no one ever does me any favors again!

He remembered the last time the Millennial Bell had awakened the napping dead. Stones had crumbled and floors had cracked in the palace far below. Here, in the very shadow of the thing, he'd be shaken to thornberry jelly. Nothing would remain but a puddle on the floor.

Finn thought of Letitia Louise. He thought of her touch, of her iridescent eyes. He thought it was quite unfair to perish in an illusion, in the midst of a sorcerer's spell.

"If the end has to be," he said aloud, "it seems only right it should happen somewhere that exists, somewhere that's real. I feel that's really the proper thing to do . . ."

FIFTY-TWO

LETITIA LOUISE COULD HEAR HER OWN HEART pounding against her chest. She prayed the Badgies couldn't hear it too, for they were scarcely inches away, just outside the narrow passageway. She could hear their gruff voices, muttering to one another as they searched the darkened hall.

She thought it was strange how one folk's language differed so much from the next. The Mycer tongue was full of whispers, murmurs, gentle sibilations. If a Badgie ever said hello—which few would ever do—it always sounded like a curse. Humans were somewhere in between. Hard and then soft. Irritating one moment, quite endearing the next. Finn was certainly capable of both.

"Finn, dear Finn, may the Fates let me find you again!"

"Don't *mumble* back there, all right? Stone carries sound everywhere, didn't anyone ever tell you that?"

Letitia felt the color rise to her face. She bit off a nasty reply, words full of brambles, thorns and sharp little tacks. This was not the time for that. Still, if one was collecting unpleasant, totally annoying sounds . . . after the Badgies, the King's daughter would be a good place to start.

If looks were all that counted, Letitia could not deny DeFloraine-Marie was easily the most breathtaking female she'd ever seen, at least as far as humans valued that sort of thing. She had never failed to notice the women who caught Finn's eye, and they *all* seemed to have those full, sensuous lips, lazy, roving eyes, impossibly long legs, and other features Letitia didn't care to list. The trouble was, this female appeared to have them all.

Of course, Finn had chosen her, a Mycer with pointy ears and downy skin, instead of a human female. She needed to remind herself of that. So why, she wondered, didn't that seem to help?

Maybe because I can smell that scent of hers, way back here. And I know it didn't all *come from a jar!*

"I just thought I'd mention," said Julia Jessica Slagg, "in passing, no offense, you have stepped on my tail twice. You might watch where you're going, and forget about our friend up there."

"I am not thinking about anything at all," Letitia said. "Besides, you have no idea what's going on in my head. You're not as good as you think you are."

"Well, of course. I am only a humble mechanical device."

"Don't start, Julia. I'm not in the mood for this."

"My snout is sealed."

"I should live to see the day."

"May it be the Fates' will. Do I have the right deities this time? I get these mythical figures Newlies and humans revere mixed up sometimes. Is it the Fates I'm thinking of? Or is that the Three Blind Lice? I can never be sure."

"Julia?"

"Right here. Scampering aside, just in the nick of time."

"Can you—sense Finn at all? Do you think he's anywhere near?"

"I had enough trouble sniffing out his trail in the hall. There is nothing in here. Certainly nothing remotely akin to Finn."

"Then what are we doing here, Julia? I mean, we've avoided the Badgies, but we don't know where she's taking us, or why."

Julia sensed the edge of desperation in Letitia's voice, the tension, the strain, the tone that said she was hanging on as best she could. Julia knew she needed all the help she could get, instead of the seven acid comments and the half dozen jibes that had just come to mind. Out of great consideration, she said nothing at all.

Letitia saw no difference in this particular section of the narrow, twisting crawlway, and the one they'd passed only moments before, but DeFloraine-Marie seemed to feel it was the right place to be.

"I cannot stop and wait for you every five minutes. You're going to *have* to keep up," the King's daughter told Letitia in that haughty, insufferable manner that seemed to be her ordinary, everyday voice.

Maybe they went to Princess School, Letitia thought. *You couldn't be that obnoxious without a little help.*

"I don't see I'm any farther back than I'm supposed to be," Letitia said. "You're our leader. I can't very well get ahead of you.

"And, while we're at it, do you think you could tell me where we're going? Could I ask why you're helping us at all? I'm sure it's not concern over me. I know better than that."

DeFloraine-Marie laughed, stretching her exquisite neck, tossing her perfect golden locks about in a manner Letitia was sure she'd practiced in a mirror a hundred times.

"Letitia Louise—such a charming name, common among the Mycer folk, I assume? If you imagine I have base designs of any sort on your male, you can put that notion to rest. If I cared, the poor dear would be stunned, paralyzed, struck completely dumb by now.

"I don't want him, I want him *out* of here. Out of this palace, out of Heldessia, out of my sight."

Letitia frowned. "Why? What has Finn done to harm you?"

DeFloraine-Marie dismissed her with a scornful glance. "That's none of your concern. There are things—matters of importance to me. His presence is a nuisance. I want all you out of here, isn't that enough for you?"

"Yes. I suppose it is. As you say, your reasons are none of my concern."

"How thoughtful of you to say so, dear. What you think means so much to me."

And there was that vain, arrogant smile, that cold, unfeeling glance that marred the princess' beauty and turned her perfect features into something ugly and profane.

"You clearly know this enormous structure better than I," Julia said, fixing DeFloraine-Marie with her bright ruby eyes. "However, I know Master Finn, and that overblown magician never brought him this way."

"Tell your disgusting machine to stay away from me," the princess said, backing off a step or so. "If that thing gets near me, I'll step on its dreadful head."

"I wouldn't" Letitia said.

"If she doesn't bite me, I won't bite her," Julia said, flicking her silver tongue. "Please pass that along if you will."

DeFloraine-Marie wrinkled her nose, as if she found something most unpleasant in the air.

"No, Oberbyght didn't bring him this way, your creature's right about that. Even that pompous oaf doesn't know about this passageway.

"When I was a child, my cousins and I found every hollow and hidey-hole in the palace. Some of them I can't even squeeze through now. We peeked on everyone.

Including Oberbyght. If they'd ever caught us, if they'd ever known we were there . . ."

For just an instant, Letitia saw the princess' features soften, the mask of contempt give way to reveal the child that lay hidden somewhere behind the woman that child had become.

"Anyway, you don't care about that. You want to know where dear, dear Finn is, right? The seer took him to his place in the south tower. You can't get near him if you go that way. There are all kinds of horrid spells and magic locks and doors. My way will take us past all that. If I recall—and I'm quite good at recalling whatever I like—we'll end up at a spot where we can get a look inside the tower room."

"Get a look?" Julia twitched her golden tail. "A look won't do us much good, as I see it. What do we have to do, break down a wall?"

DeFloraine-Marie looked past Julia as if she wasn't there. "Do I have to do everything? I'm getting you there. Don't you have a—a weapon or anything?"

"No. I've been bound up for some time. You're not aware of that?"

DeFloraine-Marie rolled her eyes. "Well, you or your monster will have to think of something. I expect you'll have to kill Oberbyght before he'll let Finn go. I'd happily do it myself, but I don't carry weapons of any sort. That's *not* what I do."

Letitia knew this was so. DeFloraine-Marie wasn't wearing enough to hide anything at all. Letitia wondered if she dressed that way all the time. A cloudy wisp of lace, a sparkle of gems here and there didn't seem the right outfit for sneaking about in drafty passageways. The palace was such a dank and dreary place, it was a wonder the princess didn't have a chronic runny nose.

"I would suggest," Julia said, "that we move along quickly in whatever direction you feel would be best."

Her silver snout was rigid, her golden scales aquiver, signs that told Letitia the lizard sensed the need for action of the most immediate kind.

"She means now. She means we don't have time to stand around."

"Oh? And why would that be?" DeFloraine-Marie flicked a mote off her bare and perfect shoulder. She was clearly bored with this venture, ready for something new.

"We are pursued," Julia said. "Badgies, and not too far behind."

"Nonsense. No one knows about these inner corridors but me. I assure you there's nobody here."

"If Julia says they're here—"

"*Julia*—and I cannot believe I am calling a machine by a name—that thing may smell Badgies, I'm certain the halls are full of them now. And yes, we will move on, as I was about to suggest myself."

"Good," Letitia said. "We are in your hands, m'lady. I'm sure you won't lead us astray."

DeFloraine-Marie left Letitia with a withering glance and stomped off ahead.

"She didn't care for that," Julia said.

"Exactly what I had in mind, then. She is truly the most annoying, irritating—"

Letitia stopped, nearly stumbled as a tremor, a quake, a deep and distant rumble shook the narrow walls. Dust rained down from above. A herd of beetles scurried across the floor and disappeared.

"When the bugs go, it's time for me to go too," Julia said. "That's never a very good sign."

"What *was* that?" Letitia braced her hands against the wall. "I think something exploded somewhere."

"Don't stand there," whispered the princess. "Do I have to tell you every time?"

She stared at Letitia, her face the color of ash. Soot smudged her nose, and a spiderweb fluttered in her hair.

Letitia noted with disgust that the soot set off her pale complexion, and the spiderweb looked nice.

"You heard that, I suppose. Is the place falling apart or what?"

The princess didn't answer. She turned quickly and raced down the corridor, past fallen stones, past ancient brick and timbered walls. Shafts of errant candlelight from royal bedrooms, ballrooms, kitchens and halls pierced the holes and cracks in the walls.

Once, Letitia heard peals of laughter. Once, she heard a woman cry.

No wonder the princess is jaded beyond her years, Letitia thought. *As a child, she must have seen* everything *from here.*

"They're coming, Letitia. I don't care what m'lady says, we've got Badgies on our tail."

"I know. Even I can hear that. Wait," Letitia said, hurrying to catch up with DeFloraine-Marie. "They're *there,* and they're not far behind us, all right?"

The princess showed Letitia a gentle, lofty smile. "We don't have to do a thing. We're there."

"What? I don't see a thing, we're where?"

"The peephole's gone, but I'm quite sure. I told you I remember anything I really want to. Obern Oberbyght's chambers are right here. Behind this wall."

Letitia stared. "You think Finn's over there? Behind *this?* What are we supposed to do now? Isn't there any way in?"

"It's a *wall,* Mycer. What did you expect, a door with a nice shiny knob?"

As the princess spoke, another tremor shook the passageway. A fine veil of ancient mortar fell between Letitia and DeFloraine-Marie.

"I hate this, I really do." The princess wiped a dainty hand across her face.

"Whatever's doing that, it's getting louder. I hope

we're not buried in here. Julia, Finn's over there. We've got to get through."

"Excellent idea," Julia said, waddling over splinters, stones and fallen bricks. "That sound, by the way, is from that Millennial Bell, the thing that wakes the royals from their naps. It sounds quite different up here than it does down below, but it's the very same. I'm sure Her Ladyship will be glad to explain."

"There's nothing to tell. Your creature's right, it's a bell."

The princess seemed uneasy. Her lovely lips twitched, and she stared at the ceiling above.

"Look. I got you here, all right? Don't complain to me, that's all I can do. You'll have to think of something yourself."

"You might help. I don't intend to stand here if my Finn's over there."

Brushing dust from her eyes, Letitia turned and picked at the debris. She found a large brick, frowned at it and tossed it away. Finally, she lifted a broken plank, a thick piece of wood nearly two feet long.

"It's not much, but it's better than nothing at all. Please stand back, lady, I don't have a lot of room."

"You're out of your mind. These walls are rotten to the core. You'll bring the whole thing down!"

"Good. That's what I had in mind."

Letitia took a breath and rammed the timber heartily against the wall. Dust rained from the ceiling. Chunks of mortar clattered to the floor.

The princess moaned and rolled her eyes.

"The odds are good she's right," Julia said. "You're likely to bring the place down. Still, our chances are somewhat better if you try. The Badgies I mentioned, the ones that aren't there? They are in this very passageway, as I mentioned before. My guess is they are somewhat less than eight minutes away."

"That's impossible, you little horror. I told you no one knows about this place but me."

"You're certain of that? No one at all."

"My cousins are dead, and there's no one else who could possibly . . . know."

DeFloraine-Marie bit her lip and frowned. "I suppose there might be. I did—meet someone here once. In this passageway, I mean. Not exactly here. . . .

"Oh, dear. I guess I forgot about that."

"And who would that be?" Letitia asked.

"Maddigern. But there's really no concern. He wouldn't hurt *me*. . . ."

FIFTY-THREE

F INN RAN.

Stumbled, fell to his knees on imaginary ground. Got up and ran again. It seemed like a foolish, useless gesture, but the only thing to do.

Where do you go when you run from an illusion, flee from a spell?

"Anywhere," Finn answered himself. "Anywhere's better than nowhere at all."

The spidery hand thundered again, pounding, crushing, grinding time to dust. The great machine clattered, ticked, hummed in the eternal sky. The horizon vanished in a blur. No way out, then, nowhere to go.

Nowhere, Finn told himself, but the worst, most horrid place he could conjure in his mind. The place where he would surely shudder into soup, porridge, mush with an odorous smell.

He ran, then, with all the speed he could muster when one is running nowhere at all, ran, and found the crawly-hole and slid under the rim of the Millennial Bell—

—promptly turned inside out, then outside in. Went to his knees. Retched. Tried to stand, fell down again.

"It's awfully hard coming out of those things. Jerks you around, makes you terribly sick. I see I don't have to tell you that."

Everything was back, everything was real. The seer's cluttered chamber, the sizable sorcerer himself.

Finn stood. Shaky, dizzy and distressed, yet determined to face the magician standing up.

"What's this, then, another sly trick? A sudden show of mercy? Couldn't you stand the thought of doing me in yourself?"

"Oh, please." The seer chuckled and shook his head. "Wherever did you get such a notion as that? If I wanted to *do you in* as you so crudely put it, there are easier ways than working up a spell. Which takes a lot out of you, in case you didn't know. I put you there to keep you out of mischief. I had a great many things to do. . . ."

The seer was interrupted by a rumble, a toll, a deep resonation that shook the chamber's walls.

". . . and not a lot of time, as I suppose you can tell. Though *time,* really, is not the proper word here. An interval, a gap, a spatial degree. At any rate, we don't want to be here when *that* thing hits the mark—my word, what's that?"

Oberbyght paused, frowning at the far wall. One of the immense, overstuffed shelves of papers and scrolls had begun to shudder, tremble and shift, as if it were trying to toss off its burdens and set itself free.

"Secondary shake, I suppose. Never seen it do that before."

"What do you mean, not much time? That bell's going to—strike, whatever it does, am I right? And you don't want to be here. But that thing isn't really here at all."

"Quite right. Good thinking, my boy." Oberbyght nodded in approval, then took it all back. "That's what you fellows who aren't in the business fail to understand. You want your little love spells, and other greedy needs, but you don't want the scary magic stuff to show."

"I'm not sure what you're trying to say. But then I never am."

"Simply that the real and the unreal are one and the same. You think the lining of your jacket is the inside, and the fuzzy part's out. In truth, there isn't any outside or in. There's only a *coat*, you see.

"When a baker makes bread, you say, 'there's a bit of dough,' you don't say 'there's a loaf.' Tomorrow, though, that's what it is, and it's flour and such before that, and before that it's in a field. Truly, it's all the same."

Finn gave the seer a wary look. "A sleeve and a jacket and a button are the dough of the tweed, and when they come together, you have a fine loaf . . ."

"Coat."

"I beg your pardon?"

"That damnable racket. I do believe that shelf is coming apart."

"I wish you wouldn't do that again. It always hurts my head."

"You're not in the trade. I wouldn't expect you to understand. The point is, you can hear the *sound*, can you not? You can feel the tremble and the quake. That's the part that leaks through, a little spot where everything's real and everything's not. Like a rip in your jacket, you see. It's neither inside nor out. . . ."

"Fine. Whatever you like. Now, Oberbyght, if you're finished fooling with spells and coats, I'd like to get out of here. I intend to free Letitia and Julia if I have to stomp every Badgie in the palace into dust. This nasty business of yours has cost me precious time. If those two are harmed in any way . . ."

"Oh, stop." The seer waved Finn away. "Don't threaten me, I'm weary of that. I told you, we don't have time. You can get another Mycer, I'm sure they're not that hard to find. And that horrid little machine—"

"What are you talking about?" Finn glared at the seer. "I'm not leaving them behind, you're out of your mind!"

"I don't think you have a lot of choice. The bell is

merely a distraction, you know. It'll set them running amok down there, but the Badgies will pull themselves together and be on our trail quite soon."

Oberbyght spread his hands wide, in surrender to the Fates. "I say *we*, my friend, for we're in this together, as it were. I cannot turn my back on Maddigern again. That's clear from the incident in the cell down there."

"I don't blame you for that. Maddigern and I were coming to this anyway. I could turn him into a wad of spit, but another of those louts would simply take his place. No, it's time for me to go, there's no doubt of that."

He winked at Finn, turned and walked quickly across the room. From behind a muddle of glasses, jugs and jars, he drew a small purple satchel, a worn and battered thing covered with mystic runes.

"Not taking much. But one must have the essentials of his trade."

"I think you're bonkers, Oberbyght, but that's no concern of mine. I'm going back for Letitia and Julia now. If you want to turn me into something, you'd best do it now."

"I do wish you hadn't said that, my boy, you don't leave me any choice—"

The case against the wall gave a shriek, gave a screech, gave an agonizing groan, then split all asunder, flinging papers, books, powdery pamphlets, ancient odes, unanswered letters, false accusations, debts, bets and dreadful poems about. Forgery, perjury, inflammatory notes, and lurid tales from ancient times.

And, out of this fluttering storm came Letitia Louise, DeFloraine-Marie, hefting a sturdy plank in her hand, and a lizard with dusty scales.

"Finn, *Finn!*" Letitia cried, and ran into her lover's arms.

"Letitia, I can't tell you how worried I've been, how much I've missed you, dear. You cannot imagine the fearsome, yet wondrous places I've been!"

"I can't wait to hear it," said Julia Jessica Slagg, nosing her way through papery debris. "First, however, I think you should know there's a horde of Badgies on our heels. We've about two minutes, maybe less than that."

"Maddigern!" Oberbyght clutched his satchel to his chest. "We're off, then, not a moment to lose."

"Off where?" Finn wanted to know. "I fear I don't see anywhere to go."

"Of course you don't. How would you know? Up there. Up that ladder. As quickly as you can."

Letitia reached down and plucked up Julia Jessica Slagg. "You know you're no good with ladders. You're not even very adept with stairs."

"I can't do everything," Julia said with a rusty croak, "though I know I'm expected to perform any sort of miracle when trouble comes along."

While Letitia was busy with Julia, DeFloraine-Marie slipped past her like wraith and pressed her slender form against Finn.

"Here, take this," she said, slipping something into his pocket, then whispering quickly in his ear.

She was there and she was gone, leaving Finn with the clean scent of her hair, the heat of her touch. "Wait," he said, "what's this all about?"

Letitia turned at his voice. The princess gave her a nearly pleasant smile.

"Wherever you're going, have a nice trip. Try not to drop in again."

She glanced over her shoulder. "I'm not an ugly little machine, but I can hear a great many Badgies down there. I think you should—*stop that, get away from me!*"

The seer moved so swiftly Finn scarcely saw more than a blur. He clutched the princess' wrist in one strong hand and dragged her roughly across the room. DeFloraine-Marie kicked and screamed to no avail.

"Here now," Finn demanded to know. "Leave her alone, what do you want with her?"

"Stay out of this, Master Finn. Tangle with me again, and I'll turn that pretty Mycer into a stone, and you can toss her at Maddigern when he comes!"

"They're coming," Julia said, "*now*."

Obern Oberbyght was halfway up the ladder at the rear of his chamber, the princess tightly in his grasp. She kicked her bare legs, and railed at the seer with curses Finn had never heard before.

"I don't see that it'll do much good to stay here," Finn said. "Please hurry, dear . . ."

Letitia didn't answer. At that very moment, Badgies spilled in through the narrow passageway, led by Maddigern himself, swinging his sword about and raging at Finn . . .

Chapter

FIFTY-FOUR

INN'S MOUTH WAS DRY AS DIRT. FOR AN INSTANT, he was too stunned to move. In less than a blink, the seer's small chamber swarmed with angry Badgies—a throng, a mob, a veritable pack of the silver-mailed creatures, cursing, howling, shouting for blood.

"Blades and Spades, it's the King's Third Sentient Guards, and every bloody one of the brutes, unless I miss my guess!"

Finn scrambled up the ladder, urging Letitia ahead, grabbing at her legs, pushing her shapely behind. Letitia told him she didn't care for this, but Finn didn't hear.

He could feel the ladder shake, and didn't dare look back to see. One step, another, two at a time when Letitia took three.

Something seized his ankle and held. Finn lashed out, felt the grip give way, heard the Guardsman fall back.

The ladder creaked, groaned. Finn pushed frantically at Letitia, nearly lifted her off the ladder and hurled her through the narrow hole above. The ladder snapped with the weight of Badgies, flinging them down in a tangle below.

Finn desperately grabbed for the rim of the hole. Letitia's strong hands clutched his wrists and held on. Finn drew up his knees, tore one hand free, got a firm grip on the tower floor and rolled himself clear.

Angry shouts rose from below. Badgies tossed bricks, stones, jugs, and ponderous tomes at the hole, while others piled chairs, cabinets, tables, anything they could find, in an effort to reach their prey above.

"That should slow them down a bit," Oberbyght said, grinning over Finn's shoulder at the rabble below. "Fools ought to think before they leap, but that's not the Badgie way."

"Let me go, you oaf," cried DeFloraine-Marie. "Get your filthy hands off me, I'm of noble birth!"

"I fear not, lady. I've become enamored with your manner, your gentle voice, your royal charm." The princess glared, her eyes bright points of fury, her golden tresses tumbling loosely down her cheeks.

Oberbyght still held her wrists in one hand, the other tightly around her slender waist. No matter how the princess squirmed, the seer refused to let her go.

"You're going to keep her?" Finn asked. "What do you intend to do with her, seer?"

"I intend to use her lovely self to keep us alive," Oberbyght said. "I can't tell you how pleased I am she dropped by."

Finn looked at the fellow, and Oberbyght met his glance, in a manner that said he was certain Finn knew full well the value of DeFloraine-Marie.

Finn turned away, then, and looked about. It was late afternoon, which surprised him a bit, for he'd lost all sense of time since his stay in the cell. That, and a venture within an illusion, where time meant nothing at all.

The open tower was surrounded by a shoulder-high wall, with the usual crenellations so soldiers could fire at their foes below.

Finn peered down from the dizzy heights. Beyond the courtyard, the bailey and the breastworks lay Heldessia Town and the vast open countryside beyond.

The walls of the tower dropped straight away, with no visible access to the ground.

"I hate to ask," Finn said, "but I hope you have a grand plan. I don't see any way off this thing."

The seer smiled. "There isn't. That's the beauty of it, you see?"

"This isn't more of that jacket and bread business, is it? I can't handle that."

"They're working awfully fast," Letitia said. "They're halfway up the wall."

"Oberbyght, isn't there a cover, a plank, something we can put over this hole?"

The seer shrugged. "I used to put a pail under the thing when it rained. Never thought about keeping Badgies out."

"You haven't answered Finn's question," Letitia said, her dark opal eyes larger than ever. "I'd like to hear what you have in mind too."

At that very moment, the deep, solemn peal of the bell resounded from somewhere, or nowhere at all. The tower shook precariously, and several large stones plummeted down the long wall.

Below, in the seer's former chamber, chaos was the order of the day. Badgies howled, and raged in fear. Bricks, plaster, and rotten timbers rattled about their heads.

Finn wondered how Maddigern had managed to bully his Guardsmen this far. The King's Third Sentient Guards were stout and valiant warriors, but they greatly feared the magician and his spells. Only a creature as fierce as Maddigern, Finn decided, could have held them under his sway.

"Finn," Letitia said, close so no one would hear, "we've found each other again and I'm grateful for that, but I fear we've followed a madman to the same dire end we faced below."

"We'll think of something," Finn said, aware that such bravado did not fool Letitia Louise. Still, he refused to admit they were doomed, for that would not bolster her courage at all.

"Yes, I'm certain we will," Letitia said, looping her arm tightly in his. "Though at the moment, I cannot see how."

"It is a peculiarity of Newlies and humankind," said Julia, who had mostly kept her silence during the recent dread events, "one I can somewhat understand, since I, too, possess an animal brain. When the situation is totally hopeless, as it clearly is now, reason says 'quit, give up, yield, resign one's self to one's fate.'

"Yet, does that foolish gray organ in our heads desist, surrender, throw in the trowel—whatever that means— does it submit, capitulate, bend? Does it—"

"Stop that thing from squawking, or by damn I'll toss it over the side!"

Oberbyght, the princess flailing about in his iron grip, was kicking at a Badgie who had suddenly appeared at the entry hole. The seer stomped on his hand and the Badgie cried out and let go.

"I don't suppose you could give me a hand over here, Finn. As you can possibly see, I *don't* have one free."

"Sorry, be right with you." Finn left Letitia and joined the seer, whose chubby features had now turned a startling shade of red. As another green-robed warrior scrambled for a hold, Finn kicked him squarely in the face, where the white streak of hair angled sharply at his brow. The soldier howled, and tumbled back below.

Still, it was only a matter of minutes before another, then another, surged up through the hole.

"I don't see how we can keep this up," Finn said. "I think Maddigern has an endless supply of these brutes."

"Won't have to," said the seer. "We can stop this nonsense soon."

"Wait, now," Finn protested, "I never said I'd quit. I certainly don't intend to give in."

"Didn't say you would. Said you wouldn't *have* to."

Oberbyght glanced over his shoulder with a grin.

"You think I'm an idiot, boy? That I climbed up here for the view?"

Finn turned, then, just as Letitia Louise cried out, leaping for joy, and waving at the sky.

"Hooks and Crooks!" Finn could scarcely believe his eyes, but it was clearly no illusion floating majestically overhead, blotting out the afternoon sky.

"Bucerius!" Finn shouted, cupping his hands about his face. "I never saw a sight more pleasing to the eye!"

"I told you one has to do business with all sorts of rogues in my trade," said the seer. "You've got to learn to listen to your betters, Master Finn. . . ."

F INN AND LETITIA DASHED ABOUT THE TOP OF the tower, chasing the tangle of ropes that dangled from the bloated craft overhead. The ropes snapped and whipped in the wind, close at hand one instant, hanging over nothing the next.

Bucerius cursed and shouted, bringing the worst of seven languages to bear, as he struggled to keep the balloon from drifting away or plummeting down to crush the creatures scurrying about below.

Obern Oberbyght did all he could, kicking angry Badgies down the hole, keeping the screaming princess intact.

The balloon dipped low, the wicker basket knocking loose stones off the wall. Letitia leaped, caught a rope and held on. Finn heard her triumphant shout, then heard it turn to a fearsome wail, as the rope yanked her off the tower and over the abyss.

Finn's heart nearly stopped. Letitia swung back, past the tower wall, just out of Finn's reach. He could see her hands slipping, quickly losing their grip. Her Mycer eyes mirrored her fear for she was clearly terrified.

Finn didn't dare stop to think. He scrambled up the wall, jumped, caught the rope just above Letitia's grip, scissored his legs about her and swung back from the dizzying heights below.

The balloon sagged beneath their weight and began to tip dangerously to one side. Bucerius bellowed, and yanked frantically on his cords. The swollen craft surged up again, and this time the Bullie's skill dropped the pair safely on the tower floor again.

Finn struggled with the rope and tied it securely through a hole in the stony wall. Bucerius tossed down two more lines, and, in a moment, the craft was riding balanced and secure, straining against the wind.

Finn lifted Letitia up, and the Bullie pulled her aboard. Finn handed Julia up next, then went to help the seer.

DeFloraine-Marie knew exactly what was coming. She screamed like a banshee, and managed to sink her teeth into Oberbyght's arm. She kicked out with her legs and struck Finn in the head.

"Enough of that, Princess, I'm losing my patience with you." Oberbyght slung her over his shoulder, stomped over to the balloon, gripped her like a sack of meal, and tossed her to Bucerius waiting there.

The Bullie caught her and dumped her to the wicker floor. In her sheltered life, DeFloraine-Marie had had little to do with Bullies. Bullies were merely Newlies who carried heavy things about. At the sight of this great, powerful creature she backed away into a corner of the basket and loosed a pitiful wail.

"Go on, get aboard," Finn shouted at the seer. "I'll finish up here."

Oberbyght paused, then nodded, and made his way up to the balloon. Bucerius flipped a short-bladed knife to Finn, and Finn began to slice the restraining ropes, one by one.

Left unchecked, the Badgies swarmed like angry hornets onto the tower floor, a blur of broad shoulders, stumpy legs and bristling jaws, silver mail and flashing blades.

With a fierce battle cry, Maddigern swept his Guardsmen aside and came at Finn, his sword cutting deadly arcs at Finn's heels, forcing him back against the tower wall.

Letitia shouted a warning, but Finn didn't hear. He knew he was but a breath away from losing it all, that everything he'd been through, everything he'd dared, could come to naught if the Badgie caught him here with nothing but the Bullie's short blade.

If he turned, and made a leap for the balloon, Maddigern would surely plunge his weapon into his back. If he stood his ground another moment, though, he could slice the final rope and let the others go.

"Don't, Finn, you cannot!" Letitia knew full well the path he would choose, knew what he had to do.

Finn didn't hesitate. He sawed frantically at the rope, slicing one layer then the next. The rope creaked and strained as each strand sprang free.

Maddigern's dark eyes glowed, for he saw his triumph near. With a growl of victory he raised his blade shoulder high and slammed one boot against the ground.

"Go on, have at it," Oberbyght shouted. "I care nothing for the wretched fellow, and you clearly have no concern for this baggage here. . . ."

Maddigern stopped, his stout frame suddenly rigid, as he stared at the hovering balloon. The seer stood at the basket's edge, his hands grasping the princess' ankles as she swung precariously over nothing but a great deal of air. She shrieked and flailed about. The most frightening moment in her life before this was when a bee stung her toe when she was twelve.

Maddigern didn't move. He glared at the seer with rage uncontained, no longer mindful that Finn was there.

Oberbyght smiled. "What does it take to get your attention, Badgie? I've got an idea, see what you think of this?"

With that, the sorcerer let go of one of the princess' an-

kles, holding her weight with a single hand. DeFloraine-
Marie cried out, a most frightening sound that was heard
by many citizens far below.

Maddigern stared, his blade still poised above his
head. Finn could see a tremor, a shudder, as the fury of indecision swept the Badgie's stout frame. For a moment
that seemed to last forever, he stood his ground, as rigid as
the cold, fossilized rulers in the Holy Place of Emperors,
Tyrants and Kings.

Then, he took a step back, lowered his blade, and
turned away from the princess, gazing at nothing at all.

Finn didn't hesitate an instant. He grabbed the nearly
severed rope and swung from the tower wall. The cord
snapped beneath his grip and the balloon jerked free,
moving swiftly in the strong evening breeze.

Bucerius hauled him in and dumped him roughly on
the wicker basket's floor.

"Finn, I wish you wouldn't do things like that," Letitia
said, as a single tear trickled down her cheek. "I will be severely upset if you ever leap off over nothing again."

"I think I can promise I will avoid such antics, my
dear."

"Where have I heard *that* before," said Julia Jessica
Slagg. . . .

INN MARVELED AT HOW SWIFTLY THE GREAT palace of Heldessia's King shrank to a speck he could hide behind his thumb. He had forgotten the perversity of balloons, which will hang without moving, and refuse to go anywhere at all, then rush through the clouds with a speed impossible for any conveyance on the ground.

Before they had drifted too far, he had seen Maddigern and his Badgies crowded on the top of the tower, watching in silence as their prey moved farther and farther away.

Finn was still watching when the great bell pealed again, its solemn tones resounding through the 'rip in the cosmic trousers,' as the seer liked to say, from the world of illusions to the deepening afternoon where the Bullie's balloon rushed away toward the west.

Either that, Finn said to himself, *or this is the illusion, and the real world's somewhere past the bell.*

And, indeed, if that were so, who could ever tell?

"If you've nothing to do," Bucerius said, "you can get your head back where it belongs and be helpin' me with them lines. You didn't learn much on the way in here, but you might be better'n some."

Finn felt a small, but honest moment of pride at the Bullie's words, for he knew this was as close as the fellow would come to granting him some station as the crewman of a balloon.

"This is really a difficult craft to master," he told Letitia Louise. "It takes enormous skill to learn the order of cords, the drift, the height, the strength of the winds, the correct amount of ballast to loose to gain the proper altitude.

"When I can find time from my work, I would like to learn more about the fascinating world of vessels of the air."

"That's wonderful, dear," Letitia said, with a sweet and haughty smile she'd learned from DeFloraine-Marie. "When you do, just give me time to pack my bags, for I'll not be living with a man who's hanging from a bag of gas, worrying me sick, instead of minding his business on the ground."

Nothing more was said on the subject after that.

PRINCESS DEFLORAINE-MARIE KEPT VERY MUCH TO herself after the craft was under way. Letitia tried to speak to her once, for she wished to thank her for doing her part in breaking through to Oberbyght's lair.

Letitia had been quite surprised to find that within that slim, near-perfect frame there was strength enough to crack stone and plaster and help bring down the ancient wall.

Still, the princess clearly didn't wish for company at all. She stayed by herself and looked wistfully back at the quickly receding hills of Heldessia Land.

"You're free to leap anytime you wish," the seer told her. "I'd not interfere with your efforts now."

Finn watched her from the far side of the basket, which was not that far away in the Bullie's craft. Bucerius had given her a blanket against the cooling afternoon, but the wrap did little to hide her lithe and graceful form.

Finn had had no chance to tell Letitia what he'd seen in the chamber of the Deeply Entombed, or, indeed, the other startling sight he'd witnessed there, though Letitia could guess some of the story herself.

Maddigern, and the daughter of the King. There was no doubt of the intimacy between them. No doubt of the look in the Badgie's eyes when he stepped back and let them all go to save the princess' life.

This enchanting, willful beauty, and the fierce, bloody-minded Badgie—a human and a Newlie who had some-how found one another despite the differences that lay between them.

Much like another odd pairing I could name. One Finn of Fyxedia, and a Mycer named Letitia Louise. . . .

Though he could not see how one of these couplings could possibly relate to the other, he could not deny that the other was there. And there were more such unions in the world this day—some, he imagined, stranger than he knew. . . .

C OME LOOK AT THIS, BOTH OF YOU," BUCERIUS said, cupping his enormous hands above his brow. "I been expectin' it, hoping it wouldn't be."

At first Finn could see nothing against the glare of the eastern sky. Then, they were there, three small brightly colored spheres, very close together, somewhat higher than Bucerius' balloon.

"They've caught a good current up there," the Bullie said, clenching his fists around a heavy rope line. "Just fool luck is what it is. Isn't a balloonist anywheres who'd know it be there."

"Anything we can do?"

The Bullie frowned at Finn. "Can't get up there, if that's what you mean. Not without tossin' all of you out, which isn't too bad an idea. I can't dump ballast, neither. Isn't enough to do much good."

"So we wait," the seer said.

"They got a wind beats the Westerlies a mile. Might be we'll get us one too."

Bucerius made no effort to pretend he thought such a miracle would happen anytime soon. . . .

W E'LL MAKE IT," FINN ASSURED LETITIA. "WE'VE come this far. Nothing can stop us now."

He was well aware how absurd such words must sound, but Letitia was kind enough to say nothing at all. Even Julia Jessica Slagg kept her silence. In respect, Finn thought, of the tragedy that was about to befall.

"Bucerius says we've passed just south of the battleground, which means we're halfway, on the other side of the Swamp of Bleak Demise. Our side, and that's good. We've a way to go, of course. . . ."

Finn paused, for the sun had disappeared behind low purple clouds, and the breeze had picked up considerably, bringing the three balloons closer still. Now, the Heldessian coat of arms was quite clear on the flanks of the racing spheres.

"If the velocity of the wind remains the same at our level and theirs," Julia said, "they will approach us less than a hundred and seven feet above us on a south-southwesterly course. In about nine minutes, I believe."

"Shut up," Finn told her. "I'm sure our captain doesn't need any navigational help from you."

"No, I don't," Bucerius said, looking somewhat appalled. "I don't, but that ugly's near right."

"I shall say no more," Julia said.

"Good. That's a splendid idea."

"Finn," the seer shouted, "over here!"

Finn moved quickly to Oberbyght's side.

"See that? In the first balloon? I'm certain that's Maddigern himself. Right below the guiding cords."

"I don't see how you can tell."

"Trust me. That's him, for sure. I'd know that brute anywhere. . . ."

A flash of bright light, then a thunderous roar reached Finn's ears. Something like an angry hornet whined by overhead.

"Damn 'em all," Bucerius said, gripping the basket's side. "It's muskets they be using. They mean to bring us down."

Another flash, and another after that. The first shot missed, but the second tore at the craft's tangle of cords. Finn could see now that Maddigern was the sole musketeer. One of his Guardsmen would hand him a loaded weapon, and take the empty back.

Another shot ripped away a section of the webbing that held the bloated sphere intact. The balloon dipped, swayed drunkenly, and righted itself again.

"He's a better than fair shooter," Finn said. "Next time he'll hit the bag itself!"

"No, he won't be doin' that." Bucerius looked grim. "He's not trying to kill us, he's trying to take us down."

Finn showed his surprise, for he failed to understand.

"He hits the bag, we'll go up in a ball of fire," Bucerius explained. "If he cuts enough of them lines—which is what he's doin' now—he knows I'll have to set her down 'fore we lose control."

The Bullie paused. "He wants his princess back, don't you see? With us stuck down in that killin' swamp, it's him that'll have the winning hand, not us.

"He can land enough louts to finish us off, 'less we give her back."

"He will, too," said DeFloraine-Marie, tossing them all a haughty glance. "You'd best do what he says, Bullie. He'll show you no mercy if you don't let me go."

Her words were nearly lost as Maddigern fired again. The wicker basket sagged dangerously, as cords parted with a whine overhead.

"That damn near does it," Bucerius cursed. "Another shot an' I got to put her down."

"And submit to him? A stinking Badgie?" The seer's face darkened with rage. "I'll give him something to ponder, he thinks he can stand up to me!"

The sorcerer raised his hands high above his head and shouted at the wind, trembled and shook, swelled up like the great bloated sphere above. From his mouth spewed a gabble, a blabber, a meaningless jabber that made Finn's hair stand on end.

Then, to Finn's horror, the balloon next to Maddigern's blossomed into a white ball of fire, a small and blinding sun. Finn heard the horrid shrieks of pain from the craft as it disappeared from sight.

"No, don't," Finn shouted. "Leave them be. We don't have to do that!"

The words were scarcely out of his mouth before the second sphere seared Finn's eyes and vanished in a wink.

He's playing with him, taunting him, saving him till the last. . . .

Oberbyght raised his hands high once more, and Finn could see Maddigern clearly, his features betraying no expression at all.

Finn gripped his hands tightly together, and brought them down soundly at the base of Oberbyght's skull. The sorcerer collapsed without a sound and fell limply to the basket's floor.

Finn glanced at the Badgie once more. Maddigern knew what had happened, but he didn't move an inch.

"Get a line 'cross her shoulders," Finn called out. "Let her down, quickly, and let that maniac see!"

Bucerius nodded. DeFloraine-Marie's eyes widened, but she didn't protest.

"We're driftin', losing it fast," the Bullie said. "I can't hold her up long."

"We don't have to. He knows that."

The princess didn't say a word as she tossed the Bullie's blanket aside and lifted her legs over the rim of the basket. She caught Finn watching and grinned. Then the Bullie lowered her slowly away, down to the dark, tangled mass of green below.

Maddigern held off to the right, watching the princess descend. Finally, she touched the ground lightly in a small clearing, loosed the line and waved, then stood there and waited, huddled against the chill.

"We can make a couple of miles," Bucerius said. "Can't promise much after that."

"You'll do what you can," Finn said. He glanced at Letitia, then turned and looked back.

"He's going down to get her. He's not concerned with us."

"Fine. *I'm* concerned with us," the Bullie said, "for there's many a craft what's gone down in the Swamp of Bleak Demise, but I never heard of one comin' out again. . . ."

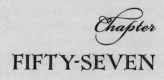

Chapter

FIFTY-SEVEN

I'LL GET YOU FOR THIS, FINN, BY DAMN, I PROMISE you that," said the seer. "My head's about to split, and I expect there's extensive damage that's yet to unfold."

"I expect you'd best save your strength," Finn said. "We've a long way to go and it's coming on night."

"A long *way*?" Bucerius gave a weary laugh. "There isn't no end to this swamp, not for more miles than you can count. And I doubt we'll last the night. Not with all the monstrous things that be roaming wild in this place."

"What kind of things would that be?"

"I just said. Monstrous things."

"I haven't seen any yet."

"You won't, neither. Not till you're inside one of their gullets lookin' out."

THE SWAMP, INDEED, WAS A STRANGE AND ALIEN place, with its enormous trees, stale black water, and great fleshy plants. Vines as thick as a man coiled around every tree in a vicious stranglehold. Yet, except for annoying swarms of bugs, no monsters had shown up in the night. And, as a new day appeared through the thicket overhead, everyone save the seer seemed no worse for wear.

"You should never have let that savage go," Oberbyght

complained, as he hunched before the small fire, eating a peculiar spotted fruit Letitia had found.

"You don't know their kind, or you'd have let me finish him off. What you have to do, boy, is get them before they get you."

"I have no love for Maddigern," Finn said, "but I don't think returning savagery with worse than savage acts makes us better than them."

The seer made a noise in his throat and waved Finn's words away.

"It's a wonder you've stayed alive with fool thoughts like that. You don't know what that cunning fellow did to me. I made a good, honest living before Maddigern came along. My great-great-grandfather came up with the bit about the Deeply Entombed, and handed the business down. It's been smooth sailing ever since.

"By damn, there was a first-class seer. I'm good, mind you, but no one was ever as great as old Unterbyght himself. No one can conjure up something like that bell anymore. Not today, they can't. 'Course *he* could figure when the fool thing'd go off. I confess, I never got the hang of that."

"Blocks and Socks," Finn said. "I'd be shamed to admit I had a hand in anything as cruel and vile!"

"What?" Oberbyght winced, as a fresh pain shot through his head. "My family performed a *service*, boy. Everyone has to believe in something, you know. And the royals love it. Always have."

"But it's not something *real*," Letitia said. "It's just something made up."

"Well, yes, but they don't know that. There's the thing about your first-rate religion, young lady. If you know what it's about, it's no good at all.

"I would have been fine, if I hadn't brought Maddigern in. I didn't exactly *bring* him in, you understand. He stumbled on the thing and I had to go for thirty percent. Offerings aren't what they used to be, I'll tell you that. This King's a miser, is what he is."

"And DeFloraine-Marie," Finn said.

The seer's mouth curled in disgust. "It was always an uneasy thing between Maddigern and me. But it wasn't too bad until she came along. That's why I had to get out.

"I know Maddigern killed Dostagio, of course, not you. I expect the poor fellow caught the Badgie with the lady somewhere. Dostagio was a loyal servant. Would have gone straight to the King."

Finn shook his head in disbelief. "And I thought Llowenkeef-Grymm was a fool for believing all that nonsense about eternal naps. I suppose he was, but they were all duped by you and your scheming kin."

"Someone's got to do it," Oberbyght said, looking hurt, looking pained, at Finn's remarks. "I don't see why it shouldn't be me. . . ."

LATE IN THE AFTERNOON, WILTED BY THE DEADLY heat eternally trapped within the great swamp, Finn stopped his party by a small patch of dry land, under the thick bole of an ancient tree. Insects whined about his head, and a very ugly fish turned lazily in the dark and fetid stream.

Across the water, deep within the shadow of a strangled grove of trees, a veil, a milky haze, rose above the dank and odorous ground.

Finn stood and watched a moment, for he was ever fascinated by the constant, smoky mist that hugged the earth in this primeval place. The world might have been this way in ancient times, or so some scholars said. There might well have been monsters here, as well, far more vicious than the ones in Bucerius' head . . .

Then, as if a cloudy mask had slipped away, he saw this misty world for what it was, a host of wispy phantoms, the specters, grisly ghosts, huddled silently across the way. Coldies, the lifeless, the husks, the lonely dead. Hundreds of them, thousands, likely more than that, simply watching from the dark.

Here, then, was the host of sorrowful wraiths, the forgotten armies of the present and the past, who had roamed the Swamp of Bleak Demise for seven hundred years.

Did they remember, he wondered, did they recall the horrors that had brought them here? Sadly, he was certain that they did, for he had learned from others of their kind that death seemed to bring small comfort from the worrisome sphere of life. . . .

Chapter FIFTY-EIGHT

I MUST SAY, MASTER FINN, I HAVE GREATLY EN-
joyed the tale of your ventures, though some of it, I feel, you
might well have left out. The parts, I mean, where people
simply talk to one another, or have some passing thought.

"Still, all in all, I commend you for your efforts.
You have carried out my command, at some little risk
to yourself, if your story is partially correct, and I must
assume it is, for it's most unseemly to lie to your Prince."

"I would not dream of doing so, Your Grace," Finn
said, bowing extra low so Aghen Aghenfleck could not
discern the expression on his face.

*Partially correct indeed! It's hardly even that, for I'm not
fool enough to reveal all to you!*

"Whatever, then," said the Prince, rolling his eyes at
the court assembled before him, "you will certainly re-
ceive a substantial reward, as promised. We shall see to
that in time.

"I hope you will recall, of course, that it was a troop of
the King's Dragoons who found your party floundering
on the edge of that dreaded swamp. *Their* efforts have to
be considered, too.

"At any rate," the Prince continued, leaning closer to
Finn, without leaving the comfort of his throne, "this ring
you have brought me from the Princess of Heldessia, this
is most helpful to me. Most helpful, indeed."

Aghen Aghenfleck paused, and a cunning smile crossed his rather unappealing features.

"There was more to your mission than was revealed to you at the time, Master Finn. I am not a simpleton, you know. I did not send you to that ghastly lair of Llowenkeef-Grymm's merely to deliver a clock. There was more at stake than that.

"I share this with you because I wish the court to hear this tale as well. I must tell you now—all of you assembled here—that there is a traitor among you. A person who is in this very chamber now."

The crowd gasped as one, and each man and woman turned to the person nearby, then backed a step away.

Finn felt suddenly numb. What was all this, now, what was this cunning fellow about? He wanted nothing more than to absent himself from this foul business as fast as he could.

"This ring tells me the traitor's name, for there are a number of rings I might have received. Each would name a man, and the ring that was sent to me would tell his name.

"I have an agent in Heldessia, you see. I will not give you that name, but it was he who gave this ring to the princess, and told her to get it to me."

The princess, DeFloraine-Marie? Finn could scarcely believe his ears.

"There is a plot, you see, a scheme that has long been in place, which I now unmask for you. The purpose of this scheme is to stop the war between Fyxedia and Heldessia, and plunge us into a disastrous peace that would ruin the economy of both our nations, undo all we've fought for, and spread chaos throughout our lands.

"People would then want to mix with those they do not know, see places different from what they've seen. Want things they do not have and don't need. Peace would be a disaster such as we've never seen before.

"Our enemies, those who plot against me, would use that peace to gain our throne, and do away with us all."

Another gasp, another murmur, swept through the crowd. Aghen Aghenfleck raised his jeweled hands to bring them to silence again.

"King Llowenkeef-Grymm is a useless old fool. He knows nothing about this business, so as usual, everything falls upon me. That's the burden of a prince, and I envy those of you who lead simple, ordinary lives, without the grave responsibilities I must bear for you every day."

The Prince sat back, weary, exhausted from the strain of all this.

"One more thing, of course. The traitor's name. It is my dear, dear brother, Lord Gherick, my own flesh and blood who would bring us to ruin."

"No!" Gherick's face went white. "I am no traitor, brother, I am ever your loyal servant, sire!"

Finn felt a chill creep up his spine, for Lord Gherick was a friend. And, shamed as he was to think of himself at such a moment, the Prince knew that as well.

The crowd moaned, moving restlessly about. Finn knew there was not a one among them now who would admit they'd even spoken to the Prince's brother at any time.

Aghen Aghenfleck folded his hands across his chest, making little effort to hide his pleasure, as his distraught and shaken brother was led away. He turned, then, and for a moment, gave Finn a puzzled, most bewildered look.

"Is there something more you wanted, Finn? Some reason you are still here? Count VanDork, would you kindly see this fellow out? I've much to do, even if this craftsman has the time to stand about. . . ."

FIFTY-NINE

I
T'S ALL A TERRIBLE MUDDLE," FINN SAID. "STICKS
and Bricks, Letitia, I know Gherick despised the Prince,
but I cannot believe he'd go so far as to betray his own
brother. Damn me, are they all daft? Clearly, forces on
both sides have kept the war going for seven hundred
years—so everyone can make money, everyone can have a
job!"

"And so many can die," Letitia sighed. "It's a terrible
kind of trade where you come home from work without a
limb, or you don't come home at all."

Finn held her close, feeling the warmth, the sweetness
of her downy flesh against his own. In the dark, her enormous Mycer eyes mirrored the buttery light of the moon
that fell across their bed.

"It is a great sorrow, Letitia, that we are led down such
a hurtful path by men such as Aghen Aghenfleck. Even
King Llowenkeef-Grymm, though I thought him a
pompous fool, had more kindness in him than the Prince.

"Someone in the palace was the Prince's agent, but I'm
perplexed as to who it might be. Certainly it wasn't
Maddigern, and I'm nearly sure it couldn't be the seer. It
had to be someone we didn't know. Some royal or noble,
perhaps. Someone who fooled the Princess DeFloraine-
Marie into passing that ring to me."

"By the way, I must remind you that it took a very long

while for you to tell me about this ring. Not the sort of thing I wished to hear in a swamp while those awful bugs were biting me to death."

"Quite frankly, I thought nothing more of the object she'd given me—or why—until we had a moment to catch our breath. Damn it all, Letitia! I'd have tossed the thing away if I'd known the dire message it contained—that my action would condemn poor Gherick!"

"You couldn't have known, my dear. Only men of a vile and treacherous nature weave such webs of sorrow and deceit."

Finn reached out to bring her closer to him.

They whispered together for a while, then her steady breathing told him she slept. He lay there with her, grateful they were together, and praying that nothing would part them again.

He dozed for a time, then woke with a start, a most unpleasant dream of Badgies bringing him out of sleep.

Taking a care not to wake Letitia, he slipped out of bed and into his trousers, pulling on a heavy shirt against the cool of the night and feeling about for his boots.

What would happen now in Heldessia? he wondered. It would surely be a most traumatic moment when the King and his family learned it was not entirely true that napping was the same as being dead.

Maybe it would simply all go on without the seer about. Maybe the Millennial Bell would peal now and then, and the Gracious Dead would go about their duties as they'd always done before.

As he made his way carefully down the stairs, he remembered he'd forgotten to tell Letitia that Obern Oberbyght had been appointed the new Grand Sorcerer of Aghen Aghenfleck's court, for there had been a vacancy in that position since the Prince had executed the last poor magician on the Chopping of May.

Not a pleasant choice, as far as Finn was concerned.

Still, since he omitted his own shortcomings in his tale to the prince, it seemed only fair—and prudent as well—to skim over other folks' misdeeds.

When he thought of misdeeds, rogues and traders and thieves, he couldn't help but grin, and wish good Bucerius luck, wherever his ventures might take him now. He was surely a fellow who was there in time of need, and more than worthy to be named a friend. . . .

"Going out, are you? I suggest you wear a cloak, Finn. It's chipper out there tonight."

Finn caught Julia's ruby eyes blinking in the dark. She sat at the foot of the stairs, no doubt pretending she could sleep.

"I'm walking out front for a moment, if that's all right with you."

"Why ask for my feelings on this, or any other matter? I am only a machine, a mechanical device, an artifice, a thing, a creature of cogs and gears and wheels . . ."

"To say nothing of a creature who talks a great deal. Be sure and mention that."

"Be sure and remember that I did not acquire this power of speech myself. I had some help in that."

"I recall that indeed," Finn said. "It's a thought that often haunts me in the night. . . ."

Chapter

SIXTY

GARPENNY STREET WAS DARK, NOT A LIGHT IN a window anywhere in sight. The rest of the town seemed quiet as well. Except for the taverns by the waterfront, and the revelry at the palace itself, the good folk of Ulster-East put themselves to bed early nearly every night.

"And why can't I find any peace?" Finn asked himself aloud. "It's not that I don't desire the rest, and it's surely not that I don't have a warm and loving companion waiting for me beneath the covers there. Yet, here I am, walking the street like a poor homeless fool, with nowhere else to go . . ."

"Up and about, I see, Master Finn. You're just as restless a fellow as I recall."

Finn started, then checked himself, for it was only a Coldie who faced him there in the dark. He truly did need a good long rest, if he was jumping at the sight of the dead. Letitia would get a laugh out of that when he—

"Kettles and Pots," he said, the hairs standing up on the back of his neck. "Koodigern! I swear I never expected to see you again!"

The phantom was little more than a wisp, a grim reminder of his mortal Badgie self, though not as ghastly as many Finn had seen.

"I expect you're surprised, though I didn't mean to startle you, sir. I arrived here by balloon but a few nights past. It's an easy way to travel, you know. We don't take up any space, and weigh next to nothing at all."

Koodigern seemed to enjoy his jest, and he laughed in that harsh, rattlesome manner that passes for a chuckle among the dead.

"I felt I should speak to you, Finn, for even those bereft of life look to whatever comfort we can get, when there's much that's left unsaid."

"I can understand that. I expect there's much I'll regret when I pass from this side to the next."

"And terribly right you are," Koodigern said, and his ghostly shape seemed to quiver at the words. "For that's why I'm here. I am sadly torn with great regret!"

Finn waited, and the specter settled into a somber veil again.

"I must tell you, sir, that great wrongs have been done, and I am the cause of many of these myself. I was in your Prince's pay, his agent in Heldessia's court. I am not proud of this betrayal, but I had a weakness for gold, as many a mortal has found to his regret.

"It was I who discovered the traitor in Aghen Aghenfleck's court. It was I who sent the ring that would identify the man to the Prince."

"This is a startling thing to hear," Finn said. "I doubt you'd know it, but Lord Gherick was a particular friend of mine. I was greatly sorrowed to learn he had plotted against his brother. Though, in truth, I can't say I greatly blame him for his feelings for that miserable lout. . . ."

"No, that's the thing, sir. It wasn't Lord Gherick. He's not the traitor at all!"

"What's that you say? I do not understand this, Koodigern. Do you tell me you falsely accused my friend?"

Once more, the grim shade trembled, each small particle of smoky substance a'shiver before coming to rest again.

"This is the guilt I bear, Master Finn. In my foolishness, I gave way to my desires for Princess DeFloraine-Marie. More foolish still, I thought she stood for the war, which her country has ever soundly supported.

"I was wrong, sir. I was cruelly taken in. I confided to the princess, shared all my secrets, for I believed she loved me as well. She said she would, indeed, see that the ring reached the Prince, in whatever manner she could.

"I gave her the proper ring, for I had learned through sources in the palace the name of the traitor in Fyxedia's court. Only she was too clever for me! She *knew* the traitor, and only used me to find the rings.

"The traitor is one Count VanDork, Master Finn. Only she sent the ring that would name Lord Gherick the guilty one . . ."

"Stones and Bones, Koodigern—a great wrong has indeed been done!"

"And then, sir, she found the perfect time to murder me. It was during the Bowser attack. Right after we'd met, and I'd given you my knife. My intention was to learn if you were close to the Prince. I would then judge if it was safe to declare myself to you.

"That never came about, of course. She killed me, in the confusion of the fight. And my death was blamed on the Bowsers.

"All along, Master Finn, it was the princess who was behind these deeds most foul. She used Maddigern, who has no kindness in his heart, the same as she used me— and any other male she so desired. She killed Dostagio, when she learned he had seen her in an intimate moment with Maddigern.

"She spread dissension between Maddigern and Oberbyght, not that she needed a great deal of work there. And Maddigern *knew* what she was after. What she is after still. She wants her father dead as well, so she can have the throne. And she'll likely get it, too, and bring the chaos of peace to Heldessia Land!"

Finn felt suddenly very tired, weary to the bone. "So the deed's not yet done. And Count VanDork holds his position still. Do you think he will try to slay the Prince? Is that his great mission in all of this?"

"I think it most likely. Most likely, indeed."

"Then I must take action. I loathe the Prince, but I will have to try to stop this insidious business if I can."

"Best you do not, sir. Leave some of this to me. For I have much to make up for in this."

"What can you do, Koodigern? No offense, but it's clear that you're dead."

"That's so. But the dead are not entirely without their wits, though we don't always recall exactly who we are or when."

"I'll not ask how this will come about. But if I can be of any help to you . . ."

"If a time should come, I will call upon you, Master Finn. Have no doubt of that."

"Well, then . . ."

"Oh," Koodigern said, just before his misty self began to fade, "good Dostagio asked me to send his regards, sir. He, too, is a victim of this sad affair."

"Yes, indeed that's so."

"In more ways than you know . . ."

"And how is that, friend?"

"The Gracious Dead. Scarcely anyone is aware of the truth of this. These servants of the King are the unwanted children of the Heldessian poor. They have been raised in secret for generations past, by Obern Oberbyght and those in his family who came before. They never knew who they were, sir, or what other lives they might have lived."

"No, that can't be. It's too great a horror to be real!"

Finn felt as if something dark and chill had coiled up within his belly. For an instant, he imagined he could hear the cries of those who'd been so sorely used through countless years.

"It can't be, but it is, sir. I fear it's sadly so . . ."

Koodigern was only a blur, now, a wisp of vapor that quickly vanished into the night.

Finn STOOD ALONE ON GARPENNY STREET, UNAWARE of the cold, or the fast-approaching dawn. When the first faint hint of the day smudged the sky, he felt a great weariness overtake him, and he walked back to his door, under the sign that read THE LIZARD SHOPPE. It needed paint, as it always had before.

Inside, Julia Jessica Slagg sat unmoving by the stairs, as she had some hours before.

"I told you to take a cloak, but you won't listen to me. Not our good and noble Master Finn."

"Don't ever call me *noble*, Julia, not even in jest. It's not a title I can bear. I shall make myself some thistle tea, now. And do not wake Letitia, let her have her sleep.

"After I've had a cup or two to bring the warmth back to my bones, you and I will have a very long talk in the quiet of the shop. There must be a way to bring a vile and dangerous sorcerer down, and I shall need a lizard with a sly ferret's brain to give me good advice. . . ."

ABOUT THE AUTHOR

NEAL BARRETT JR.'s novels and short stories span the field from mystery/suspense, fantasy, science fiction, and historical to mainstream fiction. He has been nominated for both the Nebula and Hugo awards. He has received a Western Writers of America award and the Theodore Sturgeon Memorial Award.

The Washington Post called his novel, *The Hereafter Gang*, "one of the great American novels." His current work includes a collection of short stories, *Perpetuity Blues*. His new novel, *Interstate Dreams*, received an award from the Texas Institute of Letters.

His first book featuring Finn, the Lizard-Maker, *The Prophecy Machine*, was also published by Bantam.